HARD ROAD SOUTH

SCOTT GATES

BLUE INK
PRESS

Published by Blue Ink Press, LLC

"Jamestown Homeward Bound" lyrics sourced via Public Domain

"O, For a Closer Walk with God" by William Cowper sourced via Public Domain

Cover design by Craig Gates utilizing "The Veteran in a New Field" by Winslow Homer (1865)
therealcraiggates.com

ISBN: 978-1-948449-05-2
Library of Congress Control Number 2019954965

For my family, all of whom I love dearly, and especially in memory of my father and forever mentor, Darryl Gates.

PROLOGUE

THE CLOUDS HUNG gray and heavy with snow. An occasional flake drifted, as a feather loosed from an overstuffed pillow, but the sky was not yet ready to give up its bulk. On a gentle hill overlooking a frozen cove below, a small cabin stood out, a dark smudge against the barren white landscape. The sea was still but for a small freighter steaming toward Halifax.

A man trudged up to the cabin, his arms stuffed with firewood. He flipped open the lid to a woodbin with one foot. Slightly off balance, he dumped his load in and swore under his breath. Wisps of steam rose from beneath the wraps of his knit scarf.

He knocked cakes of snow from his boots and wiped ice from his beard before pushing through the door into the small cabin. It was dark and cold inside, and it took his eyes a moment to adjust from the hazy glare outside. As he lit an oil lamp, the single room of the cabin danced with shadows. From its walls hung various implements to combat the long, heavy winter. Two pair of snowshoes, one needing mending. A few small traps. A hand drill, saw, and pole for fishing. A shovel and axe near the door, should a drift seal him in.

He pulled out of his heavy coat and hung it near his cot. He opened the inside lid of the woodbin and grabbed out a few small logs — enough to stoke the stove without being greedy. He paused a moment as the embers within glowed and closed his eyes, letting their warmth thaw his hands a bit.

It was not yet dinnertime, but he was tired. The sun wouldn't set for many hours, and his days and nights had become confused. He emptied the contents of his pockets so as to shuffle out of his trousers, their cuffs stiffened by thin crusts of ice. On a table next to his cot he tossed a pocket knife, a button that had loosed from his coat, and a tarnished oval coin bearing the worn relief of a robed man standing in a small boat.

With a deep sigh, he laid himself down and slid his legs under a ratty quilt. He stared up at the ceiling and realized he had left the lamp burning. "No matter," he muttered. "I'll just rest my eyes for a moment."

Turning on his side, he dozed as the snow began to fall in earnest outside, the first silent band of many rolling in off the coast.

PART I

SPRING

CHAPTER 1

HE HAD NEVER INTENDED to go to Virginia. Let alone the South.

Before his 26th year, he had actually never been south of Baltimore. And that had been a strange trip, now more of a fog, a collection of daguerreotypes, than a reasoned memory.

He was young and his mother was ill. She stayed home with his aunt while he and his father rode south, to Baltimore. Why, he does not remember, nor did he ever probably know. He remembers a low sky framed underneath by brown chimneys. There was an old wood floor with wide gaps, and when he looked up, his father gave him a hard candy. It was peppermint.

His mother died that winter. And that is all he knew of the South, or parts south, before the war.

And then he came to know the South intimately, for better or worse. Its back roads, swamps, and woodlands. Its wet heat and bitter cold. He had covered miles and miles on foot in Mississippi, Louisiana, and Virginia. Languished during a Georgian summer.

He despised the Deep South.

Yet from his first morning in the Shenandoah, his first emergence from tent flaps into a vast, mist-covered valley, he knew this Virginia was worth returning to. Some five years had passed since he last saw it, and it was time he made his way back. He felt its pull.

Connecticut had nothing for him anymore. Its winters were endlessly bleak, and the cold rolled in off the sea in an inhospitable way. His aunt had passed years ago, and his father, he was told, had died of gangrene during the war.

It wasn't from a battle wound of any kind, but from a card game gone wrong. His father made a bad bet, got sore over it, and kicked a blacksmith's iron. He spent the following weeks alone, at home, limping on a broken, rotting toe and slowly dying from the leg up. Stubborn to the end, likely taken quietly by a fever in his sleep. But there's no way of knowing.

He had returned to Connecticut after the war to find an empty house and a fresh grave. His plans to build a business had been buried with his father; he held no interest in his former trade. Over the years, he auctioned off his aunt's land, sold the house he and his father had built over a summer long passed, and settled the family's remaining debts.

And so it came to be that on an early April dawn in 1869, Solomon Dykes packed two bags — a leather knapsack from the war and a wood-handled satchel — and looked back on his childhood home one last time. Walking through the frost-kissed grass, he turned south once more.

South, for the moment, to Bridgeport. He caught a ride from the muddy planks along his town's main street, climbing into the back of a cart covered by a wind-whipped tarpaulin.

Before they set off the driver called over his shoulder, "Careful on the bumps there, friend. I were you I would sit on that pack."

"What's your load?"

"Bricks."

The driver snapped the reins lightly and the horses pulled to a slow trot. Dykes eased back on the angular tarp and crammed his satchel in the space under the small of his back. It was near a two-hour ride he had made many times, though never with such unforgiving cargo.

When the cart rattled up among the first houses of Bridgeport, his back was tingling and his backside was numb. One particular rut a mile outside of town had drawn blood from under his shirtsleeve, which was now wet from it at the elbow.

Dykes whistled at the driver somewhere on Barnum Street, confident that the remaining distance to the train station would be better covered on foot. The driver slowed the horses and glanced toward the back of the cart.

"This will do it for you, then?"

"Yes, this is fine. Thank you for the ride — what do I owe you?"

"Not a thing. This is my route anyway. I could take you on up a ways more if you like."

"No, thank you." Dykes lifted himself off the bricks and checked to make sure he had everything. "I could use a walk."

He slid off the back and grabbed his bags, slinging the pack over one shoulder. The driver loosely popped the reins, jostling the cart forward. He gestured a good-bye with a raised hand.

Dykes gazed up at the hulking Wheeler & Wilson building on the left side of the street. Within, hundreds of musty workers were in the third hour of their shift, toiling over sewing machines lit by shafts of morning light punching down to the factory floor. He walked the block alongside an endless row of windows thirty feet off the ground. Factory noises occasionally drifted out onto the street. The air smelled of steam and axle grease. Fresh industry.

The journey could end here in Bridgeport, he thought. He could take a job and learn a trade in any one of dozens of factories like the one he passed now. He could settle in an apartment and make a proper home, there within plaster walls swollen by the moist river air. Maybe find a wife and fill the tenement's cramped quarters with children. Start a family business with his savings and put the children to work.

But he strolled on. Past this factory and the next, down Barnum Street and through the Third Ward of the city. He could do better in Virginia.

As he went along he found the streets to be surprisingly empty for a Tuesday morning. The occasional cart would pass, but foot traffic was light. All inside, he thought. He looked up at the leaden sky, a few hours from commencing a drizzling rain with spits of snow that would likely last well into the evening. By the time the weather had cleared, he would have long been south, he thought.

He shrugged to adjust his pack and slipped both arms through the straps to better distribute the load. The walk was longer than he'd guessed it to be. He passed Washington Park to the left, the grass a muddy brown. Day-old puddles stood among the bricked paths, laid in diagonals, cutting to the park's center. He took a left a few blocks up, crossed a bridge, and spotted the tracks of the New York & New Haven Railroad, his road south. He'd head through Manhattan to Washington, and from there see what his options were. Though his mind was fixed on working a piece of land somewhere in the Shenandoah Valley, he was prepared for anything.

He arrived at the rail station with some time to spare, so he casually made his way across the platform, stopping to buy a paper along the way. There was no wait at the ticket counter. He scanned a few headlines before tucking the paper into his pack and walking up to the agent.

"One fare to Washington City, please."

The agent nodded and looked down at the counter as he flipped through a stack of vanilla-colored cards.

"You hear how the rails are south of Washington?" Dykes asked.

"Hm?" The agent briefly glanced up from the cards, his hands still working. "Seems there's new lines going in all the time, but no ticketing for them here. Where's your final destination?"

"I'm not sure. Maybe Leesburg. It's west of the capital."

"I know of it," the agent said. "You can buy fare in Washington. We can get you that far. Next train to New York leaves at nine fifteen."

"I'll take it, thank you," Dykes said.

"Fine. That will be five dollars eighty-two." The agent slid a packet with two tickets across the counter. "Your transfer to Washington is on the PRR — you'll pick that up across the river in Jersey City."

Dykes took out his billfold and thumbed out the fare. He pocketed the tickets and found his way to the platform. The station largely empty, he found a good dry bench and sunk down to read more of the paper. No news of note: an auction, a court ruling, a rather dry update on coming elections in France.

He leaned back on the bench and closed his eyes. In the sky behind him, mottled gulls wheeled above the river and cried at a garbage scow below.

* * *

DYKES PASSED MOST of the ride staring vacantly at the bleak Connecticut landscape as the train chucked along its course. His car was empty in Bridgeport, with only three additions getting on at stops between there and New York City — one old timer, by himself, boarded in Port Chester, and another man with his teenage daughter got on near New Rochelle. All were dressed in weighty wool coats, their boots spattered with mud.

This was the awkward space between seasons, when the wind still carried the bite of winter, but the right patch of sun would cause hints of sweat to appear under the folds of your coat. By the time the train began nearing New York, the car was hot and stuffy. Yet Dykes kept his coat on, as did his fellow travelers.

The scenery near New York City changed little from the rest of the ride, but Dykes knew they were on Manhattan once the train shuddered over the Harlem River. As it passed over a series of trestles, farmland was broken up by clusters of buildings, and scattered cottages were soon joined by tenements, warehouses, churches, and storefronts. The train slowed as the buildings grew taller around it, some as high as ten stories by Dykes' guess. The occasional steeple punched a gap in the brick skyline. These places of worship, once the tallest buildings, had quickly been swallowed by progress around them.

The tracks ended at a series of covered platforms on Centre Street — not far from City Hall, as Dykes remembered from passing through during the war. This was the end of the line, although schedule boards provided some guidance on what were typical transfers. He found one listing Pennsylvania Railroad southbound trains, as well as departure times for ferries to the PRR depot, and stood to check the numbers against his transfer.

The platforms were bustling with passengers. Though on the next platform over, a man sat — looking wretched on the ground — seemingly unaware of all movement around him. He had a blanket wrapped tight over his lap, and from the shape of his bulk below the waist it was clear he had little of his legs intact. He must have been drunk. At least his nodding head and loud mutterings indicated as much. Dykes couldn't make out any of what he was saying, until a man walking by, engrossed in a book, tripped on the end of his blanket.

"Watch your footing, you sonofabitch," the cripple slurred in an echo across the tracks. The passerby turned his head briefly but kept walking.

The cripple made a feeble attempt to swipe at the man's heels before doubling over with a sigh. His blanket had pulled back, exposing a flat, dingy pant leg.

"You go on, now," he spat. "I don't want to see you no more, no ways." He struggled to reposition his blanket and continued to ramble angrily, but it was low and unclear.

Dykes confirmed a departure time and stuffed his transfer

down the side of his pack. As he started the walk out from under the shed, a train steamed in on the track between Dykes and the cripple, drowning out anything more the man might be saying. Its doors opened on the side opposite Dykes, and it sat hissing as passengers unloaded. He rounded the front of the engine at the end of the tracks and peered down the platform to where the man had sat. The cripple was gone.

* * *

ON THE STREET just outside the platform buildings, freshly disembarked travelers mingled with all walks of life. Businessmen and politicians, tradesmen and factory workers, soldiers and veterans. Dykes wasn't sure where he fit in among them.

He stopped to get his bearings. Centre Street was wide here as it ran its final diagonal course to meet Broadway, with plenty of room to accommodate lines of horse-drawn taxis and all manner of other traffic, from open buckboards to fine enclosed carriages. Buildings hemmed in close around City Hall Park, and Dykes looked up and around to admire them. He found the hall itself to be fairly unremarkable, save for a single tower reaching up from the middle of the structure. On the street level facing the park were a few eating houses, an oyster house included, among various other storefronts. The oyster house had a large painted board leaned up next to its entrance: OYSTER SARNIES. TWO FOR ONE.

He could smell fried oysters from across Centre Street, a rich unseen fog wafting out from the dark quarters of the establishment. Dykes hefted his bags and jogged across the street toward the sign, watching for passing taxis and dodging a manure pile as he went. A pair of dogs had caught the scent as well, it seemed, and paced nervously near the open door.

An Englishman greeted Dykes from behind the counter when he walked in. The sound of sizzling oysters and clattering plates from behind the counter created quite a din.

"Afternoon, mate."

"Afternoon. I'll just take a pair of your sandwiches. One for now and one wrapped."

"Indeed you will, mate." He turned and deftly assembled two sandwiches from eight-inch loaves, smearing each side with butter. "Greens with it?" he shouted over his shoulder.

"Yes," Dykes answered, unsure of the type of greens in question. The Brit grabbed for a tub of cabbage slaw and forked two healthy portions onto the oysters. He wrapped one sandwich tightly in newspaper, and the other he left open on one end.

"Here you go. That'll be ten cents for the pair."

Dykes paused and stared back. "What about your sign? Two for one?"

"Right you are, mate! Sorry, sorry. A nickel, then."

Dykes paid the man and stuffed one sandwich into his bag. He started for the door but stopped short at the threshold and turned back to face the counter. "Say, what's the quickest way to the Jersey City Ferry?"

The man looked up from some knife work that he'd quickly resumed after making the sandwiches. "Going to the depot, are you?"

"Yes, for the PRR."

"Take a left out the door here, and pop down to Broadway." The man motioned with the tip of his knife as if pointing to a map in the air between them. "A few blocks down is Cortland. Right on that and hoof it to the water."

"Got it. Thank you."

The man deftly flipped the knife and gave a little salute with its butt.

Dykes left the oyster house and tore a chunk of bread from his sandwich, tossing it into the street midstride. The dogs rushed after it.

He had seen a clearing at the far end of the park, which was fixed in mind as a lunch spot. Some time before the next ferry afforded him a few minutes out in the open.

That corner of the park, as it turned out, was an active pasture — sanctioned or not — with three goats grazing at the far end. There was a relatively flat rock along the edge, under some trees near the road, so Dykes took a seat and unwrapped his sandwich. He got an oyster in the first bite, crisp with just the right amount of chewy give on the inside. Delicious.

He leaned back, wincing as his brick-bruised elbow touched the cold rock. He shifted his weight to the other elbow and gazed up through the branches. The sun had burned a hole in the otherwise cloud-covered sky.

After finishing the sandwich, he crumpled the paper wrapper and tossed it a few yards away, toward the goats. He checked his watch. Quarter of one. He worked his thumb over the watch's smooth glass face, turned it over, and smeared its brass back clean. The back was largely unadorned, but for a small eagle and the initials J.L.R. He didn't know who this was.

He often wondered if J.L.R. had ever guessed his watch would be in the hands of this stranger. Could he have known the New York sun would have one day glinted off its face? No. No more than Dykes could guess where this watch had been. Digging a ditch in Baton Rouge, passing the time before lunch. Hunting turkey in St. Charles Parish. Going to church service in New Orleans. Waiting for a train in New York. All the same to the watch.

He slipped it back into his pocket and raised up stiffly off the rock. Shouldering his bags once more, he started off toward Cortland Street, where he'd catch the ferry and another rail south.

CHAPTER 2

THE PLOW WAS CUTTING through the ground nicely, turning up rocks that had escaped notice the year before. The soil was wet and soft after three days of steady rain. Otherwise, Mosby knew this chore would take twice as long. He pulled on the reins and called to the mule plodding ahead.

"Whoa, Soupy. Ease up." The mule stopped, sighed, and stared at the ground. Mosby jumped off the back of the plow and kicked down the brake. He took off his hat, crumpled it to his waist, and surveyed his work thus far.

A good three-quarters of the ten-acre field was now fresh-turned earth. The remainder was corn stover, a low stubble, left from last year's harvest. Scattered rocks were perched on the uneven hills between rows, waiting to be collected and tossed on a wall. A job for the neighbor boy.

The rain clouds had finally raced north, but for some gray wisps lingering high enough to allow the mountains to show themselves. Mosby scanned them. To the northwest, the Shenandoah. To the southeast, the Bull Run range. Between, nothing but beautiful rolling green, fresh from the cold rain.

He was glad to be here, to say the least, but the valley didn't hold the same innocence it had when he was a younger man.

The mountains were no longer full of promise. He no longer yearned to strike out and climb one.

He had, once. As a boy, Mosby had made up his mind to climb the highest hill he could see from his family's land. Standing on the porch one morning, he just headed out, calling to his mother that he'd be back in a few days. He was back the next morning, having climbed the mountain he'd had his eye on. The top was just like everything else — dense woods — but it was the top.

He could see that hill today, some thirty years later. Paris Mountain. There it was, among the others, with clouds whisking by. But there was no mystery. He knew what was up there. Just more trees.

He took a pull of water from a canteen wedged in the frame of the plow before stepping back on.

"Hee-yah, Soupy!" The mule's head kicked up and it started off, without any further signal from his driver.

He had done another row and a half when he spotted Fannie waving to him with one arm from the east fence. He squinted at his wife and waved back without stopping. She raised the other arm and waved both.

"Damnit. Whoa, Soupy." He jumped off the back and took his hat off, running his hand through thick dark hair. "What is it?" he shouted across the field. Mosby had a Tidewater drawl, which softened even his shouted words.

Fannie shouted something back, but it was too high and faint to be heard. He looked at the mule. Looked back at Fannie. Against the backdrop of the fence line she seemed so small, her apron neat and tidy across her round waist. Her nut-brown hair pinned up for afternoon chores. He kicked the brake down and started to walk the distance between them, keeping his eyes on the ground.

"Jeb!" Mosby kept his head down and closed the remaining gap between them. "Jeb, Pappy's gone!" He looked up and saw Fannie was out of breath. "Pappy's gone."

"What does that mean? I had lunch with him an hour ago." He looked toward the house.

"Well, he's gone now. I was hanging laundry out back and he was in his chair. When I came back in he was gone and the door was open. He was just gone!"

"Damnit." Mosby spat on the ground and studied it for a moment. "He must have gone to town. There's nowhere else he would care to go." He looked back at Soupy, standing stoically where he'd left him. "Damn shame. Okay. I'll go and get him." He put his hat on and started back toward the mule. He stopped after a few steps. "Did he take the horse?"

"I don't know. I didn't check. But he couldn't have gotten far, do you think?"

Mosby started walking again and scratched at the light stubble along his jaw. "I guess we'll see."

He left the plow where it was and unhitched the mule, leading it over the rough-plowed rows and to the barn. The barn was small compared to most others in the valley, but enough to work the parcel of land they had. They kept half of its four stalls full between Soupy and Presh, and the loft could be filled with enough stacked hay to get them through a winter. There was also a small room near the front for tools and tack.

He heard Presh shift her weight when they walked into the cool darkness of the barn. He led Soupy to the empty stall on the left, next to Presh, and removed the bit and leader. He gave the mule a couple of swift smacks on the shoulder and turned to the horse.

"So you're still in here. He didn't take you along this time?" The horse whisked her tail. "Well, good for us then. The last thing I wanted to do was beg a ride into town."

He grabbed a harness from the tack room and hitched up the horse, leading it outside and around to the lean-to on the side of the barn. The cart there was looking good, sporting new side rails and a new tongue for the season. He hitched the horse to the front and climbed up onto the bench seat behind her.

Mosby snapped the reins and they pulled out, bumping over a clump of grass. He stopped in front of the house and jumped off.

Fannie had returned to hanging laundry, so he walked around back.

"Do you need anything from town?"

"Pappy would be nice."

"Agreed. Anything else while I'm there? I can save a trip tomorrow and finally get that field plowed."

"Well, we need shortening. And the roof was leaking again last night."

"That's right. I'll get some tar for it." Mosby leaned in and kissed Fannie on the cheek. "I'll be back before dark, or shortly after. The three of us will have dinner together."

"I hope so. Bye, Jeb."

He gave her a wink and went up the back steps into the house. He filled his canteen from a jug in the kitchen and tore a piece of bread from a loaf on the table. He wrapped it in a cloth and walked out through the front porch.

The horse looked his way when he walked up. "Okay, Precious. Let's make this quick." He climbed back on the bench and they started off.

* * *

MIDDLEBURG WAS ABOUT five miles down the road, so Mosby didn't expect his father to have covered the full distance to town just yet. He was likely halfway there, depending on when he had decided to wander off. Mosby kept the horse at a nice gait, bouncing along the pitted macadamized road, keeping his eyes fixed ahead.

Though the valley had seen quite a bit of fighting during the war, it hadn't taken long to get it built back to its former glory. A lack of rail had been a blessing in that case. Some other, more well-connected towns in the area hadn't been so lucky. He had made a trip to Manassas Junction in the fall and was amazed at the scars the war had left. Both Yankee and Confederate axes had made fields of stumps where serene forests once stood. Now just scrub brush and brambles. For miles and miles. It would take decades for the trees to grow back in that ravaged, pock-marked country.

But here, quiet woodlands were intact and tall windbreaks stood guard over the rolling pastures, many of which had been grazed since the 1700s. His father, Tom, had moved the family here when Mosby was a boy, up from Hampton Roads. They weren't farmers then, by any means, but fate made them so when his uncle passed and left the land to Pappy. It was a small plot, but they made it work. They had land for corn and hay, and vegetables for the table.

Mosby saw a figure a quarter mile or so ahead, walking along the roadside. He popped the reins and Presh pulled the cart at a faster clip. Within fifty yards he could tell it wasn't Pappy. The figure was too short and lithe. Likely the Stibbs boy.

He slowed the cart to reduce the clatter as he passed. It was the Stibbs boy, hands in pockets.

"John Stibbs!" he called as he pulled the cart to a stop, looking down at the boy.

"Hi, Mr. Mosby. Going into town?"

"I'm actually looking for my father. Have you passed him on the road?"

"No, sir. It's been pretty quiet today. It rained."

Mosby gazed up ahead, then turned on the bench to look back along the road. "Well, okay. I suppose I am going into town, then. Do you need a ride?"

"No, sir. I'll walk it."

"Suit yourself. Hey, John? I've got a job for you tomorrow."

The boy gazed back up at him, hands still in the pockets of his dingy pants.

"I'm plowing the Creek Field and we're turning up a lot of rocks. They could use stacking."

The boy nodded, his mouth slightly open. "I can do it. Tomorrow afternoon good?"

"Perfect. Any time after lunch. Stop by the house if you want, or just find me in the field."

"Yessir."

"Have a good walk, John." He gave the reins a shake and Precious started off.

"Bye, Mr. Mosby."

Mosby had always thought John to be somewhat dumb, though not nearly as so as the senior John Stibbs, the boy's father. The whole brood was never good for conversation, but they made decent enough neighbors. And Mrs. Stibbs had been a good friend to Fannie during the war.

ASHBY'S GAP TURNPIKE, the road on which Mosby had hoped his father was traveling, split through Middleburg running west to east. Mosby was coming from the west, so as he neared town he could see the Beveridge House up on the left. The imposing four-story stone tavern and inn had long been a roadhouse along the route, and the town had essentially sprung up around it. Mosby steered Presh to the inn's ample hitching bar and slowed the cart to a halt.

Two soldiers were standing idly at the corner of the Beveridge House, one leaning on its wooden rail post. Mosby nodded as he passed, and they did the same without shifting their positions. They each had a Sharps carbine close by — a new model. Mosby had seen more of those lately but had not yet had the opportunity to fire one. Fewer troops these days, but better equipped.

At the door of the inn, he paused to greet Mrs. Russ as she passed along the worn boards of the sidewalk. She lived a mile or so further from town than the Mosbys, and was recently widowed. Or it seemed recent enough — Mosby realized it now must have been more than a year as she was no longer wearing her weeping veil or widow's weeds.

Her husband, Nap, had been a lieutenant colonel during the war. His was a gentle death, in his own bed, far from the cannon fire of earlier years. Mosby had wept when he'd first heard the news, nonetheless. To spend years expecting death at the hands of other men, only to return and find it so soon after where you feel safest. In the moonlight, wrapped in the heavy warmth of quilts next to your sleeping wife. It seemed somehow unfair.

"Mrs. Russ," he said in greeting.

"Hi, Jeb. You're looking well."

"Why thank you. I know Fannie would disagree." He noticed she was wearing Nap's uniform jacket, a cleanly pressed gray wool that hung around her shoulders like a cape. "Have you seen my Pappy, by any chance? We think he came to town, but he didn't say before he left."

"Oh, no, sorry to say. I do hope he turns up, though. Fannie mentioned he was prone to wander."

"Just within past months, yes. Now that the weather is nicer, I'm afraid he'll be getting farther."

"It still has a ways to get nice, if you ask me," she said, pushing the top brass button through its eyelet. "Summer can't come soon enough." She patted Mosby on the shoulder. "If I see Tom, I'll be sure to get him home to you safe."

"Thank you, ma'am." Mosby nodded to her, hefted the inn's heavy door open, and stepped inside.

The inn was familiar in a comforting way, almost as much so as his own house, considering the many years Mosby had called Middleburg home. It was dimly lit but cozy. The main level's oak-beamed ceiling was low, sized to colonial travelers of another era. To the left was a dining room, and straight back past the main staircase, the tavern.

No one of the half-dozen at the inn had seen Pappy, as it turned out, and Mosby didn't have time to stay and chat. The days were getting longer, but he couldn't risk not finding Pappy before dark. He said some brief goodbyes and headed back outside.

To the side of the road in front of the inn, Mrs. Russ was talking to the soldiers. Mosby could tell she was upset. Her thin wisps of red hair danced as she looked from one soldier to the other, and her green eyes were wide and alight.

He walked over to see what the trouble was, but one of the soldiers moved toward him and put out a hand. "That'll do," he said quickly, with a trace of nervousness behind the command.

Both of the soldiers were young. Their rifles were still leaning against the Beveridge House porch.

Mosby half put his hands up. "Whoa, friend. No trouble here. Is everything okay, Mrs. Russ?"

Her head snapped toward Mosby. "It most certainly is not," she said. There was no trace of nerves in her voice. "These young men don't seem too pleased with my husband's coat."

The taller soldier, closest to her, ignored Mosby and continued speaking to her. "Ma'am, you cannot wear those insignia." Both soldiers had local accents. "I'm being more than fair. You could be shot for treason."

"Shot? For treason?" She spat the last word out at the tall soldier. She was clearly furious; her voice was raised with a slight quiver. "Well then shoot, sir! Shoot me, and be damned."

Mosby stepped past the one soldier and put his hands on Mrs. Russ' shoulders. "Easy, Gwen. No one will be shot today." He glared at the pair of soldiers. "Gentlemen, this has gone far enough. This woman needs to keep her coat. It's cold. What is it about the coat that offends you? The epaulets? The buttons?"

"It's not your place to ask such questions," the tall soldier barked. "What's your name?"

Mosby stared him in the eyes. "It is my place. And you needn't know my given name. I'm a Mosby." The soldiers cut eyes at each other but were otherwise unmoved.

"What offends us? It's those damned buttons," the shorter solider said. "Buffed to a high shine. C.S.A. glinting in the sun.

We seen them from halfway down the road and waited for her here."

The men cast eyes on the buttons as Mrs. Russ placed her hands over a pair of them.

"I see," Mosby said. "Mrs. Russ, you understand?"

She sighed. "No. But I know what needs to be done."

"Here," Mosby said, taking out his pocket knife. He gently turned her around and began cutting off the buttons, collecting them in his fist. She cried quietly as he emptied them into her small, outstretched hands. He had never seen her cry before.

Mosby sighed as he watched the scene dissipate as quickly as it had come to be. Gwen issued a defeated goodbye and was on her way; the soldiers returned to their presumed post nearby.

Such was life now, he was finding. Filled with reminders — small as they may seem — that life would not soon be returning to how he'd left it before the war.

CHAPTER 3

The Federal City was a mess.

The last time Dykes had passed through Washington, fortifications crisscrossed the surrounding countryside, and it seemed every free inch of space had been put to some sort of use. The Capitol dome had yet to be completed, but as he had marched past it with his unit, Dykes sensed there was some greatness to come. The war was over. Lincoln had done it — he had preserved the Union — and now it was time to rebuild.

But then Lincoln was shot. Momentum was lost. Dykes was shipped off to Savannah for a few sweltering months, and once mustered out, he'd returned to Connecticut.

And here, in Grant's Washington, progress seemed to have ground to a halt. The rail station was on 6th Street, just off the National Mall and west of the Capitol. Dykes had only to step outside to find a view of the newly erected Capitol dome, and it was splendid. Timeless and magnificent, reaching to the heavens.

But to the west along the river, through a smoky haze across the muddy expanse of the Mall and its scattered shanties, the pale rectangular stump of what was to be a monument to Washington sat, neglected. Some scaffolding traced its silhouette in the setting sun, although few stones had been placed in decades.

Dykes had often thought on this place, his capital, during the war. He had looked to it as a symbol of the Union that he fought for. But he had never spent much time here, and his romantic ideas of it were quickly fading as he absorbed the city around him.

He was pleased he hadn't chosen Washington as his final destination.

"Hey there, sir! Got a cab here, sir!" a nasal voice called a few feet behind him.

Dykes turned around with a sigh. "Hello, yes. Could you help me with my bearings?"

"New in town, I see. Where are you off to? I'll get you there. Got a cab just yonder." The man motioned down the street.

"No, no cab, thank you. Can you recommend a good place of lodging within a short walk?"

The man laughed and turned to approach another traveler coming from the station. Dykes glanced back in the direction of the Washington monument and studied the sun. It was low, with only a half hour or so left of good daylight. He scanned the thin crowd around the station and spotted a group of soldiers without baggage.

"Excuse me. Good evening, captain." Dykes extended a hand and the officer shook it.

"Evening."

"I've just arrived from Bridgeport," Dykes said. The officer stared back at him, blankly. "Served in the 12th Regiment, Connecticut Volunteer Infantry."

"Okay, glad to have you. Welcome back. Looking for something?"

"Yes, actually. Can you recommend a place of lodging within a short walk?"

The captain crossed his arms and looked off. "Well, I can't say you'll get the best treatment around here. You should head to Lafayette Square. There's a widow there who's kindly to veterans. Lives on Madison."

"Wonderful, thank you. How will I know her house?"

"She usually flies a naval jack until sundown. That said, it'll be dark soon. So you best be off." He pointed west. "Just head a block up to the canal and follow it until you see the President's House. On the right. Lafayette Square is just behind it."

Dykes thanked him and started the walk toward the canal. The air was cool, but Dykes was struck by the stink of sewerage carried on the breeze. He couldn't imagine the same streets under an oppressive summer heat, the city's refuse baked by the sun.

The stench grew more formidable when he reached the canal. He peered over at the canal's stagnant water, its carved banks slick with algae mats. He looked across to the other side as a woman tossed in the contents of a bucket, a brown liquid that landed with a heavy splash.

The Washington he had dreamed about on the train ride down — the triumphant capital — was not here. It had been caked over by piles of rubbish along the muddy streets, a tangle of telegraph wires sagging overhead, and the muted clatter of the masses going about the evening, oblivious to the significance of Washington's very existence.

DYKES PALMED his candle lantern along the walk as the sun gave way to dusk. He'd guessed his chances of finding the proper house were slim, but once in sight of the square he spotted the naval jack, deep blue with white stars, hanging angled toward the street. It was only halfway down the block. No need to spark the candle tonight.

The neighborhood, built around the park that gave Lafayette Square its shape, was much more pleasant than what he had found along the canal. Midsized trees created a canopy, half hanging over the cobbled street. Gas lamps lit the sidewalk along the row houses and cast his shadow long into the park as he passed.

He climbed the steps to the door of the house he'd been looking for. Leaning both bags against the carved sandstone arch framing the door, he gave the knocker three quick raps. He heard them echo within. Then quiet.

He turned to face the park again and took a deep breath of the night air. Here it was fresh. Through the dimming light he spotted the statue in the park's center — a man on horseback, hat raised in triumphant salute. Dykes did not know who it was. Perhaps Lafayette.

The latch clicked behind him and a sash of light cut across the stoop. "May I help you?" He turned to see a woman, likely in her thirties, with dark brown hair gathered and pinned on top of her head.

"Yes, ma'am." He realized he didn't know of a name to ask for. "I saw your flag. I was told at the train station that this house looks kindly on veterans."

"I suppose it depends on both the veteran and their need," she said.

"First Lieutenant Solomon Dykes." He half bowed his head, hands clasped in front of him. "A veteran of the 12th Connecticut Volunteer Infantry." She nodded with a polite half-smile. "I've traveled from Connecticut and am in need of lodging tonight. I'll leave at first light, unless you have any chores needing done."

She scanned the street behind him and eyed his bags. "Beth Tompkins. This is my house, and yes, I look kindly on veterans from time to time." She paused to study him, her eyes bright in the lamplight. "I can offer a room and breakfast, no charge or chores, but I do ask that you bring that flag in with you."

"Yes ma'am, I thank you," Dykes said. Beth opened the door further and stood by it as he unhooked the flag from its short pole and took time to fold it reverently. He didn't know its history, and he didn't want to jeopardize the hospitality shown thus far. "Your flag, Ms. Tompkins." He handed it in to her and turned to get his bags.

She closed and latched the door behind them as Dykes carried his bags into the well-lit foyer. "You can place your bags in the first room at the top of the stairs. Would you like tea?"

"Oh, no, thank you. Some hot water for a washing would be welcome, though."

"I'll put the kettle on," she said. "Take your bags on up and let me know if you'll need more blankets."

He thanked her again and headed up the narrow staircase leading from the foyer. He pushed backward through the first door on the left and found a tidy room with a four-poster bed made with crisp sheets and a worn but well-kept quilt. A rocking chair was stacked with folded blankets. The room was dark, so rather than risk knocking into any unseen furniture, Dykes dropped his bags, shed his coat, and turned to go back downstairs.

The creaking stairs announced his return, although he moved quietly through the foyer, stopping in a sitting room or parlor off the kitchen. He heard Beth filling the kettle, out of sight. He glanced around the room, crowded with shelves of books. Nautical paintings were hung over some sets of shelves. They depicted four different ships — one under sail and three steamers. Each had an engraved plaque centered on the bottom part of the frame. He began scanning titles of books on the shelves. A small table clock, made of brass and wood, sat among the books. It faintly ticked away the seconds.

"First Lieutenant Solomon Dykes," Beth announced from the kitchen. "Where did you come from today, First Lieutenant Solomon Dykes?"

"Please, call me Sol," he called. "I'm from Connecticut."

"I gathered that much, First Lieutenant." She entered the doorway, wiping her hands on an apron. "What part? I ask because my family is from Boston."

"Oh, I see. Well, I'm from Monroe. It's just north of Bridge-port. Not much to speak of, in my opinion."

"Monroe." She squinted one eye in thought. "Can't say I've heard of it. I've been through Bridgeport, which is nice. And I do have a cousin in New London."

"New London, yes. I haven't spent too much time in New London. But you're from Boston? I thought I detected an accent," Dykes said. "What brought you south?" He immediately felt he shouldn't have asked this, half knowing the answer.

"My husband was a navy surgeon. We made our home here once he left the Academy." She crossed her arms. "I apologize for not having asked: Did you have dinner? I have some stew on the stove."

"Well, I suppose that does sound good. I forgot about dinner."

"We'll get you set up, then. If you would like to retire to your room, I will bring up the stew and your washing water."

"I certainly appreciate it, Mrs. Tompkins. And do you happen to have a lamp I could take up?"

"Oh, my! I'm so sorry to have left you in the dark." She ducked into the kitchen and returned a moment later with a lit Lomax hand lamp. "This should help your situation. And call me Beth, please."

"I thank you again, Beth." He took the lamp by the finger loop somewhat awkwardly, doing his best to avoid grazing her delicate hands.

"I'll leave your dinner by the door," she said.

"Wonderful, thank you." Dykes smiled and stood for a moment as she returned to the kitchen. He turned and headed up the creaking stairs to his room, being careful not to spill any kerosene.

He left the door open a crack and placed the lamp on the bedside table. He sat down with a heavy sigh and stared blankly at his boots.

He hadn't moved in minutes when he heard the stairs

creaking softly. A shadow appeared in the crack of the doorframe.

"I'll just leave these here. Goodnight."

Dykes looked up, toward the door. "Thank you, Beth. Goodnight."

Once he heard her move down the hall and into another room, he opened the door and looked down. A tray was on the hall floor, filled to its edges with a porcelain bowl of steaming water, a neatly folded white laced towel, a bowl of beef stew, and a glass of warm milk.

Dykes sat up in the dark with a start. A stirring downstairs had awoken him. It took a moment for his mind to clear, for him to realize where he was. A row house. In Washington. That's probably the owner downstairs, he reasoned.

Still, he was on edge out of habit. He tossed back a corner of the crisp sheets. In the dark he found his trousers and pulled them up over his drawers, tucking in the bottom of his shirt. He opened the door a crack and listened. Something in the parlor. He crept to the top of the stairs and stopped, now hearing Beth singing quietly to herself.

"… the sky's as clear as the maiden's eye
Who longs for our return,
To the land where milk and honey flows
And liberty, it was born."

She sang slowly and softly, but Dykes recognized the tune.

"So fill our sails with the favoring gales,
And with shipmates all around
We'll give three cheers for our starry flag …"

The floorboard at the top of the stairs creaked loudly and the singing stopped. Dykes stood absolutely still, holding his breath.

"Solomon?" Beth cleared her throat and waited.

Dykes half considered returning to his bedroom without a

sound, but thought better of it and descended a few steps, into view. Beth was sitting at a writing desk in the parlor. "Hello, Beth. I apologize — I thought I heard a noise downstairs."

"Well, I suppose you did. And it's I who should apologize. Would you care to join me, while you're up?"

He cinched his belt and pushed up the baggy sleeves of his shirt. "Certainly, for a moment."

He creaked down the remaining stairs and stepped into the halo of light cast by the lamp on the desk. She turned it up a bit as he did so. "Please, sit down. Tea?"

"No, thank you." He sat on the edge of a claw-foot sofa against the wall opposite the desk. It was flanked by book-shelves. "I'll admit, I heard your singing. It was lovely."

She looked down at some papers on the desk. "I don't know about that. Just one of the many tunes I always have in my head. I apologize again — it's usually so quiet around here, sometimes I forget my company and just carry on as if I'm alone."

"Please, don't apologize. I know how it is. I've lived alone since the war."

"In Monroe?" she asked.

"Yes. In my father's house. Where I spent much of my youth, actually. But it's sold now and I've left it. My plan is to get a fresh start in Virginia."

"Virginia over New England?" She laughed good-naturedly. "I can't see why. How do you know Virginia?"

"I was stationed in the Shenandoah Valley for some months toward the end of the war. The roads were horrendous and there was no shortage of enemy engagements. But the ridgelines were always there in the distance, holding some promise. That's likely why I hold it so fondly in my mind."

"Well, it must be lovely then," she said. "It seemed like there was always fighting in that valley."

Dykes nodded and looked up at the bookshelves to his right. The two ships captured there, immortalized in a heavy oil paint, flew defiant banners full in the sea air. Their bows split the waves, perfectly.

"Did you collect these paintings? They're quite grand."

"No, those were my husband's. William Tompkins. He served on those four ships."

"I see."

Beth cleared her throat again, lightly. "He died on one of them."

"I see," Dykes said. "I have great respect for surgeons and seamen alike. I'm sure he was a great man."

"He was. But he was young when he died. He had a great career ahead of him. And a loving family, I like to think. But it wasn't meant to be." She straightened the stack of papers on the desk and then folded her hands in her lap, turning back to Dykes. "He served on blockade ships along the coast."

"Then it was his work that made mine all the easier on the ground," Dykes said. "I am so sorry for your loss."

"Thank you, but there was so much loss. No need to feel any sorrow for mine. I've no doubt you have felt your share as well." She stood up, suddenly. "My, but isn't this a way to treat a guest. I should let you rest."

Dykes followed her lead and stood up. "I'll be fine with whatever rest I get. And thank you for the fine meal earlier."

"I wish I could have offered more than stew, but you're welcome." She paused. "I don't want to keep you, but I do have one question," she said, placing a hand on the back of her chair.

"Please. Do ask," he said.

"You're going to Virginia. But where? How do you make up your mind where to settle in such a vast place? With no kin?"

He thought a moment. "Well, I'm not quite sure, to be honest. I suppose I'll be off to Leesburg tomorrow, where I hope to purchase a map. Between that and word of mouth, I'll find my way. I'll settle somewhere."

"Leesburg." She let the name hang in the air for a moment. "I may be able to help there. William collected an awful many local maps once we moved south. If you can stay a moment longer I may have luck finding one for you."

Dykes nodded again. "I can think of nothing that would be of greater aid at this point. Thank you, Beth."

"Let me find it before you go thanking me." She moved from the parlor, through the foyer and down a hall into a back room, lighting a wall lamp as she went.

Dykes could hear her opening drawers and riffling through papers down the hall. He sat down again, folded his hands behind his head and leaned back against the carved top ridge of the sofa, letting his eyes drift across the ceiling. Fine cracks ran across the off-white plaster, like fissures tracing February pond ice.

She hurried back in after a few minutes carrying a rolled piece of linen, folded over and tied in the middle. "Found it!" She gave his shoulder a light double tap with the map as she walked back to her desk. She pushed some papers to the edges of the desk and moved the lamp to the safety of a rear corner. Dykes stood up and joined her side.

"Loudoun County," she announced, unrolling the linen. "This is an older map, from before the war, but I do remember it having a great amount of detail." It was large; its front edge hung off the desk.

Dykes studied it over her shoulder. The detail was impressive, with homeowner names scattered across the county. Along the edges of the map, its maker had sketched scenes from the area, intertwined with crops and livestock.

"Leesburg," she said, proudly tapping a cluster of lines and small squares.

"This is incredible. Perfect, Beth. I don't know how to thank you."

"Oh, think nothing of it. What else am I to do with a map of Loudoun County? Just take care of yourself down there."

"I will do my best."

She eyed the map for a bit longer before rolling its edges back in. She folded it over itself and handed it to Dykes. "Now I've kept you up too long. You must be exhausted."

"I'll be fine."

"Do you need another light for your way back upstairs?"

"No, I can manage. And thank you again." He placed his hand on her arm as he said this, and then turned and started up the creaking stairs, into the darkness.

Beth sat back down at the desk with him gone and gazed expressionless at the sofa cushion where he'd sat.

The room was silent aside from the small clock, which chimed weakly from its shelf.

CHAPTER 4

THE AFTERNOON SUN sparked off patches of water between tree shadows. All was still, save for a narrow canal boat approaching from the east, sitting high on the water. This water was muddied but clean, not like that of the derelict canal running through the capital city's core. It was fed by the Potomac, and ran alongside the wide river's winding path west.

A mule plodded along a dirt track running parallel to the canal. It walked just ahead of the boat, tethered to it with a thick and twisted rope. A figure was standing on the bow, helping the craft along with a long pole, while a man on shore led the mule with loose reins.

"Here!" the man on the bow called out. The other pulled the mule to a stop. The man with the pole heaved on it off the port side, easing the boat tight to the shoreline.

A third man, shorter but solidly built, emerged from a midship open hold and tossed two bags ahead of him onto shore. He followed with a short leap. He was clean-cut, with side-parted ash-blond hair and a light anchor beard, a few days of stubble blending it up to his sideburns: Solomon Dykes, now standing at a time and place long sought, but a short river crossing from Virginia.

Dykes had slipped away from Beth's house early that morning, before sunup. He assumed she'd been off to bed late given the way he'd left her. Catching up on correspondence, he'd thought.

After he washed up and dressed he made his way down the creaky stairs as quietly as possible. Before leaving he found her dip pen on the writing desk and scratched out a brief note on a scrap of paper.

Dear Beth,

Your hospitality has been humbling.

Sincerely,

1st Lt. S. Dykes

He wiped the nib clean between his thumb and forefinger and returned the pen to where he'd found it, placing the note next to it.

He heard the latch catch as he pulled the front door behind him. A thin blueish light was already permeating the city, allowing him to study the house number for a moment before trotting down the steps.

The next leg of his trip was less certain than the first. Closer to his goal now, his options opened up. He could return to the station and catch a train into Virginia, leading to any number of decent rail towns. He also knew there was a toll bridge from Georgetown that he could cross on foot, but he wasn't sure where exactly he would end up. Too far east from Leesburg, he knew.

But he had tired of trains from yesterday's journey, so even an uncertain walk sounded more appealing. He hefted his bags and turned in the direction of Georgetown, or best he could reckon from memory. He had at least a general sense of direction from when he had passed through with his unit, now some four years ago.

His walk took him past the specter of the President's House, pale in the morning light. At the end of the street that ran parallel to its vast manicured lawn, he saw Pennsylvania

Avenue. This was familiar to him. A wide thoroughfare that led northwest from Lafayette Square and straight into the heart of Georgetown.

The sun cast its first strong light over rooftops behind him as he loped up Pennsylvania, past a mix of dirt, gravel, and cobbled side streets. Within twenty minutes he crossed the bridge over Rock Creek and into Georgetown. At the bridge's midpoint he glanced downstream, his eye catching a crew maneuvering a narrow canal boat from the mouth of the creek into the Chesapeake & Ohio Canal. Although he'd heard the first rooster not a quarter hour ago, these men were already beginning a day's journey on the water. They'd negotiate a series of locks in Georgetown, then pole up the still waters into the highlands of West Virginia.

Georgetown's residents were more active than those of Washington. He was amazed at the number of colored people who were up and about — block after block, he passed all manner of working-class freedmen, off to paying jobs. Off to their fair and honest lives. Working of their own will, for their own profit.

He walked due west on Bridge Street, making good time on his way to the footbridge across the Potomac. He stopped briefly at a bakery, drawn in by the heavy aroma of fresh morning bread, but otherwise moved quickly. His mind was fairly made up to cross here into Virginia, and he was fingering a nickel in his pocket for the toll when he spotted it: the same canal boat he'd seen from the Rock Creek Bridge.

The crew was negotiating a final lock before they reached the flat haul out of the city. Dykes had to walk along the lock's edge in order to reach the toll bridge, which shared space with a grand aqueduct made to transport canal boats over the swift current of the Potomac. Man's ingenuity at its best.

An oarsman cast a lingering gaze at him as he neared the lock. Dykes raised a hand and shouted a good morning.

"Hello," the oarsman called back. Dykes stopped and watched the crew for a moment. The oarsman stayed on deck as one of the crew worked the lock gates. A third man helped a mule along the path up ahead. Dykes looked west along their route. A thought struck him, and he strode closer to the edge of the canal.

"Excuse me!" The crew, save the mule driver, looked his way. "Is there a good crossing up river from here?"

The oarsman looked off toward the aqueduct. "They don't come much better than that. Just a few other crossings between here and Harpers Ferry." His voice had a soft twang to it.

"Any near Leesburg?"

He nodded again. "White's Ferry. About thirty miles up. A long walk."

Dykes considered his options for a moment. To cross here would put him at least a day's walk from Leesburg, along uncertain roads. Tracking the canal west from here would provide more guidance. Still a long walk, though.

Dykes studied the boat as it idled in the lock. He called back to the oarsman, "How long a trip by boat?"

* * *

THE RIDE WAS a peaceful respite from the road Dykes had traveled thus far. He nestled in among his bags in an open hold, its plank floor and walls covered in a fine black dust. A few chunks of coal lay clustered in the corners. Fishing into his knapsack, he pushed a pistol to the side and took out the map Beth had given him. He folded it out over his other bag — a makeshift desk to keep the linen document off the dusty floor.

Scanning the town names, he found Leesburg just south of the Potomac. A ferry crossing was marked nearby, but not White's. Conrad's. Dykes searched around for White's, but it wasn't on the map. He looked up suspiciously at the oarsman, who stood with his back to the hold.

"Sir?" Dykes called. "I believe Conrad's Ferry will better suit my needs. How far up to that crossing?"

The oarsman turned and looked down at him. "What's that?"

"Conrad's Ferry. Near Leesburg."

The oarsman chuckled. "Old Coonrad's? It's no more. That's White's now. Been bought up and renamed." He spotted the map and gathered it was the source of the error. "Where'd you get that old thing? Don't know how useful it'll be if it's marked with Coonrad's."

Dykes squinted down at the mislabeled ferry crossing. "A friend. And it will do fine, I have no doubt."

"Okay. Well, off to Coonrad's then." The oarsman chuckled again and looked back upstream.

Dykes traced a finger from Conrad's Ferry to Leesburg along a straight road. He could be there by nightfall. He leaned back against the hold wall, crossed his legs at the ankles, and gazed up at the clear sky above.

* * *

THE RIDE WAS UNEVENTFUL, and the crew asked nothing of Dykes. He stayed out of their way, and they acted as if he was any other bit of cargo. He passed the time studying the map and reading one of a few books he'd brought along. Around midday he unwrapped the second oyster sandwich. Not as good after a day. The oysters had lost their snap, and their flavor was stronger. Pungent.

Several hours passed before the oarsman turned and called down to Dykes. "Your crossing. Coming up!"

Dykes gathered his things and stretched his legs, standing against the side of the hold as the crew worked the boat up along shore. Once steadied, he leapt off the deck down to the towpath and gave the crew a final wave. Traffic on the canal was light at the moment; within a few hours it would be clogged with boats floating loads of coal down from the Cumberland mines and east to Washington. They'd unload after the locks in Georgetown, only to start the journey over again after a brief night of rest.

Dykes crossed a small arched footbridge over the canal to the tree-lined northern bank of the Potomac. A rutted path led down through the woods, past a stone grain elevator to the shaded water's edge of the ferry crossing.

Two men on horseback were waiting just to the side of a short gravel ramp where the ferry sat, a sturdy raft about ten feet wide and twenty feet long. It was uncovered but for a frame and tarpaulin that created shade for its operator. A wooden sign across the frame read in bold white letters: Gen. Jubal A. Early. What this crossing had to do with the Confederate general, Dykes did not know.

A ferryman worked onboard under cover of the craft's canopy. Dykes approached him, nodding to the men on horseback as he passed.

"Next crossing?" Dykes asked.

"Could be now," he responded. "Five cents if you've got no horse or cart."

As the ferryman turned a wheel, the raft clinked along a fixed chain stretched across the expanse of the Potomac. The leafy canopy overhead rolled back to expose a clear blue sky as they pulled away from the bank. It was a perfect early spring day. Just as Dykes had remembered. This was it — this was the Virginia he had been longing for. He placed his hand on a rail to steady himself and gazed up, watching songbirds flit overhead. The sun warmed his face. The river was quiet, other than the steady slosh of water against the underside of the raft and the methodical crank of the ferry mechanism. Drawing him farther south, ratchet by ratchet.

The cranks slowed as the Jubal Early neared the southern bank, eventually easing to a stop against a short pier jutting into the water.

The ferryman locked his crank in place and threw a few ropes to the pier, where a colored man was waiting to tie the raft off. The ferryman dropped the loading gate, coughed, and called into the air, "Aa-ll off!"

Dykes filed out onto the dock behind the other passengers and took a first step back onto Virginian soil. He had arrived, the bleak North relegated to fading memories.

* * *

HAVING ALREADY STUDIED Beth's map at length, Dykes knew the walk from the ferry to Leesburg well. He figured it to be about four miles. It was a pleasant afternoon, nearing dinner time. Dykes took deep breaths of the clean air as he strode along the wide road, past rolling pastureland and fields, some freshly plowed, some freshly planted.

Houses clustered closer to the road as he neared town, and traffic picked up. He studied passersby with a heightened interest, musing through future acquaintances he might make. Though he had not yet been in Virginia for an hour, he felt his roots were taking hold.

Downtown Leesburg was crowned by the county courthouse, square and brick in the federal style. It was situated on a grassy plot, fenced from busy streets on its four sides. Dykes was immediately drawn to it. Its benches seemed as suitable a place as any to pause and get his bearings.

He tossed his bags to the side of a bench in the shade of a tall oak tree. The sun was beginning to sink lower but was still high enough to be caught in the branches above. Dykes sat down with a sigh and leaned over to retie one of his boots.

"Evening," a man croaked from the opposite end of the bench.

Dykes turned his head while still hunched over and reciprocated the greeting. The man was old and weather-worn, his bushy gray beard showing signs of recent neglect. He stared off into the town's streets and offered no further conversation.

Dykes sat up. "I'm new in town. Do you live nearby?"

"No."

"Passing through?"

"No." The man maintained his fixed gaze.

"Well, this sure is a beautiful town," Dykes said. The man gave no response. Dykes leaned toward him and offered a friendly handshake. "I'm Solomon Dykes. Fresh from a long journey from up north."

"Pleased to meet you." The man fixed his blue-gray eyes on him and shook his hand with a brittle grip. "The name's Tom Mosby."

CHAPTER 5

WHITE FEATHERS WERE STREWN across the ground, tracing a path out from the chicken pen.

"Ah, now don't tell me that," Mosby muttered. "Well, hell."

He ducked through a splayed hole in the thin wire fence and peered inside the coop. One hen was tucked in a dark corner, nestled over a patch of straw. Another was alive but crumpled on the floor, its wing fixed at an unnatural angle. Two hens and the rooster, missing.

He pulled his head out and surveyed the yard. The rooster was scratching at a piece of ground a dozen yards away. All else was quiet. The feathers were likely the only mementos of the other hens.

Mosby slipped through the hole in the fence and bent it back as best he could, crimping the edges over each other. He fixed his gaze on the rooster and hoisted his pants up. He went into a half squat and crept toward the oblivious bird. Within a few feet of it, he leapt, arms outstretched.

He landed squarely on the rooster, which shrieked in surprise and immediately started working its spurs into his chest. Mosby sprang up, holding the writhing bird at arm's length by its feet.

"And just what were you doing last night when those dogs

made off with our hens?" The rooster, unmoved by the rebuke, continued to thrash. Mosby walked back into the pen, through the gate this time, and tossed the rooster into a far corner. He ducked in and grabbed the injured hen by the feet and turned back toward the house, latching the gate behind him.

He paused at the wood pile by the porch and studied a few logs. He hefted a medium-sized piece and held it up for further inspection. Pleased with it, he lifted the bird and with a quick, hard swing, struck it in the head with the log. He put the log back and walked in through the porch.

Fannie was making breakfast in the kitchen when Mosby walked in.

"The dogs were back last night," he said.

"Oh, Lord. What did they do?"

"Made a mess of the chicken coop and supped on two of our hens." He hoisted the third up by its legs. "Looks like this one goes to us. She was badly broken when I found her."

"Chicken dinner?"

"Consider it a surprise treat."

"But without Pappy." Her eyes tracked the limp chicken as Mosby tossed it onto the table.

"I'm hopeful, Fannie. I know it looks bad, but I'm hopeful."

"He's never been out through a night before. Where would he sleep if he's not in town?"

"I don't know, but he'll make do, Butternut. I spread word in town, and he's bound to come across someone before too long. They'll get him back safely to us." Fannie didn't look convinced. "Okay, look. After I'm done with the Creek Field I'll hitch up Presh and take another look around."

Fannie sighed. "And I suppose I get to pluck this hen today?"

"I'll plow, you pluck. Deal?"

She wrinkled her nose. "Fine. But I want Pappy at the table tonight."

"I shall do my best." Mosby kissed her on a rosy cheek. "I'll be in for breakfast after I finish a few more chores." He turned and went back outside through the porch.

* * *

HE AND FANNIE had been up late the night before, waiting. Mosby had just assumed Pappy would turn up in town that afternoon. But he found not a trace of him. Mosby had lingered as long as possible — running his errands, spreading word of Pappy's wandering — but in the end returned home empty handed.

It had been years since Mosby had gone to bed with that kind of worry on his mind. And never about Pappy.

Pappy would disappear from time to time, but typically either walk in for dinner or turn up before sundown in the barn or a close field. Once, last fall, he had wandered a piece down the road, toward town, but never any further. This was the longest he'd been out, and Mosby knew his father's mind was faded and ill-equipped for any kind of long journey.

He likely carried nothing with him. Not a possession, a plan, or even a song to travel by, for he could no longer remember the words to his favorite hymns.

After breakfast, Mosby led Soupy out of the barn half hoping to find Pappy asleep in a stall. But no luck. The barn had been empty all night, but for the horse and the mule. Mosby shook his head as they passed the pillaged chicken pen. Feral dogs had been a growing problem since the war, and they roved the county in loose packs at night. Their usual wildings amounted to little more than toppled fences and missing chickens, but Mosby feared Pappy to be unexpected and easy prey.

Mosby passed the morning hours cutting rows and worrying about Pappy. His eyes were either fixed ahead in a vacant gaze or scanning the edges of the field for signs of familiar movement. His distraction led to several direct strikes on larger rocks, which served to jolt him back to the task at hand for a few moments but otherwise left him unfazed. Soupy was growing agitated.

He had packed a lunch of bread, cheese, and fatback left from breakfast and was finishing it against the plow when young John Stibbs began picking his way across the field. Mosby raised a hand in greeting but remained seated, forearms perched on knees before him.

The boy stopped halfway across the field and crouched over. He picked something up and was still examining it when he reached the plow.

"Hello, John. What did you find there?"

"Bird point." He held out his palm and displayed a small bit of flint chipped into a half-inch-long arrowhead.

"So it is! Look at that. You haven't even stacked a stone and you've already collected a day's wages."

The boy squinted down at him and dropped his hand to his side.

"I may be able to add to that, though," Mosby said. "We'll see how far you get."

He stood up and set the boy about his task, instructing him to get a cart and pointing out which rocks he wanted where. Goose Creek ran through the woods to the west of this field, and Mosby liked to maintain a short wall along that tree line. To the south of the Mosby plot was a similarly sized parcel owned by the Stibbs family. To the north was the turnpike.

Within a few more hours Soupy reached the end of the last row. "Whoa, boy." Mosby set the brake and stepped off, fishing a few bits of carrot out of his breast pocket. He palmed them out for the mule and gave him a few smacks on the neck. "Good work, Soup. I knew we could get through it."

The Stibbs boy was filling the cart midfield, so Mosby cupped his hands and shouted to him. "John!" The boy stopped and looked up. "I'm done here! Take a break when you need it, and come to the house after you finish two more rows!"

Mosby assumed the boy understood, as he went back to

work without pause or question. "Half-wit," Mosby muttered to himself. He lifted the plow blades and began leading the mule back to the barn.

* * *

MOSBY HAD FINISHED BRUSHING Soupy down and was about to hitch up Presh when the thought struck him to right a piece of fence that had fallen in the night. It was a part of what ringed the garden near the house — not a big job at all, but it had been bugging him since he'd noticed it this morning. Better to do it now before heading out, he thought.

He had hefted the end of the fallen crosspiece back between its posts when he heard a voice in the distance. He looked down their short drive to the road. Nothing. He squinted and kept his gaze fixed there for a moment. A man's head sprang up above a short rise. Then another, more slowly. Pappy, he thought.

"Pappy!" Mosby raised his arms in a wide wave. He trotted over toward them and suspiciously eyed his father's companion as the pair came into better view. He was clearly a traveler, stocky and carrying two sizable bags. The man steadied Pappy with an outstretched arm as they walked.

Mosby slowed a few yards away. "What in the hell, Pappy? Where did you get off to?"

The old man limped forward and patted him on the shoulder, walking on by toward the house. His beard was dusty on one side. Mosby studied him for a moment before turning to the stranger.

"Well, I can't imagine you'd planned on coming here today, but I thank you." He held his hand out and the stranger shook it.

"Not a problem, sir. Your father?"

"Yes. He doesn't usually wander from home like this."

"It's no trouble, but your father just had a fall here in the road. He hadn't been limping before now."

"Oh, my, I'll help him in then." Mosby turned and started

after Pappy. "You're welcome to join us for a spell," he called over his shoulder. "Please come on in."

"I will, thank you."

By the time they reached the porch Fannie had heard the exchange and was already at Pappy's side, wiping tears from the corners of her eyes. "My God, Pappy, where did you get off to?" Pappy kept walking, through the front door, and Fannie followed him in to his chair. He sat down and closed his eyes with a heavy sigh.

"I asked the same and got the same answer," Mosby said. He looked at Fannie and shrugged. "He just took a fall out front. Look him over and see if he needs mending."

She kneeled in front of Pappy's chair and felt his thin legs through his pants. He winced when she touched his knee. "Did you bang yourself up? You're lucky you made it back here in one piece. You realize you were gone all night?"

Pappy opened his eyes and looked down at her. "Gone all night? My ass I was gone all night. Does it look like morning to you?"

"No. No it don't, Pappy." She rose up stiffly to start for the kitchen and spotted the stranger just outside the open door. "Jeb! What are you doing, leaving that kind man idling out on the porch?"

"I didn't tell him to stay out there."

"Well, bring him in and introduce me! My Lord." She shook her head.

The man stepped in, gently leaned his bags against the door frame, and gave a slight bow to Fannie. "I apologize for not making myself known," he said. "I'm Solomon Dykes. Thank you for inviting me into your home."

"We should be thanking you!" Fannie said. "Pardon my husband. He has clearly forgotten his manners after being on a plow all morning."

"Okay, okay. I think he'll understand, given the circumstances," Mosby said, holding out his hand again. "And pardon me for not properly introducing myself. Jeb Mosby." They shook a second time. "And this is my wife, Fannie."

"Pleased to meet you, and I hope your father is all right," Dykes said "We met in Leesburg and have been traveling since breakfast."

"Leesburg?" Mosby near shouted. "What in the hell were you doing in Leesburg?"

"Leesburg?" Pappy parroted. "I went for a walk! Can't a man go for a walk without everyone getting all up in arms?"

Mosby sighed and looked back at Dykes. "Well I honestly can't thank you enough. I don't want to think what would have happened if he had been left to his own devices out there. We don't know anyone in Leesburg anymore."

"I think we were glad to have found each other," Dykes said. "I just crossed into Virginia yesterday evening, and I didn't have much of a sense of where I was going. Your father helped me with that."

Fannie came back in from the kitchen with a bowl of water and a washcloth. She rolled up Pappy's pant leg and started dabbing at his skinned knee. "How did you find us, anyway?" she asked.

"It was quite lucky, actually," Dykes said. "I introduced myself to your father, and once we got to talking I realized he was lost and not in the best shape to be getting found again."

Mosby laughed. "Well said."

"I asked where he was from, and he said Middleburg."

"So did someone in town point you our way?" Fannie asked.

"No, actually. We came straight here."

Pappy yelped as Fannie pressed the cloth against his wound. "My pant leg's gone wet. Why is my pant leg all wet?"

"This will help, Pappy." She blew gently on his knee to ease the sting. "So he led you here? I'm amazed!"

"Well, no, not exactly," Dykes said. "I have a map. Once your father said Middleburg I took it out to study, and lo and behold if his name isn't clearly marked on the bottom edge of the map."

"That a county map?" Mosby asked.

"Yes, an older one. I've noticed some of the river crossings and mills are wrong. But your land is clearly marked: 'Tho. Mosby.' He had introduced himself as Tom Mosby, so I put two and two together."

"God bless," Mosby said. "I remember when he paid to be put on that map. A man was going farm to farm asking families if they wanted to be marked. My mother was cross at him for days after that — saw it as a vain waste of money."

"It was of some merit in the end, I suppose," Dykes said.

"You hear that, Pappy?" Fannie said. "Did you see your name on Mr. Dykes' map?"

Pappy closed his eyes again and rested his head against the high back of his chair.

"I apologize for how he's acting," Fannie said. "He gets foggy when he's tired."

"Oh, it's quite alright, ma'am. We did some talking on the road. I know he means well."

"That's about as kind as it can be put," Mosby said. "I know it's early yet, but would you care to stay for supper? I'd say a little celebration is in order, and we happen to have a chicken in the pot. How is that coming, Fannie?"

"Out of the pot and over the fire, now," she answered.

"Then we have a chicken on the spit," he said, giving Dykes a wink.

"I appreciate the offer, but I should get on the road before dark," Dykes said. "Where would you recommend I stay for the night? Is there a decent patch of woods nearby?"

"Patch of woods?" Fannie said.

"Well, yes — I don't have much in the way of kit, but certainly enough to make for a comfortable night or two out-of-doors."

"You will do nothing of the sort!" Fannie said. "What kind of hosts would we be if we fed you and sent you off into the night, fare-thee-well?"

"Fine hosts," Mosby said. "There's a nice patch of trees five miles up the road." He grinned and cast a testing eye toward Fannie. She was not smiling. "Ah, I kid too much. Our hay loft is all yours. I would offer you a bed if we had a spare."

Dykes considered the offer a moment. "The loft would be more than welcome, thank you. I really can't thank you enough. For everything."

Mosby shook his head in protest. "Say no more, friend. You've made us rich in bringing Pappy home. It's the least we can do." He looked to Fannie, who nodded in agreement.

"Sounds wonderful, then. I could use a proper introduction to your county, anyway. Tom and I saw some of it today, and I'm ever amazed at the beauty in this valley."

"Excellent!" Mosby said. "Fannie, I told you we'd have reason for chicken tonight."

She smiled and walked back into the kitchen.

"Come, I'll show you to the loft. I've spent some nights up there myself," Mosby said. He hefted one of the bags over his shoulder, and the pair walked out through the porch and across to the whitewashed barn.

CHAPTER 6

WITH THE TABLE now set for four, Fannie had reason to make more of supper than the chicken stew she had considered. While the chicken was roasting nicely over the fire, she gathered some spring vegetables from the garden and dipped into a tin of cornmeal she'd been rationing. Cut and simmered asparagus, a salad of raw greens, and fry bread made good company for the tender meat. She nestled a cast-iron oven in the coals of the fireplace and, using the last few apples from cold storage, worked up a quick cobbler for dessert.

The men were seated in the living room, washed up and ready for supper, when Fannie set the last plate on the table. "Come on, then," she called into the next room. "You've all been stewing in there long enough."

Mosby was the first to get up and strode in to the table. "Well it's hard to keep away, Fannie. We smelled your chicken a half mile out from the house."

Dykes walked in after, followed by the senior Mosby. "This looks just wonderful," Dykes said. "It certainly was good fortune to have met your father how I did."

The four took their seats and Mosby motioned to pray, bowing his head and lightly clearing his throat. "Lord, thank you for the blessings you have granted us today. Send us anywhere, though accompany us. Lay any burden upon us, though sustain us. Sever any ties but those that bind us to thine heart. Bless this food to the nourishment of our bodies and our souls to the service of Christ. Amen."

"Amen," the others echoed.

Dykes felt he had barely eaten in days and didn't quite know where to start. After the disappointing sandwich he'd had on the canal, he had hoped for a decent meal in Leesburg. But looking after Tom had proved taxing, and the pair were barely able to have a cup of soup at the ordinary they'd found for the night. Breakfast hadn't been much more filling — a biscuit for each topped with thin gravy. Lunch had been forgotten once Tom was returned home.

He pushed up his sleeves and started with a bite of the fry bread. Warm and buttery, with a welcome soft grit to it.

"I feel I spent all afternoon talking about our land," Mosby said. He looked to Fannie. "We must have walked near abouts every inch of the place."

She nodded and carved a piece of the chicken. "Mr. Dykes, please have the bosom."

"Why, thank you," Dykes said. "I enjoyed the walk. This kind of country is what brought me to Virginia in the first place. Most recently, I should say."

"So where are you coming from, anyway?" Mosby asked. "I feel a fool having not already asked, but I think I've proven I'm not the most thoughtful of hosts."

"Connecticut. North of Bridgeport, if you know it. I came down by train through New York the day before last, stopping in Washington for the night."

"Washington!" Mosby said. "Filthy place, isn't it?"

"From what I saw, yes. For the most part."

Pappy glanced up as he hovered over his plate, chicken skin dangling from his clinched teeth. "It is filthy. A filthy place."

"It's not as I had remembered it," Dykes said. "Seems the basic infrastructure has been ignored."

"Well, you may find that to be true in a lot of parts down here," Mosby said. "Seems if you get your infrastructure shot to hell for four years it takes some time to bounce back. Who knew?"

"What ground your father and I covered this morning was lovely. Your county has fared well, wouldn't you say?"

"Compared to others, yes," Mosby said.

Dykes turned the piece of chicken in his hands before taking a bite. It was lean but succulent. Gamey but expertly seasoned. "This is a fine meal, ma'am."

Fannie waved him off. "I'm just glad to be able to cook for a full table. Hard to justify a meal like this when it's just these two."

Mosby nodded. "Another reason I'm thankful for your arrival, Solomon."

Dykes took a drink of water and gazed off thoughtfully for a moment. "I've been meaning to ask you folks," he started. "Are you all kin to John Mosby?"

Mosby rested a forkful of food on the edge of his plate and sat back.

Dykes knew of John Mosby from newspapers and word of mouth during the war. He was a lawyer from Warrenton, in the next county over. He grew up further south, near Charlottesville, and graduated with high marks from the University of Virginia — Thomas Jefferson's own jewel of higher learning. He was smart, well-liked, widely respected, and headstrong, all of which served him well in the war.

Very well, in fact, to the chagrin of occupying Union forces. Mosby became a colonel with Jeb Stewart's cavalry, but soon took to his own style of fighting. He and his men would prey upon those enemies who let their guard down, using guerrilla tactics to cripple supply lines and confound Union commanders. Their attacks became more brazen as time passed. It was widely told that Mosby once snuck into the quarters of a sleeping enemy officer, smacking him soundly on his naked back to wake him and take him prisoner. He and his Raiders were legend.

"Nossir." Jeb said flatly. "Wrong Mosby."

"A fair question and an honest mistake," Fannie said patiently.

Mosby raised his hand to quiet her. "Don't think I'm going to jump all over him, Fannie. I have manners enough to do right by a guest in my home, though I know you think otherwise." He turned to look at Dykes. "I will put it this way. I am a Virginian. John Mosby is a Republican."

Pappy nodded in agreement. "I seen him speak up for Grant."

"He's doing more than that, Pappy," Mosby said. "Point is, our family — me and Pappy and my mother, that is — came up from Newport News in the '30s. Our name is of French descent. Pappy changed the spelling so people would get the pronunciation right. So, no. Hope not to disappoint, but no kin to the Gray Ghost here."

"I had to ask," Dykes said. "When I met your father, it's the first thing that came to mind, especially being in Leesburg. I've heard many a tale about Mosby. I had assumed he was still spoken of fondly here."

"You'll find assorted opinions around these parts," Mosby said. "He served his allegiance well during the war. Just seems his allegiances have since changed."

"Jeb, I did not cook all afternoon to hear your views of John Mosby," Fannie said. "Mr. Dykes, why don't you tell us more about where you're from."

"There's not much to tell, really. That's why I'm here. I wanted to start a new life, away from the cold of Connecticut."

"It gets cold here, you know," Mosby said.

"It's a different kind of cold. This land is rich, and it comforts me. The land of Washington, Jefferson, Madison. I see why they all loved it so. I want to be a part of it."

"Well, you've done that," Mosby said. "You spent a night and a morning with Tom Mosby. I think that grants anyone honorary citizenship on account of good works. And ungodly patience."

"We love our Pappy," Fannie said as she leaned over and patted her father-in-law on the arm. He looked up from his plate, somewhat confused.

"I didn't vote for Grant," he said.

Fannie sighed. "Who wants cobbler?"

*   *   *

THEY TOOK their cobbler in the sitting room, by a fire Mosby kindled from a cooking coal. As they sat, Mosby poured two tin cups of whiskey for himself and Dykes. He cooled his with a splash of creek water and hovered the jug over Dykes' cup.

"Branch?" he asked.

"Yes, thank you." Mosby splashed some water in the cup and passed it over.

"Cheers." He raised his tin cup. Dykes did the same and nodded before he took a drink. The whisky was smooth and earthy.

"So you've seen our county, and you love every bit of it," Mosby said. "You plan to settle nearby?"

Dykes thought for a moment, savoring a spoonful of warm cobbler. "I suppose," he said. "Funny, but I had never thought through this part. The in-between part. Traveling comes naturally, so that was no trouble. And my future is clear in my mind: working a piece of ground as you do here. Mountains over my shoulder, a family across the field in a saltbox house."

"The in-between part is a stinker," Mosby said. "There's a lot between this here cobbler by the fire and that life you're thinking on. And that's if things go smoothly."

Fannie chimed in. "I think he'll manage just fine, Jeb. Think of how you had it starting out up here. Didn't know a soul." She leaned toward Dykes. "When I met him, all I knew him for was talking to goats."

Dykes looked at Mosby, puzzled.

"I had things to say, and the goats weren't going nowhere," Mosby said.

"It was strange," Fannie continued. "My mother thought I had lost my mind when I brought him home."

"Pappy, are you going to help me out? Tell this kind man about your upstanding son."

"You milked the goats. Every day," Pappy said into his cobbler dish.

"I can assure you there was no milking going on when I saw him chatting it up with that goat," Fannie said. "He was squatting on a rock, eye to eye with the beast. Just talking away. Motioning and carrying on — you would have thought they were locked in debate." She and Dykes exchanged a glance and laughed.

"Okay, fine," Mosby said. "I could have made better friends. But back to the topic at hand. Where do you plan on settling, Solomon?"

"Where would you recommend?" Dykes asked.

"Well this valley is just fine," Mosby said. "Spared a good bit during the war, as we've discussed. That's relative, of course. But I think a man could do a lot worse than Loudoun. There's Middleburg down the road, Aldie, Waterford, Leesburg. All nice towns. Good spread of mills and churches. Yes, a man could do worse."

"And Washington isn't but a day's trip away," Dykes added.

"You can keep Washington and those big bugs in the capitol building. Winchester. There's a better use of your time on the road," Mosby said. "That said, there's always the valley. Over the mountains you see to the west there. You can get through the ridge through a gap not too far off, along the turnpike you came in on today. And the Shenandoah Valley is just beautiful. I'd be there, if it weren't for our land here."

"I have a lot to consider," Dykes said. "Were you to find yourself in my position, where would you start? How does one move from being a guest in a hayloft to a landowner in these parts?"

Mosby considered the question and rolled a sip of whisky around with his tongue, relishing its burn. "Yes, a fine question. Thankfully one I don't have to answer for myself, but a fine one nonetheless. I hate to say it, but I believe where you came from yesterday was as good a spot as any. The Leesburg courthouse would have news of any land auctions of interest to you. Assuming you have funds for that sort of thing. Otherwise, find a town you like and work a job."

"Thankfully the funds shouldn't be an issue," Dykes said. "Leesburg. That is a help. At least I know the road between here and there."

* * *

DYKES AND MOSBY finished their drinks while Fannie cleared the table and Pappy went off to bed. As the fire died down, Mosby lit a lantern and walked Dykes out across the yard to the barn. It was a clear night, and chilly. He pointed out the privy along the way, a small outhouse set several paces out from the kitchen door.

Soupy and Presh were standing in their stalls but remained still when the men walked in. The animals took little notice as the lantern sent a warm light spilling across the barn floor.

Mosby motioned to a ladder toward the back of the room. "That's you," he said. "Plenty of hay up there to keep you warm, and you've got the blankets Fannie readied for you."

"I'm all set. Thank you, Jeb."

"I'm glad we can accommodate. You take this lantern on up — there's a hook for it up there, and I can find my way back. Just be careful up there with the fire."

"Of course. I'll shut it soon after you leave, anyway."

"Okay then. Well, have a good night's sleep. Holler if you need anything."

"Will do. Goodnight."

Mosby handed him the lantern and walked into the night. There was a half-moon out. It cast enough light to dim the stars and highlight faint wisps of breath as Mosby walked back to the house. From the porch, he looked back to the barn. Light shone softly through its upper vent for a moment, and then the lantern went out.

CHAPTER 7

Tuesday, January 13, 1863

I have lapsed in my entries, and since last writing a new year has arrived — it has been a long year, indeed, since leaving Connecticut for the war. A bit of good news, though: I am now a freshly minted second lieutenant, awarded citing actions during an engagement with the rebels at Georgia Landing. Though I am honored, it is what I am learning to be a standard promotion, part through only very minor heroics of my own and part through the bad luck in combat of those above me in rank.

Our time spent occupying New Orleans was interesting, as mentioned in past entries, but the bayous surrounding it afford little to my liking. The winter months do somewhat lessen the oppression of the swamp, but I wouldn't go so far as to say the weather provides any relief. It creates an odd sort of balminess, where one wakes to a chill in the morning but soon breaks a clammy sweat under any physical labor. The sky is a perpetual and glaring bright-gray, the trees bare and dark in relief against it but for draperies of Spanish moss. An odd land, Louisiana.

We've recently reorganized into the 19ᵗʰ Corps, under a Major-General Banks, who I have not yet seen. From my understanding, our corps is to be grown by others new to the Western front, making us the veterans. Experts in the lay of the land, so to speak.

It is all water and spongy ground between, so a large part of our duty has become support of river vessels. As such, today was notable. Our current camp is cut from the supply line by the Bayou Teche — a river with raggedly defined boundaries, creeping into the surrounding woodlands and crisscrossed by all manner of rivulets. At times it can be difficult to discern where the river edge ends, although at one portion free of trees, a complement of engineers constructed a respectable seawall along the embankments, creating a means for reliable ferry crossing. This morning I was paired with an aide-de-camp and two enlisted men to make the crossing and deliver a list of needed supplies to the depot on the eastern side. I was pleased with the orders. A break from the regiment at large would do me good.

And it did, to a point. Although at the moment it may have become too much of a break. Our small cohort, having made a fruitful trip of delivering orders to the supply depot, was returning to the river crossing when there came a commotion from the river. It was out of sight, a thick stand of cypress between us and the river, but there came a series of whoops and taunts, followed by musket fire and a volley of what sounded like small cannon. We quickly armed ourselves and, hunkered low, made our way through the cypress to a view of the river.

There before us lay a wreckage of smoldering wood that had been the ferry landing, a few injured men and others running downriver along the bank, in pursuit of a sidewheel steamer churning up the muddy water behind it. The craft was what I learned this evening to be a cottonclad — I admit I had to laugh at the absurdity of the concept when I first heard the term. It was a large ship, but fast and lightly armored, protected by bales of cotton stacked wherever possible, presumably to absorb some amount of fire. A makeshift casemate topped her deck between two tall smokestacks, again made out of a ring of cotton bales from which her crew could fire. A tall flagpole tipped its stern, flying the rebel Navy ensign — a flag that has puzzled me for its rather striking resemblance to Old Glory herself. Its crew made quite a ruckus as it steamed away, firing shots at the shoreline, seemingly indiscriminately, and peering out around the bales.

We ran to the aid of those injured and helped them back away from the water's edge, to safety. We are presently bivouacked on a patch of dry ground in the cypress stand, awaiting passage on a transport ship coming from upriver.

All has been quiet since the Confederate steamer made its presence known, but it has us admittedly spooked. The swamp has an unnatural stillness about it, and I fear its bogs and marshlands hide enemies all too easily overlooked. I shall be glad to have the sun up once more, and to make passage back to camp on the morrow.

CHAPTER 8

DYKES ROSE EARLY, jolted awake as a storm rolled through the valley. He backed down the ladder and neared the open door to take in a better view of the rain. It was coming in hard and diagonally, blasted by a violent wind in the gray morning light. The mule rested lazily, but the small horse was agitated and fidgeting in her stall.

He stood with arms crossed and breathed deeply as the rain hammered at the barn's tin roof. A chilly mist blew in and wet his face. He heard thunder roll far off at the head of the storm, maybe five miles away. It was moving fast. Within a few minutes the rain slacked and turned to a drizzle.

Dykes neared the horse and held his hand out, trying to reassure it. "It's okay, girl. It's passed." Her nostrils flared lightly and she jerked from his open palm. He turned and climbed back up to change clothes and collect his things.

On the front porch, Dykes stamped his boots free of mud and rested his bags by the door. He opened it slightly and rapped a knuckle on the wood, peering inside. "Mrs. Mosby?" he called back into the kitchen, sensing activity.

"Come on in," she answered. "Jeb's gone to walk a few fences."

Dykes walked in and gave her a nod. "Good morning."

" 'Morning, Mr. Dykes! That was quite a blow we had there."

"It served well in getting me out of bed." Dykes took a seat at the table as she busied herself by the fire. The senior Mosby must have still been in bed. "Jeb didn't want to take the horse?"

"No, he usually walks the lines when they need checking," she said. "He likes the activity in the morning."

"Does he think the storm did any damage?"

"He's taking a look to be safe, but it was through here so fast. We should be alright." She turned and wiped her hands on an apron tied around her thick waist. "How about some breakfast?"

"That sounds fine, thank you. You and Jeb are spoiling me."

"Hardly." She forked two eggs out of a skillet and put them on a plate, along with a biscuit. "Milk?"

"Why yes, thank you. Do you have goats?"

"We do. They usually stick to the field behind the house, keeping scarce. We have three. Mary, Moses, and Job." She put the plate down in front of him and poured a glass of milk from a heavy jug.

Dykes took a bite of biscuit and sat back, smiling. "Mrs. Mosby, I have a question for you."

"Please."

"The horse, the mule, your goats. They all have such wonderful names."

"It's like they're family, isn't it?"

"I think it's wonderful. Does that come from you or Jeb?"

"Neither. We're not so creative as to come up with all those names." She sat down at the end of the table and took a bite of a biscuit. "Those names came from our daughter. Maybelle."

Dykes studied her face and knew he had broached a sore subject. "Maybelle. That is a pretty name." He eyed her and let that hang in the air for a moment. "How old is Maybelle?"

"She would have been twenty-one. Can you believe that? Twenty-one years old." She put her half-eaten biscuit on the table. "But the Lord took her from us. During the war."

"I am so sorry, ma'am," Dykes said. "That is so sad to hear."

She leaned over and patted the back of his hand. "It is sad. Thank you."

The front door swung open and smacked the wall behind it. Fannie sat up with a start as Jeb pounded into the kitchen in muddy boots. "Well damnation, Fannie."

"Jebediah, the language! We have company, and need I remind you there is a lady present?"

"Okay then." He stared at the floor and pursed his lips. "Cuss it. We've got a tree down in the High Field. A big one."

"Can't you plant around it?"

"I would like nothing better than to plant around it, Fannie, but it's landed square in my irrigation ditch. Right down the goddamned middle of it. Got to be bucked. Damn pain in my ass."

Dykes stared into his milk glass, now saddled with an unspoken obligation that he wasn't sure he wanted to take on. He had planned to return to Leesburg after breakfast.

"My luck Stibbs is still laid up with a sore back," Mosby muttered.

"We'll you could always pay John Junior to help," Fannie said.

"I swear, that Stibbs boy. It would take twice the time and I would be twice as dumb for it. That boy has rocks in his head, Fannie."

Dykes took a sip of milk and cleared his throat. "Jeb, you realize you've got an able pair of hands here at your breakfast table?"

"I'm sure you have better things to do than buck a tree in the mud."

"It's no problem, really." Dykes wiped his mouth with the back of his cuff. "Maybe you could share a bit more with me about the county as we work. I could stand to get a primer on my new surroundings."

Jeb grabbed his hat off his head and straightened up taller. "A winning take for me, then! If you really wouldn't mind, I would be grateful. I'll pay with more than verbiage, too."

"It would be my pleasure," Dykes said. "But no need for any payment. Let's just get this thing done."

"I like the way this man works, Fannie."

"You are a lucky man, Jeb," she said. "Found your Pappy and now cleaning up your mess. This one is a keeper."

Dykes shook his head and sopped up a bit of egg yolk with his biscuit. "Just glad to help."

* * *

THE MORNING SUN had burned through any remaining clouds by the time Dykes and Mosby had gathered the handful of necessary tools and carted them up the slope behind the house to the High Field. As they walked, the wet grass passed its chill up their pant cuffs.

The source of Jeb's frustration became clear when they stepped within view of the toppled poplar. At the eastern edge of the field, a massive ball of earth and tangled roots jutted some fifteen feet into the air, leaving a crater of clay and loose stone beneath it. The girth of the tree—an easy three feet in diameter—filled a long span of an irrigation ditch running down the middle of the field.

"Isn't that a sonofabitch?" Mosby said. He put his hands on his hips and eyed the tree. "I dug that ditch some years back. It runs through to a spring and keeps this portion of the field in production. Water runs off otherwise and my corn dries up midseason."

"So how do you want to do this?" Dykes asked. He had no timbering experience, aside from splitting firewood.

"We buck it with that crosscut saw you're carrying, wedging it as we go to keep the blade from binding up. We can limb it as we go. Once it's all to bits, I'll hitch Soupy and haul it into the woods. But that's another day."

"Buck it?"

"Cut it into sections. Do I need to get the Stibbs boy?" Mosby grinned.

"I'll manage fine," Dykes said. "But I admit this will be my first bit of sawyering."

Mosby walked on ahead toward the root ball. "I bet they don't grow them like this in Connecticut." He stood and surveyed the lower span of the tree, angled off the ground where it connected at the roots. He walked up to it and patted a spot low on the trunk. "We'll start here. Hand me that saw. And come around the other side of the tree."

Dykes did as instructed and watched as Mosby made a few initial cuts across the trunk, etching a groove in the bark. Once he had cut a half inch or so down, he nodded toward the handle of the saw on Dykes' side of the tree.

"Okay, you grab that and hold it steady when I pull. This blade cuts on the pull. Just go loose when I pull, and I'll do the same on your pulls."

"No pushing?"

"No, it could warp the blade. You don't want to push, anyway. That will wear your ass out before lunch." Dykes put both hands on the wooden handle and Mosby started in with his first good pull. The blade skipped out of the groove and grazed the bark. "Okay then." He reset the blade in the groove and hauled back again. This time it cut along the track he'd made. "That's better."

Dykes pulled back and sawdust spat out below the blade on his side of the trunk.

"That's it," Mosby said. "And away we go." The two leaned back and forth on the saw in a slowly speeding rhythm. The long teeth of the blade steadily chewed through the tree as they worked, making a satisfyingly throaty hum on each pull. Once the blade was halfway through the trunk, Mosby hammered a wedge in at the top portion of the cut. Within what seemed like five minutes or so the blade neared the bottom of the trunk. Quicker than Dykes had expected.

"Okay, it'll likely fall when we cut through," Mosby said. "Just drop the blade down with it." He pulled back with one more, hard cut, and it was through. The trunk fell free from the section still attached to the roots and sagged toward the ground. Its limbs rustled all the way up its length, bracing it from lying flat along the muddy ground.

Dykes surprised himself with a shout. "Ha! Look at that."

"Nicely done. Now how many more cuts do you reckon?" Mosby stretched his back and gazed toward the crown of the tree. He sighed. "Pain in my ass."

Over the next hour or so they repeated the steps, cutting several more chunks to be strapped up to Soupy and dragged into the nearby woods. When they had cut their way up to the first lower branches of the tree, Mosby sized up their progress.

"We're making good time," he said. He walked over and rustled one of the closest branches. He held his hand on it for a moment and looked up at the sky. "You know what?"

Dykes left it as a rhetorical question.

"We don't have a damn hand saw."

"Take a break and I'll get it from the barn. Where do you keep it?"

Mosby shook his head. "Just so happens we don't have a hand saw, as in I lent it to Stibbs a week ago yesterday and still haven't seen it come back. What do you think he could be cutting down there, anyway?" He spat and thought a moment. "Okay, well. I'll go fetch it from him. You can take a break here."

"I'll join you, if you wouldn't mind the company."

"Shoot, no. Suit yourself. It's not a bad walk. Just the next house down the road."

The pair stowed their tools under the fallen tree and turned to go back down the hill, past the house and to the road. They took a right and walked for a few minutes under the cover of a tree canopy, which grew denser over the road past the Mosby house. It was colder in the shadows of the trees, and an occasional breeze rustled raindrops out of the top branches, wetting them lightly on the walk.

Unlike the Mosby house, which was hidden from the road, the Stibbs place was only a few dozen yards off. It was a two-story cube of cut stone, with two chimneys flanking its sides. The trim was a dingy white, and aside from the clutter in the yard surrounding it — scattered broken tools, a half-fallen clothesline — the smallish house looked quite grand for its size. As they approached the front door, Dykes noticed the rank smell of hogs hanging heavy in the air. A few chickens scattered aimlessly away from them.

"He just lets them roam free," Mosby said. "Miracle dogs, raccoons, and foxes haven't made off with the lot of them."

Mosby took his hat off and knocked loudly on the door. All was quiet. He looked over his shoulder at Dykes. "Probably trying to find a hiding place for that saw." Dykes chuckled.

He raised his hand to knock again and the door swung open. A tall man with a bushy black beard and greasy, parted hair greeted them. His shirtfront strained to contain the paunch of his belly. He nodded at Mosby. "Jeb."

"John," Mosby greeted in reply. "I seen more of your son than you lately. How's your back?"

"Keeping me from work." He eyed Dykes.

"This is a friend passing through," Mosby said. "Sol Dykes, down all the way from Connecticut. Helping me with a tree that fell in the High Field."

Dykes nodded and shook Stibbs' meaty hand.

"I said he's helping me with a tree that fell," Mosby said. Stibbs stared blankly at him. "Only one way I know to fix a tree that fell." Still nothing. "Damnit, John, you've got my saw."

Stibbs scratched his chin through his beard. "So I do. Sure, sure. Sorry about that, Jeb. One minute and I'll fetch it for you." He shuffled back into the house and left the door open. Dykes could make out some ratty furniture in the darkness within. The floor was good solid plank, though, and had a polished sheen to it. A faint musty smell drifted out into the fresh air. Cabbage, maybe. Some type of old vegetable.

Stibbs reappeared with the handsaw, a fine looking tool with a fairly ornate carved handle.

"Thank you for the loan, Jeb. Did the trick."

"What were you cutting, anyway?"

"We had a sow that died on us."

"Jesus, John. This is a woodcutting saw." He thumbed the blade. "Well, I thank you for cleaning it, I suppose. Tell Dottie and John Junior hello for me. He did a good job picking rocks for me yesterday, you know. He's a hard worker."

"He's not a bad boy. Send our best to Fannie, now."

Jeb gave a half-salute with the saw's handle and stepped back out into the yard. After the door shut he motioned to some outbuildings and a pen to the side of the house.

"They keep pigs. I can't say he's ever seemed to have had much luck with them. They're either scrawny or dying whenever I get word of them."

"How much land does he have here?" Dykes asked as they neared the road.

"Same plot size as us — about a hundred acres. Just right if you ask me. He doesn't do much with his fields, though. Mainly grows alfalfa for the pigs."

"The place does seem a bit run-down."

"Yeah, it's a shame," Mosby said. "It's a nice old place. Family that was in before the Stibbs kept it up right, and you should have seen their wheat. But they're good folks. Quiet and keep to themselves. Best kind of neighbors to have."

They walked back along the road in silence. Dykes occasionally gazed off into the woods to their left, studying the old-growth trees and the clean, rolling earth beneath them. This was good country.

CHAPTER 9

Dykes slipped out of the barn before first light the next day, being careful to straighten the loft behind him as he'd found it. He gave the animals a fistful of hay each and reached again for Presh. She conceded this time and leaned in as he rested his hand against the warm velvet of her muzzle. "That's a girl," he whispered. She closed her eyes.

He purposefully avoided the house, feeling as though he'd imposed enough on the Mosbys, but did want to get another look around from what they called the High Field. He had paid little attention to the sweeping views it afforded during the previous day's work. By the time he had trudged up to the open expanse of the field, the sun was beginning to cast its long arms out across the valley. Stepping through firming mud trodden with sawdust, he hoisted himself up on one of the taller portions of the fallen poplar. Wind and rain had toppled what was once girth to height.

The foothills of Middleburg and it surrounds rolled out between the mighty Shenandoah Ridge and the smaller, though still formidable, Bull Run Range. It was fertile ground, fed by eons of runoff from the pair of ranges hemming it in. It reminded Dykes of parts of Massachusetts he'd visited, although the speckled greens of spring seemed more lush. The fields older, but cleaner.

Over the ridge to the west, the broad Shenandoah Valley gave way to the wilds of what was now West Virginia. To the east, the foothills spread to piedmont and the bottomlands of the Potomac. This part of the county had escaped him during the war, but he felt more tied to it than any other he'd seen.

He cut across country to the turnpike, following Jeb's description of the property so as to avoid the possibility of being spotted from the house. When he reached the road he stopped to have a bit of cheese and bread for breakfast. He screwed off the cap to his canteen with one hand while unfolding Beth's map with the other.

Although he had hoped to find a better route to Leesburg than what had brought him to the Mosby plot, it didn't seem to exist. He thought it best to head east, through Aldie, before picking his way north to the Old Carolina Road — a straight shot to Leesburg, its courthouse, and his next order of business. The route took him along two major roads, providing more opportunities to hitch a ride. Two seats in a miller's wagon had made all the difference when he had traveled with Tom Mosby.

The walk to Middleburg was quiet this morning but went quickly enough. The road was good for walking, the air was cool, and Dykes was able to cover the distance through the rolling countryside in just over an hour. As he neared town an impressive stone wall that he had been following for half a mile or so cut at an angle away from the road. In its place ran a raised plank sidewalk, so Dykes stepped up onto it. His boots tamped out a rapid and satisfying beat as he walked briskly over the planks.

Though he had not passed through Middleburg before a few days ago, he knew it had weathered a good deal of skirmishing during the war. As was the case with many towns in this fringe south of the Potomac, it had changed hands many times. A home might be a Union field hospital one day, a rebel map room the next. An acquaintance from Connecticut had served in the 8th Regiment Infantry and spoken of Middleburg. Dykes thought of him as he squinted through the rising sun at a tall stone inn up ahead.

"We approached the town from the southwest, just at dawn," his friend had started. The two had been passing a bottle of whisky one chilly November night after the war. "The rebs were holding the town then, and we weren't looking to take it — a few from my platoon had heard tale of some hogs kept fenced at the town's edge. Livestock had been all but culled in the countryside." He pulled from the bottle. "Oh, and we found those hogs, alright. Three fat sows. We slipped that gate open and leashed two of them, sneaking out with a pair of us on each. I could taste the bacon. We decide to move back from town single file, along the roadbed. The boys ahead of us made it just fine, so we followed in their tracks. But our sow got ornery, squealed and bucked out into the road. Goldblum, the guy I was with, stumbled out with her and cursed. And that was it." He stopped.

"That was what?" Dykes asked.

"That was the worst I ever saw. There was a shot, and the sow grunted and went down. I turned to look up the road but was met square in the face with the rising sun. Still, I swear I saw it. I saw a glint up on the second tier of an inn's balcony. A sharpshooter reloading fast. I looked back and locked eyes with Goldblum, and time stopped. I yelled something. I have no idea what, but it doesn't matter. It was the last words he heard, but it doesn't matter. It's trivial. His face — forehead, eyes, nose — just ... and the worst was the sound he made. He didn't fall over straight out, he let out a bleat, like that sow. Staggered. Then fell. That was the worst I ever saw."

Dykes looked up at the inn's balcony as he walked. It was empty. Quiet. The sound of some chickens fussing somewhere nearby. A hammer doing work far down the road.

He didn't care to stop in town, but as he walked he took in the sights of a community getting about its day. It was peaceful.

A shopkeeper unlatching his door, an old woman sweeping her stoop. Moving forward in time, away from the blood that had once soaked this thoroughfare. Some soldiers loitered in an alley between two storefronts, and Dykes gave them a nod as he passed. They looked like schoolboys.

Traffic was picking up on the other side of town, and Dykes began scanning for potential rides. He felt he could be picky, and let several loaded carts pass without glancing up at the drivers. Before too long he heard the light rattle of an empty wagon behind him. He turned and walked backward for a moment as he eyed the driver.

He was a colored man, probably about his age and clean shaven.

Dykes raised a hand and the driver slowed. " 'Morning," Dykes called to him.

"Good morning, sir. Need assistance?"

"I'm traveling to Leesburg. If you could spare the room, I would be obliged for any distance you could take me."

The driver pulled his buckboard to a stop and looked down at Dykes. "Leesburg?" He took a breath and considered the stranger before him. "Well come on up, then. I'm heading just north of there."

"Many thanks," Dykes tossed his bags into the back of the wagon and hoisted himself up next to the driver on a worn wooden bench. "I'm Solomon Dykes." He held out his hand and the driver shook it.

"Pleasure, Mr. Dykes. My name is Cassius Freeman." He wore silver-rimmed spectacles and a nice gray jacket of tightly knit wool over a flannel shirt.

"The pleasure is mine." Dykes smiled and settled against the stiff back of his seat.

* * *

THE PAIR JOSTLED along the turnpike through Aldie before

turning north onto the hard-packed earth of the Old Carolina Road.

Freeman held his back straight and tipped his chin up slightly, keeping his eyes on the road. "So you're not from here," he said matter-of-factly. "Massachusetts?"

"You're good, but no. Connecticut. My accent is that strong?"

"That and your kit." He motioned toward the luggage with a jerk of his head. "Folks don't carry things like that around here."

Dykes looked back at his black leather knapsack, its US brand face up, and his patterned double-handled satchel. "I suppose I might stand out."

"To those with the right eyes you do."

They rode in silence for a mile or so through thickening trees marked with scattered boulders. A slope in the woods gave tell of the west face of the Bull Run range. They passed a narrow side road that wound up the hill. It seemed seldom used. A sign where it split was marked "Negro Mountain." Dykes reached back for his bag and riffled through it with one hand until he felt the soft folds of the map. He unfolded it gently on his lap and studied it, tracing his finger east from Middleburg to find their present location.

Freeman eyed the map while keeping his head straight. "Nice map. You lost?"

"No, just like to get my bearings as we go. This land is all new to me."

They rode along a little further.

Freeman broke the silence again. "That is a real fine map you've got. One of the best. Where'd you come by it?"

"A friend. You sound as if you're familiar with it."

"Well sure — that's Mr. Taylor's map."

Dykes glanced down at the map's title: Loudoun County Virginia, from Actual Surveys, by Yardley Taylor. "You know Yardley Taylor?"

"Sure, I do. He lives in Lincoln. Goose Creek to some. Not too far from here."

Dykes sat back, impressed. "I'll be. That's something else! His map sure has been a help to me. So are you familiar with Negro Mountain? I thought that was Bull Run Mountain."

"Yes, it is that. Negro Mountain is a community up on the ridge there. Real kind folks," Freeman said. "I've passed through a time or two. It was actually where I stayed when I first came through the county. That was fifteen years back. Hasn't changed much."

"I'm finding this county does have its share of kind folks," Dykes said.

Freeman smiled. "It's a nice place. There's bad apples, like anywhere, but better than most."

A cart loaded with sacks of flour passed on the left. Freeman nodded and Dykes raised a hand. "There's a mill up ahead," Freeman said. "One thing you won't find around here is a shortage of mills. If you want work, that's a good bet. Not to say I know your business."

"No, I thank you for the tip. I actually have my mind set on farming. So I may be on the business end of those mills, if I'm lucky."

"Good land for it here. You farm back up North?"

"Not to speak of. My father had a bit of land and we grew vegetables, but we made no money from it. We worked in plate and Britannia ware. Tea sets and the like."

"Britannia ware? Has a silver-type sheen to it?"

"That's the stuff. We worked for my uncle. My father never had a taste for bookwork, so I was to take over the business. It wasn't for me, though. After the war, I had no real ties up there and certainly didn't want to spend the rest of my days turning out tea kettles."

"So you served." Freeman maintained his fixed gaze ahead.

"I did. First Lieutenant, 12th Connecticut Infantry."

"I thank you for your service, sir. Strange times we live in. Amazing times."

"They are indeed."

"What made you come back South?"

Dykes stared off into the woods. The terrain was flattening out as they rounded a pass through the ridge. "I like it here. And I wanted to do some good." He chose his next words carefully. "I imagine in these times your people need advocates. Just want to be here to help."

"We have good folks down here who have long looked out for our interests. They stick their necks out when they need to, but they have families here. Friends in the community. They have roots. You afraid you might draw the wrong kind of attention?"

Dykes searched for the right answer, but Freeman began again before he could speak.

"No offense, sir, but I do want to tell it to you straight — you're a Yankee. Fish out of water," Freeman said. "Some may misjudge your being here as motivated by opportunity, despite your noble intentions. Unfortunately, men have come before you seeking to profit from the South's present transitory state."

"I know the stigma. But I feel it's something I need to do. I need to be here at this time. I don't know how else to put it. I've seen horrible things over these past years, things I never could have imagined. I've also seen your people treated in ways I never could have imagined. I wasn't an abolitionist before the war, and for that I am ashamed."

Freeman turned his head toward Dykes. "Now why would you be ashamed for a thing like that? You never left Connecticut, I'm guessing?"

"Not this far south, no. Not before the war."

"You can't be ashamed for that," Freeman said. Dykes nodded and considered the thought as the cart clattered on. Freeman looked ahead and grinned. "You can be embarrassed for that. I don't know about ashamed. Damned ignorance is what that is."

Dykes chuckled and nodded again. "That's why I'm here. We'll leave it at that." He had yet to truly talk through his motives with anyone and felt he deserved the ribbing. "So what do you do, Cassius? What cause drives you?"

"What cause? I don't know about any cause. I do intend to take advantage of this opportunity we've been given. Help those who can't help themselves." He jostled the reins lightly. The mill he had mentioned passed to the left. It was situated at a fork in the road, adjacent to a ramshackle post office. "I see it as a payback, almost. I had help once, too."

"We all have," Dykes said.

"You seem like a good man, Mr. Dykes." They rode on a bit more in silence before Freeman spoke again. "It's like this. I wasn't born with this name. I took it. I took it before Mr. Lincoln made it my legal right to take, too."

Dykes studied his face, but it remained expressionless and fixed ahead.

"I come up through here just before the war and had help from those who sympathized with the likes of me. They got me north. To where I was no one's property. Like you, I'm here to help. I came back to help as the dust settles all around us in these amazing, confusing times. White folk don't know what to think. Colored folk don't know what to think. We're all just being polite at this point. Most of us, at least. But you can only be polite so long. We'll straighten it all out in the end, but it won't come easy. So I thank you again for your service, and I thank you for your intentions."

Dykes gazed off into the woods as they rolled along. The first of the dogwood blooms had opened, creating a lacy petticoat under the green-bud-speckled canopy above.

"How do you help those who need helping?" he asked.

"Me? In recent years, I've found merit in the Freedmen's Bureau. I work in a school west of here. On the road today to fetch a load of books, as a matter of fact."

"Freedmen's Bureau. You wouldn't believe it, but a man from my regiment laid some groundwork for that effort during the war. Has it been a success here?"

"I'd say it has," Freeman said. "We've educated many folks, reunited many families. Mr. Grant could find no better cause to fund if you ask me. Times are lean, but we've done a lot with a little and have plenty more to do."

"I was through Washington earlier this week," Dykes said. "They could use your ambition up there." He had meant it to get a laugh, but it fell flat.

"I don't know about Washington — there's plenty to do here. You should consider it, if you want to help as you say."

Dykes nodded as the cart rolled along.

* * *

He knew they were nearing Leesburg when traffic began to pick up. Just south of town, what looked like picnickers were gathering in the shade along an open field. Freeman turned his head for what may have only been the second time since they'd started out from Middleburg. "You in a hurry to get to town?"

"Not in any particular way. Why do you ask?"

He motioned to the field. "Thought you might find this interesting. Looks like a ball game could start before too long."

Dykes looked past the picnickers and saw that further in the field a few men in uniform, striped blue shirts with white caps, were moving about in a relatively active manner. One of them broke out into a run and dashed into the open as another lobbed a ball toward him with an underhanded arch. The runner caught it with both hands and slowed to a trot.

"This is interesting," Dykes said. "I've seen a game or two played in Connecticut. Does Leesburg have a club?"

"They do indeed," Freeman said. He edged the horse to the right and pulled him to a stop along a fence. A quiet settled over them as the clatter of the cart ceased; the muted din of the picnickers carried on the breeze. "These here are the newly minted Tuscaroras. Can't say I know who they aim to play today, but by the gathering crowd I'd say it's more than a practice."

Dykes studied the field for a moment and turned to Freeman. "I believe I will watch for a bit. Care to join?"

"No, sir, I should be heading along. But if you want to walk it in from here it's not far. Another quarter mile and you're in the thick of things."

"Sounds fine, thank you." Dykes reached over for a handshake. "I am interested in what we discussed, though. How can I look you up?"

"If you're in Lincoln, that's where I stay. Do look me up. Cassius Freeman."

"I certainly will. Thank you for the ride, and I wish you the best on the remainder of your journey." Dykes hopped down and reached for his bags.

"Same to you, sir. It was a pleasure meeting someone of like interests. Take care, now." Freeman watched as Dykes moved back from the cart with his bags, then gave a nod and popped the reins. The cart jostled back onto the road and kicked up a light dust.

Dykes leaned his bags against a fencepost and edged himself up on the highest of its sagging split rails. He watched quietly as more ball players took to the field in practice. It seemed only the Tuscarora ball club was present at the moment. One of the players produced a lean bat and took some swings at the air. Another lined up from him some twenty yards further into the field and steadied himself with the ball in hand. After a pause, he tossed the ball toward the batter with a floating underhanded arch. The batter swung and connected, and with a dull *thud* sent the ball low and off to the left. Several men scampered toward it.

A few spectators took notice of the action and clapped their hands.

CHAPTER 10

THE BEVERIDGE HOUSE was rarely vacant. It had long been a natural resting spot for travelers moving between Alexandria and Winchester or parts further west. Through the years its low-ceilinged public area had played host to royalty and presidents — both for the Union and against it. During the war it had been a natural strategic safe house, and as the town changed hands its thick oak bar had been covered by both battle maps and blood spilled by amputees to the doctor's saw. Where there were now rubbish bins in the back alley, not six years ago there had been piles of splintered and rotting limbs.

After dinner each night, the tavern typically played host to both locals and travelers, and tonight was no different. Mosby scanned the crowd for familiar faces as he picked his way through tables to the bar at the back of the room. He had been in town late for errands and decided to stop in for a meal and a pint of beer. The ceiling was thick with cigar smoke, which mingled with the smell of stale ale and sawdust to create a familiar comfort to Mosby.

He placed his order at the bar and had a seat at a small table in the corner. His presence was soon acknowledged by a man standing tall and holding court a few tables over, who pointed at him with a thick finger.

"Mosby knows how it is," he said into the air between them. "That right, Mosby?"

"You're going to have to catch me up, Harlan," he replied.

"Luke here was just saying wheat is the only way to turn a profit. You grow corn, don't you, Mosby?"

"Yes, I've been trying it three seasons now. Wheat sounds fine to me, though. Corn worms about gave me fits last season."

"I say corn is only going to grow in demand. Worms or no, corn is it. Mark it — you'll see less gold and more green in the fields in this valley."

"Fine," Mosby said. He pulled out an Almanac and began thumbing through its thin pages in order to extract himself from the conversation. He had learned that engaging Harlan Kirkbride was not worth the breath, regardless of where you stood on the issues he bloviated about.

Kirkbride had become a bit of a rudderless ship since the war. Before emancipation, he had been the largest land owner in the valley, with some fifty slaves working his fields. Although he still cultivated a large swath of farmland north of town, his economic might had slipped and his estate had eroded. Former slaves had banded together to purchase a cluster of tenant houses and a patch of surrounding acreage, which had since grown to become a thriving negro community. Another parcel had been ceded to the county to settle a tax matter. His manor house remained, but his pride was nonetheless deflated.

He would never admit it, though, and he maintained a band of devoted social hangers-on who still took his word as law. They surrounded him now at the table, laughing and nodding as he gestured broadly. Between his teeth he clenched the tip of an ornate cheroot holder, its meerschaum body depicting a hound pinning a fox by its throat. He was gruff but handsome, sporting mutton chops trimmed tight to his jawline to meet at a well-kept mustache.

"Yes, wheat is the Old South. Dead and gone. Corn is how we'll fill our silos and feed our Yankee occupiers." A few men laughed.

"Dead and gone, eh, Harlan?" Jim Duncan was Mercer Township Constable. Although he sat a few tables over he was clearly part of the group. "The Old South is here. You keep it yourself with those hounds you run."

"I can run hounds and hunt fox in a foreign country as easily as I can across my own land," Kirkbride said. "The Commonwealth has changed, Jim, and you know it. People have changed." He put a boot on his chair for effect. "We've been broke by our captors, damnit. The lot of us. We may call our home Virginia, but for how long will we tolerate being reduced to a 'military district'? That sordid moniker remains years after our surrender. We may be born Virginians, but our captive hides are forever sullied by the brand of General Schofield."

"You're being a bit dramatic, I'd say," Duncan said. "I've been North, and I'm not impressed. They talk quick and forget their manners. They have no passions. Industry and growth drives their decisions. It's different here and that can't be taken."

"Different is right," someone said. "They've got 'colored folk.' We've got uppity freedmen." The crowd of them chuckled.

Kirkbride took his cheroot holder between thumb and forefinger and blew a line of smoke into the air. "You'll see that industry and growth here soon enough, Jim. It'll arrive at your doorstep in a carpet bag. I see more and more Yankees poking around every day. They had never given us notice before, but now we're a land of opportunity. We're the new frontier. We're ripe for cultivation." He sat down heavily and took a pull of beer.

A night watchman entered the room and approached Duncan. The scruffy man leaned over and said something low into his ear. It was no secret the constable did most of his policing from or within earshot of the bar, a small band of watchmen keeping him abreast of goings on out in the world.

Duncan nodded at whatever was said and waved the man off before turning back to Kirkbride.

"You work on hearsay, Harlan. Where I see Virginians building their home back up to former glory, you see opportunists cloaked in blue."

"Damn right I do."

"Well open your eyes and join in, Harlan," Duncan said. "We could use you."

Kirkbride took another drink from the pint glass before him and stewed for a moment. His eyes rested on Mosby. "Mosby knows what I say firsthand."

Jeb looked up from the Almanac with a blank expression. "Sorry?"

"You've been housing a Yankee, haven't you? Come to pick over what his brethren trampled and burned?"

"Now where would you hear a thing like that?" He tossed the open Almanac facedown on the table.

"Stibbs met the both of you the other day, from what I heard. Short, quiet fella not from around here. A friend, did you say he was?"

"Stibbs has too much time on his hands if he's making gossip of that," Mosby said. "We housed a traveler, and yes, he was a Yankee. He did us a good turn and we did him one back. He's up and gone. That's the end of it. No more to tell."

"Did he fight?" Kirkbride asked.

"We did not discuss the war."

"He fought," another man said. They all laughed heartily at that, although Mosby was unimpressed.

"It's not my business whether he did or didn't fight," he said. "What's done is done. We got licked. Let's move on."

"Did you make it your business to find out what he was up to?" Duncan asked.

"He was upfront about it. Looking to settle around here. But hell, I don't blame him. You said it yourself, Jim: The North is all a mess of industry. Give me the fields of Loudoun any day."

"Goddamit, that's what I'm talking about," Kirkbride said. "He'll settle right on in, to our detriment. He'll take our jobs, send our money back north, and invite his Yankee cousins down to join in the fun. We're getting it from them like a heifer in heat."

The barkeep brought a plate and a glass of beer over to Mosby's table.

"What he does is not my business," Mosby said. "If he's a good man, we could use him. If he means trouble, the constable could use him. That right, Jim?"

"I'll put his ass to work if he steps out of line," Duncan said. "We need more on the chain gang these days."

Someone asked about where his gang was working and the conversation took a turn. Mosby used the opportunity to return to his book and supper; that kind of prying made him uncomfortable. Tensions ran high after the war, and he found it best to keep out of local drama. The last thing he wanted was to have his name tied to a migrant carpetbagger.

He had been surprised and a bit hurt to find the hay loft empty without a parting word from Dykes, but in retrospect it was best. A clean break. He could carry on with business as usual, however thankful he was to have Pappy safe at home and a tree bucked, ready for hauling.

WITH HIS SUPPER finished and the tab settled, Mosby was about to push away from the table when Kirkbride rose and walked over to him. He pulled out the chair across from him and took a seat, leaning in.

"I may be running my dogs your way in the next few days. You alright if I have to chase them across your land?"

"Never been a problem before," Mosby said. "But know that I've had issues with wild dogs as of late. If you flush them, I'd be obliged if you laid them out."

"I'll keep an eye out." Kirkbride stared into his hands, open on the table. "And you keep an eye out for that Yankee. If he comes calling again, I'd be obliged if you laid him out." He looked up and grinned at Mosby.

"You're quick but crass, Harlan. He seemed a fine man, like any of us. But I can say I've seen the last of him. He's moved on. Rest easy."

"I won't be resting easy any time soon, and I recommend the same for you."

Mosby sighed and shook his head. "Okay, Harlan. I'll stay vigilant." Mosby rose and gave him a solid pat on his broad shoulder. "Good night to you."

He motioned a good night to a few others as he moved back toward the door. The outside evening air was cool, but a gentle mugginess hinted at hotter weather ahead. Summer would come, and with it persistent weeds, smothering heat, and violent storms, but for now the world was relatively quiet and in order.

He walked through the lamplight to unhitch Presh and offered the horse a hunk of biscuit he had saved from his meal. "That's a girl," he whispered.

CHAPTER 11

Mosby was a few strides out the back door when he abruptly turned and marched back up the steps. Fannie looked up from cutting vegetables for a soup as he walked back in through the kitchen.

"Damn cold out there," he said as he passed. She watched him walk through into the next room and returned to her cutting. Pappy was at the table, having finished breakfast, and took a loud sip of coffee.

"Can I get you a warm cup, Pappy?" she asked.

He turned slightly in his chair. "What's that, dear?"

"Can I pour you a warm cup of coffee?"

"No, no. Don't trouble over me." He took another sip and stared out the window at the fog-covered yard.

Mosby walked back in wearing a canvas barn coat. He stopped and gave Fannie a quick kiss. "It's cold out there! I thought we were done with it. Cold out there, Pappy."

"There are two buttons loose on that coat, you know," Fannie said.

He grabbed a biscuit off the table by Pappy and opened the door. "I saw. I'll mind them." He took a bite of the biscuit and let the door shut loudly behind him.

"You'll lose them is what you'll do." Fannie shook her head and scraped her cuttings into a pot.

* * *

CHUNKS of the felled tree were still sitting heavy in the High Field, but Mosby didn't care to haul them today. With the tree cut, he felt no rush. He could clear it in the coming weeks and still have time to ready the field and irrigation ditch for planting. He walked to the barn and grabbed a hoe from where he'd left it leaning just inside the door. It would be a good morning to prep the kitchen garden. Easy work that would keep him warm.

The garden was in a nice patch of full sun not far from the house, about fifteen feet by thirty feet, surrounded by a low split-rail fence stacked two rails high. Mosby had set all the posts in the ground, two side by side, and threaded the rails through them to keep the fence orderly without taking up too much space. There was no gate, so he stepped over to get into the plot.

He gazed out over the misty yard before taking his first chop with the hoe. There was a large oak tree between here and the barn with a rope swing still attached. Fannie would sit there every now and again, but for the most part it went unused. Soon the rope would rot out, and Mosby would cut it down.

But looking at it now, he could almost hear the kitchen door slam as a lively little girl came tearing out of the house and over to the swing. Maybelle loved to play outside while her daddy worked near the house. During the summer, he would pull a few carrots out of the ground and surprise her with them. They would brush them off and, holding a few by their wispy greens, snap into them with a gritty crunch. He loved her little smile, especially in those months when she had some teeth missing up front.

As she grew older, Maybelle still used that swing. She would sit there on nice days and read or knit. Legs crossed at the ankles, gently rocking in the shade. If he was working near enough, she might read some passages to him or sing a song. She made a game of Bible study, often taking breaks to formulate tunes for her favorite Psalms. Mosby always said she was a true beauty, with his strong, lean frame and Fannie's soft features. The best of both of them, with a sparkling wit. Work was always easier with her out on the swing.

He used his cuff to wipe some wet from the corner of each eye and stared at the packed earth of the garden before him. He took a swing and the hoe broke loose a piece of crust, though not as easily as he'd imagined.

"Well," he said aloud. "I can only blame myself for picking this chore." He sighed and took another few good swings, turning to make a row and find his rhythm.

* * *

BEFORE LUNCH, Mosby took a moment to look over his work before leaning the hoe against a corner of the fence. He saw Fannie was back in the kitchen. He walked over and gave the door a quick knock before opening so as not to startle her.

He stuck his head in through the frame. "I'm heading to the Stibbs' before lunch. Got to pay the boy for some stone clearing work."

"Alright. Does ham sound good for lunch?"

"Does ham sound good for … well hell yes it does, Butternut. I shall return forthwith."

"Send Dottie my regards."

"I shall do it."

He had taken the coat off during the hoeing work but put it back on, unbuttoned, for the walk. It was warming up a bit though the breeze still carried a chill. He walked quickly out to the road and along the stretch between his and the Stibbs' property, jingling a few coins in his pocket as he did. He hoped Dottie would be home. He loathed dealing with the men of the house as of late.

Fate was not on Mosby's side. As he neared the house he could see Stibbs dragging a log from the roadside toward the house. It was a hefty piece of wood, heavy even for a man of his stature, and he stooped as he pulled it awkwardly, arms dangling below his knees.

"Well shoot, John," Mosby spoke loudly from the road. "Sure you should be doing that what with your back and all?"

Stibbs dropped the log with a hollow *thump* and stood up straight, returning the comment with a blank stare. "It ain't heavy."

"Can I give you a hand?" Mosby walked up into the yard and stopped short of the log, surveying it with hands on hips.

"I'll be able to manage. What can I do you for, Jeb?"

"Well I owe John Junior for some work he's done for me. Is he around?"

"Can't say he is. Him and his mama went into town."

"Well, I'll leave it with you then." Mosby pulled a few coins from his pocket and placed them in Stibbs' meaty palm. Stibbs crammed them in a breast pocket. Mosby wondered if they'd ever make it to their intended beneficiary. "He does good work."

"So you've said." Stibbs looked down at the log and back toward the house, agitated. Mosby ignored the subtle plea to end the exchange. "Say, John. I was down at the Beveridge House the other night, and Harlan mentioned you were a little uncomfortable with my bringing that visitor around. That Mr. Dykes fellow."

Stibbs looked a bit surprised, but his expression quickly returned to an emotionless stare. "He did, did he? Well he's right then. Don't know what made you think any of that was a good idea."

"Any of what?"

"Your bringing a Yankee around and all. I don't want his kind on my property."

Mosby took a step back. " 'His kind on your property?' What on earth kind do you think he is? He seemed an honest man passing through. Helped me and helped my pappy out of a tight spot."

"I don't care what he helped. He looked a damned carpet-bagger and if he's down here he's up to no good."

"I don't know where you get that, John."

"I read the papers. And you should know better, Jeb. Any good he did for you was a ruse, you can believe it. A wolf in sheep's clothing."

"Alright then. Well my sincerest apologies for any offense the visit caused." Mosby gave a mock half-bow. "He's long gone, anyway, so you and Harlan and whoever else can rest easy. Long gone with no ill deeds to show for it."

"We'll see about that."

"Okay then, John. Good luck with your log. Fannie sends her regards to Dottie, by the way."

Stibbs replied with a short snort and planted his feet to resume log-hauling. Mosby turned and walked back out to the road, jaw locked. He felt a compulsion to say something else in parting, to end on a more polite note, but worked to stifle it and marched on.

* * *

AT LUNCH, Mosby, Fannie, and Pappy sat around the table with little conversation passed. Mosby knew the silence was stirring curiosity in Fannie, and he knew she would ask what was bothering him. It wasn't until Pappy finished and stiffly pushed his chair away from the table that she said something.

"Mighty quiet, Jeb. Everything go alright with John?"

He looked up from his plate, scraping at the last remaining bit of beans. "With John? Fine. He was alone, though, so I didn't see Dottie. Lord knows if the boy will ever see that payment."

"You left it with John Senior?"

"I did. I need to pay that boy on the spot. Next time I'll have the coins at the ready."

"That's not what's bothering you, is it?"

"The payment? No, that's on the Stibbs." He sat back from the table after taking the last bite. "And I'm not bothered, Fannie. Just thinking a lot this morning, is all."

"Thinking about Maybelle?"

"Yes, of course. And Pappy. I had a dream about him last night."

"What kind of dream?"

"Well, not much of anything special. I was working out in the barn, and I was me — the same age and all — but Pappy was a lot younger. He was like how when you and I met."

Fannie smiled. "Well that's nice."

"Yeah, it was. He was walking in from doing some chores all puffed up like he'd get, holding a pitchfork at his waist with those strong arms. He had all his hair!" Fannie laughed. "So I saw him come in and stopped what I was doing. I put down a bucket and sat down before him, cross-legged. He sat down right with me, pitchfork across his lap. He stared at me and asked what was on my mind. I told him about that Yankee who visited us. Asked him what he made of it."

"So what did he say?"

"He didn't say anything at first. He stood up and grinned real big. And shook his head like he thought me a fool. And then, as he started to walk out of the barn, he turned and said what you could guess he'd say."

Fannie thought a moment. "To thine own self … ?"

"You got it. 'This above all, to thine own self be true.' "

Fannie laughed again. "Well of course he would. He told me the same a half-dozen times before we got married."

"Oh, I can't tell you how many times he trotted that old chestnut out when I was in the throes of juvenile angst. But it was good to hear it again. And to see him as he was."

"Sounds nice. I miss the old Pappy." She suddenly noticed his coat, which he'd left on during lunch. "Jeb. Your buttons."

He looked down to see a set of frayed threads where two

buttons had been fixed last he'd checked. "Well shoot. I guess that means we're due for some warmer weather."

Fannie patted the back of his hand and stood up from the table, a slight grin escaping as she cleared the empty plates.

CHAPTER 12

DYKES STUDIED his map as if by habit. He had become familiar with the general lay of the county, but now his eyes scanned its roads and streams as a breeder would a foal at market. Leesburg and its surrounds was active and close to the river, but Middleburg and Aldie were nestled in the most beautiful hills and forests he could remember. If he was to settle somewhere and lay down roots, he preferred it be fitting with his mind's eye view of Virginia: pristine, fertile, rejuvenating.

A round man with bushy gray burnsides and suspenders entered the room, his feet falling heavy on the hollow wooden floor. "Solomon Dykes?" he asked.

"Yes, that's me." Dykes stood and folded the map with a few quick motions.

"Come on in then," the man said.

The room — this man's office — was small with high ceilings and vertical pine board walls. Although the room was square, an encroaching pile of books and stacked papers reduced the size of the space and left it cramped, rather like a long casket turned on end. A ladder was leaned against the back wall to provide access to the upper reaches of the pile.

The man sat behind a cluttered desk and opened a ledger. "So you are looking to buy land," he said.

"Yes. Best to start here, no?"

"It's one way to do it. What are your requirements?"

"I would prefer within a short ride of a mill or town, with acreage to farm. Fifty at the least."

The man scratched a few notes in the ledger. "What part of the county are you looking in?"

"South. Middleburg is preferred."

"Middleburg? Nice town, but a lot of that land is claimed and paid for." He thought a moment. "But let me see what I can do. I'll need a moment. You can wait here if you like."

Dykes nodded and sat back in his chair. He was satisfied with how quickly he seemed to be settling in. This was already his second visit to the county seat. He was laying history in a part of the world that had been foreign to him but a few days ago. The courthouse where he sat was where he had met Tom Mosby and where he would, with some luck, stake a claim to a future of honest work and possible fortune. He looked up at the room around him, thinking on what business he might have in this very building. Auctions, hearings. Maybe an occasional trial.

The man licked his thumb as he leafed through a second, larger ledger. He scanned its entries with a stubby finger and muttered to himself. After a few minutes of this he stopped and called into the air, "Penny!"

Dykes sat up. "Pardon?"

The man eyed him and shook his head from side to side. His bushy jowls shuddered with the gesture. "Penny?"

A slight young colored woman walked in. "Yes, sir?"

"Penny, I need the latest records from Mercer Township. I believe it's somewhere up there." He waved toward the top right corner of the pile of documents behind him.

"Yes, sir," she said with a nod, already repositioning the ladder. She tested its stability and leaned back, squinting to make out titles of the upper tier of books. Satisfied, she climbed and quickly put her hand on what seemed to be the book in question. She pulled it out, cracked it open and nodded to herself, tucking it under her arm for the descent. She wore a heavy wool skirt and a white cotton blouse that billowed out behind her at the waist.

"Here, sir." She placed it on the desk and waited for another request.

"That's fine, thank you, Miss Penny," the man said. "That'll do." She nodded again and left the room.

He sighed as he opened the book, turned to its midsection. "So where are you from, Mr. Dykes?"

"Connecticut. I'm glad to have it behind me."

"I had a cousin up that ways. Delaware," the man said.

"Had? Did he move south?"

"You might say that. He died in Second Bull Run. So, yes, we're practically neighbors now."

"I'm sorry to hear that," Dykes said.

"No matter. I'm sure he had it coming. Growing up he would always be the one to start trouble. That stayed with him into adulthood, and no doubt led him into the hands of our maker on the battlefield."

"Many good men died, cautious or no." Dykes said.

"Mm-hm." The man exhaled loudly through his nose and turned a few more pages. He stopped and planted his finger squarely on a line item flagged with red ink. "This looks promising." He leaned in to read the entry. "One hundred acres, four improvements — one stone house and three outbuildings. Agricultural land. Road access to Ashby's Gap Turnpike." He looked up at Dykes. "That runs through Middleburg."

"I know of it," Dykes said.

The man returned to the entry. "Eleven years of back taxes." He exhaled from his nose again and leaned back. "This may be what you're after, Mr. Dykes."

"What do you mean by the back taxes? Would that complicate things?"

"Complicate? Why, no! It makes it easy from where you sit."

"I'm afraid I don't follow you," Dykes said.

"Well, it's not for sale and not yet reclaimed by the county. But now that I have this here on my desk, and I have this note of outstanding debt, and I have what I presume to be a willing settler of said debt ..."

"Is the property occupied?" Dykes asked.

"Seems to be. But not legally from the county's perspective. You might call it an oversight up to this point."

"What happens to the current occupier?"

"They'll receive notice of the amount owed, but it likely won't change a thing. So we call them squatters and they move on. Clearly with this history of debt they're not likely to have many possessions to speak of. I've seen it before. Probably inherited the property — may not even use it as a primary residence. Possession is clearly not a priority, whatever the case."

"Well how would the process work?"

"You settle the tax bill and pay some fees, and we transfer the deed to your name. Fairly simple. The occupant is notified and given a modest amount of time to vacate the property. By the time you arrive they'll be long gone. Goes pretty smoothly."

Dykes thought on the proposition for a moment. "What kind of taxes and fees are we talking about?"

The man turned the book to Dykes and pointed to a number. "There are your taxes. Figure another ten percent for fees."

"Can I have a look at the place?"

"I wouldn't recommend it if you're serious," the man said. "In matters like this I find it best to settle the business and remain as distanced from the other party as possible. There can be sore feelings, you understand."

"Sure, I understand." Dykes thought for a moment and leaned toward the open book. "Does it have any ponds or creek access?"

The man returned to the entry. "No and yes. It's on Goose Creek. Sounds like a lovely spot, actually."

"Well. This is all very interesting," Dykes said. "I didn't expect such an immediate opportunity."

"These don't often come along," the man said. "As I said, it was an oversight. This property should have been possessed by the county and auctioned years back. So count yourself lucky in this case."

Dykes leaned back and smoothed his mustache with his thumb and forefinger. "Okay. When and how do you take payment?"

"It depends. How will you be making payment?"

"Do you take cash?"

The man grinned. "We most certainly do." He paused in thought. "There's typically a waiting period while we notify the present occupier, but I doubt in this case it's entirely necessary. Add another, say, one percent to those fees and we can get things moving right along for you."

"That sounds fair," Dykes said.

After a half hour or so of Miss Penny retrieving various papers from adjacent rooms, the man presented Dykes with a series of forms to be signed. After Dykes thumbed out a stack of bills, the man presented the deed, which he pressed with a metal seal after it was signed.

"Congratulations, Mr. Dykes, and welcome to Loudoun County." He extended a chubby arm across the desk and came to a half-stand to shake Dykes' hand.

"Thank you, sir. And I thank you for your assistance today. I have to admit, I didn't expect it to go so smoothly."

"It usually doesn't. Like I said, this was an oversight that you profited from," the man said.

Dykes stood and collected his papers, tucking them into his satchel. "One question: Who was the former owner?"

"Hm. Well, let's see." The man looked back down at his book and traced his finger across the page. "John P. Stibbs, Sr."

Dykes paused. "I'm sorry?"

"Stibbs. John Stibbs."

Dykes stared down at the folded deed jutting out from his carpet bag. He repeated the name to himself. "Stibbs."

PART II

SUMMER

CHAPTER 13

IF SPRING WAS for plowing and planting, summer was for hoeing and weeding. And Mosby hated it. It was not yet July but the late morning heat was already sweltering, the humidity a drag on his tired body like a sack of wet flour. Yet onward he hoed, cutting more defined lines between the rows of young Indian corn. In the evenings he would have Fannie come out and help with some of his light work — as he would have had Maybelle, were she still alive.

He arched his back to crack out some kinks, reaching his hands to the sky. He gazed up. The humid air blurred the horizon up to the firmament above, making the sky indiscernible from clouds. It was all just a haze of blue-gray. The glare was formidable, though, and he had to squint to make out a hawk circling above the tree line, lazily. It dipped suddenly as two jay birds flitted up and made passes at it. Mosby chuckled. "Hoo, you better get out of there, boy."

He sighed and looked down the row. There must have been another few hundred yards to go before he reached the edge of the field. Taking a pull from his canteen, he made up his mind to break for lunch after he finished the row.

He wiped his hands on his pants and grabbed up the hoe,

beginning a shallow swing to chop at the ground. Along he shuffled, chopping and stepping back. Chopping and stepping back. Every now and again he would half-sing a little tune between the chops.

"No more picking of corn for me." *Chop chop chop.* "No more, no more, no more." *Chop chop.* "No more picking of corn." *Chop chop chop.*

Between steps and chops he would occasionally wipe his brow with the back of his hand, but it all worked as parts of one fluid operation.

The end of the row took him by surprise — startled by the tall grass under his feet, he lost his balance. He recovered by standing upright and whooping into the air. He tossed the hoe, sending its worn handle through a double flip into the fresh-turned row. "Hoo, damn!" He yelled. "Lord, it's hot."

"Okay," he muttered, putting his hands on his hips. "Lunchtime."

This end of the field was abutted by a raised bald scattered with small boulders. It was too steep to cultivate, so he left it unplanted year after year. It did afford a nice view of the surrounding countryside, though. He scrambled up to its top and flopped down for lunch beneath a scraggly tree.

He had stuffed lunch into a small satchel he wore slung across his chest. He fished out a cold biscuit wrapped in a cloth, some cheese, and a tomato he had picked that morning. After some quick work with his pocket knife, he had assembled a respectable sandwich.

He followed a bite with a sip from his canteen and gazed off across his land. From here he could see parts of the Stibbs plot off to the south, laying fallow. The fields, long neglected by John Senior, were growing wild. He could only imagine what was becoming of the house, now with the family gone.

He caught his breath as a shadow of a figure moved into view. It was walking a ramshackle fence along a bit of an old

Stibbs field. Mosby stood up, slowly. He squinted through the midday haze but didn't recognize the figure.

He watched as the figure moved down the fence line. It stopped, stooped over, then continued its walk. Mosby cupped his hands along either side of his mouth. He waited a moment and dropped them back to his side. "Aw, come on now," he muttered to himself. He cleared his throat and brought his hands back up.

"Hey!" It didn't seem to hear. "HEY!" It continued walking the fence, without pause. Mosby continued watching but sat back down. Within a few minutes, the figure was out of view. He finished his lunch quietly in the thin shade of the tree.

* * *

HE WAS WASHING up on the front porch when Fannie came outside. She dried her hands on an apron tied around her hips and stood waiting for him to look up. After a few splashes in the bowl he did, his face dripping.

"It was hotter than hell out there today."

"But humid, too. I was worried about you," she said.

"I'd have come in if I got too hot, you know that. There's some work to be done in the barn."

"Maybe you can do that tomorrow." She sat down on the opposite end of the bench from where Mosby had placed the bowl. He went back to washing.

"Maybe, yeah," he said between splashes. "I saw something interesting today, from the High Field."

"Another ball of fire?"

Mosby stared at her. "You still think I'm a fool, don't you?"

"I would never," she said, smiling.

"As a matter of fact, I saw someone down on the Stibbs' land."

"Did you? Well I suppose it was only a matter of time before someone moved in. Or do you think they're with the county?"

"I have no idea, Fannie. I called out but they didn't hear me, or chose not to. It looked like they were checking a fence line, so I suppose it could be a surveyor with the county." He reached for a dry cloth on the bench and dried his face. "I suppose I'll take a look tomorrow."

"Being nosy?"

"Nosy my ass, I'm being rational! What if squatters take up there?"

"Lordy, I hadn't thought of squatters. That would be horrid."

"Right you are, Butternut. So as I was saying, I suppose I'll take a look tomorrow. And if it's still hot as blazes I'll finish the day in the barn. Sound good?"

"Fine by me." She stood up and gazed out down the drive. "When are you going to town next? I need some material. Pappy has worn through another pair of britches."

Mosby barked a short laugh. "Worn through? Doing what?"

"I don't know, Jeb, you know he gets into things. Looks like he's been walking through briars or some such."

"Briars. Well maybe I can take him with me later in the week. If he needs to wander so much, he can wander around town and do a few errands while he's at it."

"Okay then." She patted him on the shoulder. "When you're done out here I have supper about ready."

"What are we having?"

"Beans and cornbread, with what's left of the pork."

"Sounds fine. I'll be in shortly."

When he'd finished washing up he leaned back against the planks of the house and gazed off into the yard. He had been sitting right here when all the Stibbs rolled by that final time a month or so ago. Mosby had heard the unmistakable clatter of their old wagon and the squeezing huffs of their hogs. Walking down to investigate, he found them passing in their rig: the wagon loaded with furniture and piles of clothes and blankets, the hogs in tow in an old cart hitched to the wagon.

"John? Where are you off to?" Mosby had called as he trotted down to the road.

The Stibbs clan all looked in his direction. John pulled their old mule to a halt and glared at him. "You tell me, you sonofabitch."

"I'm sorry? What's this all about?"

"Seems we've been booted by the county. They took everything from us. The house, the land."

"Oh — oh, my. That's a damned shame, John. Damned shame." He looked to Mrs. Stibbs. "I'm so sorry, Dottie." She nodded solemnly. "But I don't follow your tone with me, John."

"Just funny, is all." His wife put a hand on his arm. "All is well one day, next you bring some stranger around I don't know from Adam, and before I know it, the county shows up and starts asking questions. Can you explain that to me, Jeb?"

"It's a shame, John, but I hardly see how one has to do with the other. That man is long gone, anyway. Was just passing through and did some work for me."

Stibbs spat a stream of tobacco juice at the ground between them. "If you say so." He gazed ahead down the road. "I hope it was worth it to you. Given what John Junior's done for you through the years. Given what mama's done for you and yours through the years." Mrs. Stibbs looked down. He popped the reins and the mule startled to a walk. "Careful who you friend, Jeb, is all I'll say. I fear your hospitality has gone and got you in some trouble."

Mosby furrowed his brow and surveyed the wagon as they passed. Junior was nestled among some blankets in back and was now hiding his face among them. The hogs were in a state, packed into that rickety cart with some lengths of old fence lashed to its sides. Mosby stared after them, arms crossed, until they were several cart lengths down the road. Dust settled around him. He looked down and kicked dirt over the streak of brown spit at his feet.

"Goddamn shame."

* * *

THE NEXT MORNING Mosby bided his time before sunrise by cleaning his hunting rifle, Pappy's old two-triggered Hawken. It was muzzle-loaded, but Jeb preferred it to his newer breech-loader because it could be set with a hair trigger. After he'd reassembled it, he loaded it and packed extra powder and balls in his satchel. He left before Fannie or Pappy were up, closing the door softly behind him.

It was already hot outside, the sun barely up. The cyclical thrum of cicadas drowned out whatever stillness the morning might have offered otherwise. He noticed a few flying awkwardly overhead as he walked down from the house to the road.

Mosby thought about his intentions for this errand as he walked under the dark of the tree canopy toward the old Stibbs place. As he saw it, if they had a new neighbor, he needed to properly introduce himself. That made plenty of sense. If it was a surveyor with the county who was staying there for a spell, he might be able to get some news from Leesburg, or otherwise.

The third possibility left him less sure of an outcome. Say it was someone who had bad intentions, or who at least was there unlawfully. He could confront them — given some authority by the Hawken slung over his shoulder — or report them to the constable. He supposed he would know what to do when the time came.

He slowed his walk when he came within view of the stone house. He stopped to scan the property. The yard had been cleared of some junk and the stench of the hogs had lifted, but it was otherwise as the Stibbs had left it. There was no sign of the house being occupied, that he could tell. No open windows, at least on the front of the house. He continued to walk and stepped into the yard. Paused. He took a few more long, quiet steps further onto the property.

"This is ridiculous," he muttered to himself. He straightened up and strode up to the front door, giving it three loud raps. He listened for any activity within, but heard nothing. He was about to give it another knock when he heard what sounded like a bucket being kicked around the corner of the house. Mosby snapped around to face the side of the house and listened.

There was a light shuffling and a few huffs. "Hello there!" Mosby called. No reply. The shuffling grew heavier and Mosby froze. As he started to work the rifle off from around his shoulder, a soft brown muzzle eased around the corner. Then an unblinking eye and a broad, spotted neck.

"You're kidding me," he said aloud. "Anyone there?" The horse turned the corner to face him. "You don't have a rider? Well what are you doing up and about?" Mosby held his hand out and clicked his tongue. "Come on, now."

The horse walked closer. It was a pretty paint mare with no saddle but a bit and half-fastened bridle. Reins dragged loosely on the ground between its front legs.

"Did you lose your rider? That's a bad way to start the day, girl." Mosby reached out and touched the horse's face, adjusting her bridle with his other hand. He gave the yard another scan. "Let's find that rider of yours."

CHAPTER 14

DYKES HAD NEVER KEPT up more than one building on a property, and he was only slowly warming to the prospect. The barn was a wreck. Scattered about inside was a jumble of scrap lumber, rotting hay, and broken furniture. He assumed it had been the dumping place for anything the previous tenants wanted cleared out of the main house but didn't care to haul off with them.

Between the barn and the house, which were on a diagonal from each other, was a spring house, a lean-to built to one side of what had been a hog pen, a ramshackle chicken coop, and a privy. They were all relatively close together, which Dykes rather liked. Somehow the proximity gave him a sense of organization, or at least the potential for organization.

The privy itself was in fine shape, although the pit it sat over was filled to being useless and foul. Rather than dig a new one, it seemed the Stibbs had been moved to take relief in the spring house, at least for a time. Cleaning that out was a priority due to his need to frequently access the spring, although the current heat and humidity was making the chore a formidable one.

He had hoped a break in the weather would come, but it had been nearly two weeks since he'd moved in and it had only grown hotter.

Dykes rose early one morning to get a start on it before sunup. At the first feeble crows of a distant rooster he swung his legs over the edge of the bed and willed himself to get dressed and make his way to the barn, where he had rigged a sled the evening before. He planned to shovel the offending pile onto the sled, hitch it to his horse, a lovely mare he'd acquired in Lincoln, and haul it back off into the woods.

He had hoped his initial sense of disgust would ease after the first few times he slid his shovel into the rank mess, but it did not. The task was slow going, the various layers of excrement nauseating. Once the waste was cleared he dug deeper into the earth to be sure it was properly cleaned.

The sun was inching up when he emerged with one last load for the sled. He leaned the shovel against the door frame and brushed his hands on his pants. He glanced over toward the barn and noticed that he'd left the door open. "Ah, hell," he said aloud.

He trotted over to verify his suspicion that the horse was gone. The small open stall he had cleaned out for her was empty. "Damnit." He turned back and stood in the doorway, scanning the yard in the morning light. He strained to hear anything that could be her.

There was the low hum of insects. And then he heard a voice.

He had grown accustomed to being alone over the past several days and froze at the sound. He heard it again, by the house. Dykes quickly looked around the entrance to the barn and found a rusted meat hook in a corner. He held it tight in his fist and walked slowly toward the house. Before he had closed the gap he saw a man with a long-barreled gun holding his horse by the reins.

"You, sir!" He shouted, firmly. "State your business!"

The man looked back at him across the yard and tilted his head slightly. "Sol Dykes?"

Dykes recognized the soft drawl immediately. "Jeb?" He

strode forward and raised his hand in a greeting. "My! I do apologize, you gave me a start."

"Likewise. You plan on hooking me or this runaway mare of yours?"

Dykes looked down at the hook and tossed it aside. "Neither, long as you leave your rifle shouldered."

The pair shook hands, and Mosby passed the reins to Dykes, giving him a firm smack on the shoulder in the process. Dykes became suddenly aware of the mighty stench about him, but Mosby didn't seem to notice.

"Well don't that beat the Dutch? I was out for a morning hunt and thought I'd check in on the place. And here I have a new neighbor. Been mighty quiet over here."

"I've meant to visit with you and Mrs. Mosby," Dykes said.

"No worries, I know how it is." Mosby peered around the immediate property. "I know you have your work cut out for you, settling in and all. How long since you've moved in?"

"Oh, a few weeks back now. I thought we would have crossed paths by now."

"A few weeks? I feel downright unneighborly." Mosby grabbed the back of his neck and looked at the ground between them. He cocked an eye at Dykes. "So did you strike a deal with the Stibbs?"

"I wish I had. It was unfortunate, really. The county made the property available, so I moved in. The Stibbs were gone before I arrived."

"They did leave in a hurry. And none too happy about it. It was a shame to see them go," Mosby said. "But I'm glad to see a familiar face. I'll bet you clean this place up nice." He glanced toward the spring house. "Looks like you've started already. What's that rig you've got there?"

Dykes looked back at the pile. "A sled, of sorts."

"Are you loading or unloading?"

"Loading," Dykes sighed. "Loaded, thankfully. The Stibbs had filled their privy. Now I've emptied their spring house."

"Ah ha. I thought I smelled something rank."

"It's a full sled."

"It certainly is. Have you moved the privy?"

"No, not yet. I still have the hole to dig."

"Well give me a shout when you need to move it and I can lend a hand. That's a job easier done by two."

"I do appreciate it, Jeb."

"Not a thing — I'm always glad to lend a hand." Mosby looked up at the brightening sky. "I should be getting along, but it's real good to see you, Sol."

"Agreed! And thank you for wrangling the horse." He nodded toward the mare.

"Glad to help. What's her name?"

"No name yet," Dykes said.

"No name. Well, it'll come." He reached out for another handshake. "Take care, and holler if you need anything."

"Likewise, Jeb."

Dykes watched for a moment as Mosby walked toward the road. He patted the horse's neck and gazed back at the sled. "Come on, girl."

* * *

MOSBY TREAD quietly on his walk home in case he came across any game. He'd loaded the gun and would have to discharge it anyway, so he hoped to put the shot to some use. Sure enough, he heard a rustle off the road to the right before he'd reached home. He stopped and peered into the woods. A doe and her spotted fawn were nibbling ferns a short distance away.

"My, my," he whispered. "You're a pretty pair. Where's your daddy?"

He walked on but didn't see anything else. When he was back at the porch he grabbed an old jug and walked it over to a post near the garden. He took fifteen long paces back toward the house and turned, shrugging the Hawken off his shoulder. He fished into his shirt pocket and fingered out a percussion cap, pressing it firmly onto the firing mechanism. He hefted the gun's octagonal barrel and took aim at the brown jug. He squeezed the rear trigger to set the primary trigger with a click. He took a breath and eased his finger onto the primary. The gun went off with a crack; the top of the jug disappeared into mist.

"Ahhh," he breathed, displeased. Mosby studied the largely intact jug for a moment before reshouldering the rifle.

When he'd returned to the house Fannie had laid out break-fast and was pouring a glass of goat's milk. "What were you shooting at?"

"Not dinner," Mosby said. He took a seat. "You won't believe who I found at the old Stibbs place."

"I couldn't even guess."

"Not even with a clue?"

"Oh, okay, give me one." She sat and closed her eyes for him to pray. He took the cue.

"Lord, bless this food to the nourishment of our bodies and our souls to the service of Christ. Amen." Mosby looked up. "He found what we'd lost."

"That's my clue? Then I guess the gentleman who found Pappy."

"Right you are, my bride! Can you believe it? I met his horse out in front of the house, and he was around by the barn. Said he moved in weeks ago."

"My goodness. Did he mention how the Stibbs family left?"

"He didn't seem to know a thing about it. John Stibbs was part right, though. The county may have runned them off, but if I hadn't brought Sol around I can bet you it wouldn't have happened that way."

"You don't know that."

"I sure do." He chewed some salt pork for a moment. "I'm glad to not have had to tangle with squatters over there, but I sure do wish Sol Dykes had moved on down the road. He kept talking about Leesburg, which would be fine by me."

"I thought you took a shine to him! While he was here you certainly did carry on together. And he saved you having to hire help for that tree."

"Sure, he's a nice man. Polite. Seems smart. I just don't know, though. Times seem a little ... fresh ... to have a damyankee around."

"Jeb Mosby, I have never heard you talk so about a Northerner. And what do you mean, fresh?"

"Soon is what I mean. I don't rightly know what to think these days, Fannie. We've been over this, I know, but a part of me still wants to hold it against the lot of them. What happened to Maybelle, that is."

"You can't fault the whole for the actions of the few," Fannie said quietly.

"I know, Butternut. Still. It wasn't that long ago I would have been shooting at him, not that jug out there."

"You did not shoot at the jug I had set out on the porch."

"Yes, but missed. Mostly."

"Jeb, that was to return to Mrs. Russ. Land sakes." She crumpled her napkin on the table. "And since when are you talking about shooting your neighbor?"

"Since never. That's not what I'm aiming to say ... it just seems like trouble to me. People's emotions can run high these days."

"All the more reason for us to set the example, then. So you really shot that jug?"

"I nicked it. I'll take a new one up to her tomorrow, okay? Do we have one or do I need to fetch one from town?"

She glared at him, he hoped playfully. "We have. I'll find if you deliver. You can take a few jars of sweetbread with it."

"Fine." He wiped his mouth and stood up. "I'll excuse myself then. I'll be in the barn today, so holler if you need anything."

"Don't shoot at any more jugs."

"My rifle is safe on the wall. There shall be no more shooting today." He pushed his chair in and walked out the back door to the barn.

It was getting hot outside, but the barn was still dark and cool. Presh and Soupy looked up as he passed. " 'Morning, all," he said into the air between them. He gazed up into the loft. There was old hay up there he wanted to clear before harvest to make room for new stores. He figured he would back the cart up out front and pitch the hay down from above. There were some spots near the house and garden that were washing out where he could spread it.

With his head still back, he sighed and stretched his arms out to each side. He took a deep breath. Harlan Kirkbride's words from months ago were now fresh on his mind. He'd essentially befriended a stranger, a Northerner, and now he found him as his neighbor. A few thin rays of light were slanting in through the loft, illuminating specks of dust hovering above. He dropped his arms and looked to the horse.

"Strange times, Presh. What do you and Soupy think?"

The horse stared ahead and swished a fly with its tail.

"I figured as much." He gave the horse's ear a scratch as he walked out to push the cart into position. The sun seemed somehow higher already.

CHAPTER 15

Goose Creek was too wide to ford but too narrow to be anything more than a creek by name. Its shallows frequently gave way to deep pools that would catch a man off guard if he tried to cross, tugging him down and into the lazy current. Brown trout flashed in the shallows, brim and crappie hid in the pools.

Dykes could feel the rocky bottom if he reached a leg down. He ran his fingers through his hair to let the cool water in and immediately wished he'd brought a cake of soap. He had dumped the feculent load downstream, and only after a long soak did he feel he was entirely clean of it. The horse was tied up in the shade by the bank, in the only stand of trees along this piece of the property.

Compared with Jeb Mosby's land, Dykes felt his was decidedly less cultivated. Whoever had cleared it, generations ago, had cut a field from the west side of the barn all the way to the creek. It was hemmed in by a stone wall nearest the barn, ramshackle fence and deep woods to the south, and a patchwork of stone wall and fence to the north, along the Mosby plot. A smaller field had been cleared along the road south of the house.

Dykes was calling that the Front Field. Where he was now, or not far from where he was, lay the Long Field.

The Long Field was overgrown with weeds and neglect. The more Dykes saw of the place, the greater the distaste he had for the Stibbs family. Or at least its patriarch. He had been left with little to impress him after meeting the man, and the state he had left the property in bordered on disgraceful.

The wooded part of his land — near half of the plot, from what he could tell — remained a mystery.

A cloud moved to cover the sun overhead, and Dykes took the moment of shade to paddle back to the bank and step out of the creek. After he had dried off and put on fresh clothes, he untied the horse and let her trot off among the weeds to graze while he took some time to explore the woods.

He walked quietly among the oak and poplar trees, glad to be fully hidden from the midday sun. The forest was relatively old growth, perhaps having taken root before the land was first settled. He paused at the base of a massive poplar that was at least an arm's spread across. Its canopy reached high to gather light from far above. Who might have paused at this very tree? An English colonist? A wandering Powhatan? Dykes traced his hand over the ridges of its bark.

He kept a loose southerly course, with the creek to his right, scanning deeper off to the left for any sight of structure. He half expected to find a still left by Stibbs or some prior bootlegger. But there was nothing but trees and the rolling forest floor.

A large black woodpecker, the size of a crow, caught his eye, dropping down from the canopy above. It lighted on a low oak limb and flashed a raised red crest. Dykes watched it as he walked, and fell swiftly and flatly on his face.

His chin stung. An arm hurt. He smelled decaying leaves. Pushing up to brush himself off, he looked around. All was still. The woodpecker was gone. And at his feet was an oblong patch of sunken earth. He glanced around to see another, and another sunken patch. There were at least a dozen in a natural clearing.

He knew these; he had seen plenty fringing cooled battlefields during the war. Graves.

There were no markings, no other indication of burial, but the grave sites were unmistakable. Years old and clearly forgotten. He looked for some sign of memorial, some means for the gravedigger to find the spot, but there was none. He rubbed his chin and checked for blood. His hand was clean.

A thin-tailed chipmunk scampered across the site and darted for its den, dug under a log to the side of the clearing. An unnatural glint there caught his eye. He stepped around the graves and kneeled down near the log to have a closer look. Pushing bits of pinecone to the side, he found a tarnished brass buckle, turned face down.

Curious to read any insignia, he fingered it front-side up and quickly drew back — underneath was a fragment of jawbone, two browned teeth still intact. The buckle was stamped "US," of a fallen former Union compatriot. The provenance of the bone, he'd never know. Dykes stood up and looked around, suddenly sensing a heavy solitude in the woods. No birds sang. No leaves rustled. He turned and quickly traced his path back out to the field.

* * *

DYKES WAS tense with unease on the walk back to his grazing horse. He owned this land outright, but it felt strange to him. The house full of neglect, the land full of unknown history. The graves were only a part of it — the land was beautiful but not yet home.

Leading the horse back to the barn, Dykes made up his mind to turn his attentions to the house and its cleaning, a chore that would keep him out of the sun and inch him closer to taking a true stake in the property. The Stibbs had left their now too-familiar hoof prints inside as well as out. The house was strewn with toppled furniture, piles of clothes, broken dishes. It looked as if the family had left in a hurry, perhaps even in a half-rage. Nothing of value remained as far as Dykes could tell, but he intended to pick through the mess and burn what he could in the Front Field.

He had started a small pile in the parlor, near the fireplace, of items to keep. So far it contained a few tin plates and cups; books, mostly hymnals; a sewing kit, more substantial than the housewife he carried in the war; tinned essence of coffee; a broom; and a nearly complete set of checkers.

The prize of the house, to this point, had bypassed the pile and was by his bed upstairs: what he assumed to be Stibbs' pistol, somehow forgotten.

Dykes had found it in the kitchen, of all places, wrapped in cloth and stashed in a dented copper pot on a high shelf. It was in fine shape but an older model, making his Navy Colt look quite advanced. Heavy, single-shot with a curved, brass-wrapped grip — Dykes had seen the model before but had never handled one. This piece seemed to have some custom flourishes as well, including a worn brass lion head adorning the butt. He was eager to shoot it but needed powder and shot, which he had added to a mental tally of provisions to collect from town.

After a few hours of fruitless sifting, he had cleared out the downstairs bedroom and relegated all of its items to the burn pile. He decided to break for a lunch of bread and canned apple butter.

Upstairs there were two bedrooms. One he had made his own, and the second was relatively empty. It did contain what Dykes assumed was a narrow closet door he had not checked, so after lunch he marched up the steep staircase to see what might be tucked inside. Turning the peeling door's brass knob, he pulled it open to reveal an expansive room — no mere closet — filled from wall to wall with piled, broken furniture.

"Lord Almighty," Dykes said. He put his hands on his head and studied the mess for a moment. A fly was buzzing some-where among the rubbish, which seemed to intensify the heat of the crowded upstairs room. There was a window that opened to the back of the house, its sill peppered with dead and dried lady-bugs. Dykes pried it open and heaved a nearby chair down into the yard. It landed with a splintering crunch. Satisfied, he tossed another, as well as some musty couch pillows. His afternoon's task had become apparent.

The contents of the room seemed very old, perhaps from before the Stibbs family had moved in. Dykes saw value in none of it and made no ceremony of slowly transferring it all to the hard-packed dirt below. He did pause to inspect a desk that still had two drawers intact. In one, an old newspaper dated 1847. Amid its numerous headlines, "Gen. Taylor Triumphant at Buena Vista" stood out in bold. He closed the drawer and opened the other, exposing a vacated mouse nest and a tin box that looked relatively new. It was wrapped tight with twine, but he took it out and set it aside by the doorway.

Most of the furniture broke easily into bits that would fit through the open window, and within an hour the room was empty but for the desk and couch. He pushed them to the middle of the room and fetched an axe from the woodpile outside.

For the desk, he trimmed off the legs and splintered the body down the middle. As he heaved it outside a drawer opened and let loose the yellowed leaves of newspaper. For the couch, he raised the axe high and, after several strong blows, cleaved its frame in two. Its thin upholstery gave easily and waved like tattered streamers as the bulk of each half fell to the earth. Sweating and exhausted, he laid down flat on the gritty wood floor.

He wanted to be done with this purging process, so after a rest and some water he loaded the pile of debris onto a cart to be hauled to the Front Field. It took two loads to clear the furniture, and on the second he added the additional burn pile he'd gath-ered from the various rooms. He fetched the tin box, which he had already assumed to be junk, and unwrapped the twine in the shadow of the loaded cart. It popped open, stuffed tight with blue-backed Confederate bills. Its bottom was lined with a tintype: a barrel-chested man — Stibbs, from what he could remember — holding two large flintlock pistols crossed over his chest.

"Pathetic ass," Dykes muttered. The man's clothes were simple but had an orderly appearance, as if serving as a home-spun uniform. The pistols were of the same type as the one that had been stowed in the kitchen. Dykes tossed the tin and its contents onto the rubbish heap.

* * *

THAT EVENING as the sun lay low, he walked out to the Front Field with a bottle of kerosene, a lucifer match, and a flask of whiskey. Lightning bugs flashed near the tree line in the dusk. He splashed the kerosene around the lower rim of the pile and looked around. The field was quiet. Above, the evening star stood out against the Union blue sky.

He struck the lucifer to direct its sparks toward the wet of the kerosene. Flames spread quickly, licking up through the heap. Once the furniture caught, the fire towered brightly into the night air, casting its embers high. The blaze called to mind his service in bayou country. He sat in the grass nearby and uncorked his flask.

He took a sip and mused over this new home. He held out hope that once the season had cycled through, he would be able to make a proper farm of the place. His plan was to use the remainder of the summer and fall to clean up the house and outbuildings, and prepare the fields for planting in the spring.

Maybe tonight, with most of the house's rubbish burning into the sky, he would sleep easier in his bed.

The burn pile slowly leaned and toppled into itself, and the high flames turned to glowing embers. Dykes stretched out on the ground and gazed up at the stars above. It was the same night sky he had marveled at as a boy. The same he had taken for granted as a young man. The same he had found escape in during the war.

Laying in silence but for the occasional pop and hiss of coals, his thoughts turned to Beth and her guest house in the Federal City. She had been lovely to him.

He fixed his gaze on a small star and closed one eye, musing over how it seemed to bobble and weave from its perch in the sky.

* * *

A DOZE TURNED into a deep sleep in the dewy grass for much of that night. He dreamed that Beth came to him where he lay and took his hand, drawing him up and silently leading him to the house. She was wearing a green dress that made her seemingly glide ahead of him. At the door she was gone. He opened it hoping to find her inside.

A glow came from the kitchen. He followed. There, around his table lit by dim lamplight, sat several Union soldiers, pale and sallow cheeked. There were more standing off in the shadows. Dykes knew them, almost intuitively, from the shallow graves in his woods. Risen from the dried leaves. One, at the table, turned and looked to him. Where his eyes should have been shone two black orbs — Dykes drew back and awoke with a start.

CHAPTER 16

Mosby hitched his cart to the side of the Beveridge House, but walked past its door and into town. As much as he would like to hole up under the cool of its rafters, he had been tasked by Fannie to right a wrong: he was to replace the shot jug, to be returned to Mrs. Russ forthwith. The Mosbys did not, as it happened, have a spare jug, leaving him sorely regretful of not unloading his shot into something more worthy of his aim.

He also was to acquire some calico, so that Mrs. Russ might make him a new shirt. Fannie had some agreement with her to this end from what Mosby gathered.

There was really only one reliable source of useful provisions in town, owned by Jim Cogg. Cogg's General had been a mainstay in town for years, staying open through the war with Jim behind the counter all the way — he had one arm and hadn't taken up fighting. He functioned so naturally with just the one, though, Mosby guessed he had been born that way or lost it as a child.

Mosby walked into Cogg's and nodded to the counter. "Morning, Lilly." One of Jim's three daughters often worked the counter.

"Good morning, Mr. Mosby." Lilly had been a friend of

Maybelle's, although Mosby had never really known her otherwise.

Jeb browsed the racks of preserves at the front of the store. Food and like provisions were arranged to the right of the store, among a few rows of stand-alone shelves and along the wall. Cloth and similar home wares lined the left wall. In a back room was the hardware and shooting supplies. He palmed a jar of berry preserves and walked over to Lilly.

"I have been sent to fetch a jug and three yards of fabric," he said matter-of-factly. "I suppose I'll also have to take these preserves and some crackers to help get me home."

Lilly smiled. "What kind of fabric?"

"I was told calico, but it's for a shirt for me. I trust you know the latest fashion, so I leave the decision to you."

"Well I shall do my best, Mr. Mosby," she said. "Just give me a few minutes to measure and cut it."

"Yes ma'am. Give a holler when it's ready. I'll be in the back." Mosby ducked through the low doorframe to the back room. There was a table on the back wall that Cogg used for gun cleaning and such. He was seated there, and Sol Dykes was perusing ammunition nearby.

"Sol, you're everywhere these days," Mosby said. "Morning, Jim."

Jim nodded and Dykes spoke without turning. "Well hello, Jeb. What brings you to town?"

"Some sundries for Fannie. You?"

"A few necessities came to light as I was cleaning up the property."

"He's got a helluva pistol here I'm working on," Cogg said. He looked at Dykes. "Hope I'm not out of line, but it's fairly unique is all. Older cavalry model."

Mosby walked back to take a look and whistled at the sight of the gun. "Aston/Johnson. That is one elegant firearm, Sol. Reminds me of bygone days."

"Well, it needs a cleaning and some shot, so here I am."

"I'm here for a jug," Mosby said. "After I saw you the other day I had a little target practice back at the house. Turns out it was with a borrowed jug."

Cogg chuckled. "Well at least you hit it," he said.

"Did I ever."

"You still got your daddy's old Hawkin?" Cogg asked.

"I do indeed! 'Twas the Hawkin that slew the jug, as a matter of fact."

"That's a fine piece," Cogg said. He threaded a wire and a wad of cloth through the barrel of Dykes' pistol.

"Fine indeed," Mosby looked down his nose at a jig saw he'd plucked from a nearby shelf. He thought a moment and then huffed out a breath, as if having made up his mind about something. "Hey Sol?" He kept inspecting the saw as he spoke.

"Yes, Jeb?"

"You still need that privy dug and moved?"

"I do."

"How's about you keep me company on an errand and then I aid you with the privy work this evening?"

"Well, I'd planned on doing some shooting once Mr. Cogg finished up."

"We can shoot where I'm going. Come on, now. How you gonna make it much longer without a privy?"

"There are woods."

Lilly peeked in and cleared her throat. "I have you ready, Mr. Mosby."

"Sol! Such vulgarities in front of Lilly?" Mosby smacked Dykes on the shoulder. "I'll wait for you out front."

Mosby followed Lilly back to the front room and was surprised to see Harlan Kirkbride carrying a sack of flour to a box on the counter. "I didn't know you'd come in, Harlan. 'Morning."

"Hello, Jeb. Shopping day?"

"Fannie sent me." He pointed to a smooth, light brown jug behind the counter. "Could you wrap that for me please, Lilly?"

"Yes sir."

"And I'll take what's in the box here on credit," Kirkbride said.

"Yes sir."

"I haven't seen much of you lately, Jeb," Kirkbride said.

"I've been busy on the farm. It's a hell of a summer. I feel like every chore takes me twice as long in this heat."

"It has been uncommon hot." Kirkbride picked through his box to ensure it contents were as expected. "Hey." He stopped and looked at Mosby. "You ever hear from that mudsill Yankee friend of yours again?"

Dykes stepped through from the back, turning the cleaned and oiled pistol over in his hands. "Okay, Jeb. Mr. Cogg has it cleaned up and ready for shooting," he said. "Where are we off to?"

"I'll be ready shortly," Jeb said. He sighed and swept his hand toward Kirkbride. "Have you met Harlan Kirkbride? Sol, this is Harlan. Harlan, Solomon Dykes."

Harlan's eyes tracked the pistol as Dykes tucked it into his knapsack and held out his hand. "Pleasure."

Harlan stared at him, then Mosby. "You're shittin' me, Mosby. Is this the one?"

"I'm sorry?"

"Is this that carpetbagger you were cozying up to?"

"Carpetbagger?" Dykes said. "Sir, I don't know where you get your information, but I am a landowner in this county."

Harlan looked him up and down. "A landowner. Well ain't that a sign of the times." His voice had risen indignantly. He hefted his box off the counter and strode toward the door, calling over his shoulder, "You best watch your ass around friends like that, Mosby." He spat on the dusty wood floor. "Can't trust these goddamn interlopers."

The three of them, Dykes, Mosby, and Lilly, stared at the empty space in the doorway that Kirkbride left behind. Mosby sighed. "Dang, Sol. I am sorry about that. Harlan is a damned hothead, so don't pay any mind. You could say he carries a chip on his shoulder."

Cogg appeared in the back doorway wiping his hands on his apron. "What's the trouble, Lilly?"

"Don't know, Papa."

Jeb put a roll of candy on the counter. "It was Harlan up to his usual peacocking. Sorry about that, Jim."

"It ain't the peacocking that bothers me, it's the profanity. Lilly, clean up in the back, please. I'll settle Mr. Mosby's purchase." He stepped behind the counter and added the candy to the bill. "Anything else, Jeb?"

"That does it, thank you. Awful sorry for all the fuss."

"Just keep that nonsense to the tavern. The last thing I need is the constable or blue jackets taking an interest in my store."

"I'm afraid my presence has stirred the pot," Dykes said. "Thank you for your services, Mr. Cogg."

"You're welcome here anytime," he said. "And let me know when you want that watch cleaned and serviced." Dykes bowed his head, collected a sack of items from the counter, and walked out to wait for Mosby on the front porch.

THE PAIR SAT TOGETHER in Mosby's cart, jostling over the hard road with Dykes' horse tied and trailing behind. Mosby fingered a pale green candy disc out of the waxed paper wrapper and offered it to Dykes.

"No thank you. I've had enough of Necco's wafers to last a lifetime."

"Were they part of your rations? I'd heard such."

"You heard right. I fancied them then but have since lost my taste for them. So where are we off to?" Dykes asked.

"Shame on me for keeping you in the dark — that run-in with Harlan left me forgetting to share the details. You showed great forbearance there, I might add. He's known for getting the best of folks and I know he prides himself on it."

"What's his story?"

"He used to be a somebody and got knocked down a few pegs after the war. You might say he's having more difficulty adjusting to the times than most. Still walks around like he's some-pumpkins. But regarding the errand at hand ..." He patted the brown parcel tucked behind the seat. "We are to deliver this here jug to Mrs. Gwendolyn Russ. She lives just over the Goose Creek Bridge, and no finer citizen will you find in the county. If you're here to stay, it is high time the pair of you met."

"I shall be pleased to meet her," Dykes said. "Not to mention pleased to have a partner in testing the aim of this relic from the Stibbs' estate."

"I might have guessed he had left it behind. I wonder how the Stibbs family is getting along. I'll have to ask around next time I'm at the Beveridge House."

Mosby kept to the left of the road to take advantage of any patches of shade they came across. Most fields were full of rolling young crops, fast on their journey to the fall harvest. A mile or so before the turnoff for their properties, they passed a more dilapidated patch of cropland to the right. Dykes gazed out across the field, ratty with tall weeds choking out whatever crop had been planted in the spring.

"Whose property is that?" Dykes asked. "They had prepared it so nicely in the spring — plowed, rowed, and planted just as any of these other fields that are thriving."

"That's the Jenkins' property. Bob Jenkins. He does that every year and it breaks my heart. In the spring he plows that patch to its full beautiful, fruitful potential. He seeds it, with what I don't know, and then proceeds to let it go to what you see. Every damn year."

"How does he make a living?"

"I couldn't tell you," Mosby said. "I will say that before the war he cared for his crops through the season and always turned a good yield. Could be that the war broke that in him. You just never know with some men."

The cart clattered on and in good time they came to Goose Creek Bridge. It was a wide stone bridge with the macadam of the road continuing over it, standing high above the creek below. Dykes had last crossed the bridge from the other side, coming from the town of Lincoln to claim his purchased property, once taxes were paid and processed and the county papers were settled.

"You cross this bridge much?" Mosby asked. "I don't often have business this way."

"In past months I did spend some time in Lincoln, which took me this way."

"Lincoln? You must mean the town of Goose Creek," Mosby said.

"They're going by Lincoln now."

"It'll always be Goose Creek to me. You meet some Quakers or something?"

"I did, as a matter of fact. They're fine folk. I can't say I'd had any experience with Quakers in Connecticut."

The cart shuffled a bit as it crossed the transition from bridge back to road. "Well I've never mingled with them. I hear they're fine people, though." Mosby sat in silence for a few moments, and Dykes didn't care to fill it with any more on the people of Lincoln.

They were on a treeless run of road after the bridge, and the sun was coming at them from a merciless angle. Dykes could hear cicadas off in the grass, humming above the din of the wagon.

"So let me tell you about Mrs. Russ," Mosby said. "So as to prepare you some."

"Should I be worried?"

"Worried? Sakes no, but she can be a bit eccentric in her widowhood. She was fairly reserved for as long as we knew her, but once her husband died, a fierce independent streak rose up in her. Just be ready to take what you've got coming with her."

"Meaning?"

"Meaning she says it like she sees it."

"Well I can respect that," said Dykes. "Maybe I'll learn something."

* * *

THE RUSS PLACE was up on a rise with a green field sloping down to the road, clumped with grass and unmoved stones creating a pastoral, almost English, scene. Unlike the Mosby and Dykes properties, the house faced west with a view of the mountains. Behind it, the rise tapered back down through looming hardwood to the west bank of Goose Creek.

"This is a beautiful plot of land," Dykes said as they rattled up the drive to the stone house.

"Indeed it is. I am of course grateful for what my father left me, but I've always been envious of a few properties on this side of the creek. The Russ place is right up there with them."

Mosby pulled the wagon under the shade of a tree and unhitched Presh and Dykes' horse, leading them to a post where Mrs. Russ had a trough of water waiting for just such visitors. He patted Presh on the shoulder and gazed out at the view.

"Grab that package with the jug before you hop down," he called to Dykes. Dykes did as instructed and fell into step with Mosby in an approach to the front door.

Mrs. Russ had it open in a welcome as they neared the base of the steps. A small pair of glasses was hiding among her curls, and she held a book with one hand protruding from casually crossed arms. "Well good afternoon, Jeb. To what do I owe the pleasure?"

Jeb removed his hat and gave a little bow from his shoulders. "Trust that the pleasure is mine, Mrs. Russ. And I am here to right a wrong." He motioned to the brown paper parcel tucked under Dykes' arm. "Fannie had borrowed one of your jugs, if you recall. Unfortunately I rendered it unserviceable with my rifle and have come begging forgiveness. And with one of Jim Cogg's finest jugs."

"Well come on in," Mrs. Russ said. She paused and eyed Dykes. Mosby took the hint.

"Let me introduce our new neighbor, Solomon Dykes."

Dykes mimicked Mosby's bow. "It is a pleasure."

She smiled. "Gwendolyn Russ. Very nice to meet you, and do come in."

The inside of the house was cool despite the heat of the day. It was just as neat and tidy as the yard, with claw-footed furniture toeing Oriental rugs.

She put the book on a table and offered them a seat in one of the front rooms. "Would either of you care for tea or a nice glass of water?"

"I will take some water, thank you," Mosby said. "Sol?"

"The same, thank you."

"I'll be back in a tick," she said. "And I'll put that jug in the kitchen, thank you." Dykes handed it to her.

As she walked into the kitchen she called over a shoulder, "You really didn't have to do this, Jeb. I hadn't expected the jug back."

"Well you know Fannie," he said, realizing that to leave it at that might sound too careless. "And I felt horrible about mistreating it, so I'm glad to make things right."

Dykes gazed around the room as his eyes adjusted to the lower light. There was a portrait of a uniformed man above the fireplace and several framed tintypes on tables and shelves. An oil rendering of a bowl of fruit hung above the high-backed sofa they were both on. A pendulum grandfather clock stood in one corner, quietly swinging out the seconds.

Mrs. Russ returned with two glasses of water, handed them to the men, and took one of two seats flanking a small table opposite them. She smoothed her dress as she sat.

"So, Mr. Dykes. When did you move in?"

"A few weeks back now. I am on the property just south of Jeb's land. This is a truly beautiful part of the country."

"He's on what was John Stibbs' place," Mosby said. Mrs. Russ nodded.

"I came here from Connecticut in the spring and have spent some time in Lincoln ahead of moving in."

"Connecticut?" Mrs. Russ took the glasses from her head and folded them on the table, on top of the book she had left there. "Did you serve?"

Dykes leaned forward to fold his hands, resting his forearms on his knees. "I did. I served in the 12th Regiment, Connecticut Volunteer Infantry."

"Did you see fighting in Virginia?" she asked.

"I did." He left it at that.

"Sol and I haven't discussed the war much," Mosby said. "We've found more pressing talk in maintaining our properties and such. Sol, what do you think to plant next year?"

Mrs. Russ dodged the conversational parry. "I think wartime is very pressing talk. It still bears the county with quite a weight, you know. The Commonwealth as a whole, for that matter."

"It does that, yes," said Mosby. He was regretting the invite for Dykes to join him. A real live Yankee in the hall of Gwen Russ.

"I was stationed in Virginia, but most of my deployment was further south. In Mississippi and Louisiana. Some time in Georgia. My time here in the Commonwealth was late in the war and blessedly peaceful, at least as compared to earlier times," Dykes said.

"Blessedly peaceful," Mrs. Russ repeated. "It was not so for our community here, I'm afraid. The Mosbys can tell you as much."

"It was hard and sad times, yes," Mosby said. "I wish I had been here to help. I was too far from home to protect what we all hold dear. But it was hard for everyone, Gwen. Even our friend from Connecticut, I'm sure."

"Why did you enlist, Mr. Dykes?" Mrs. Russ asked, stiffening her posture. He took a sip of water before answering.

"I joined to preserve our Union." He said it sincerely and into her eyes.

"And you, Mr. Mosby?"

"To protect my home. But as I said, that aim didn't work out as I hoped."

"Well I can speak for the Lieutenant Colonel in saying that he joined for the Commonwealth." She nodded toward the portrait above the fireplace. "He stood by Virginia against Northern aggression, and I am proud of him for it. But you see, Mr. Dykes, whether fighting to defend Virginia or your own home, the Confederacy and its armies had a very noble cause that went beyond political ideals. We were fighting off an invasion. We were protecting our way of life on the lands we have called home for generations. We have just met, and I do want to be a good hostess, but I find it interesting that those Yankee veterans I have spoken to sound very much like yourself. They have fought for a political ideal. We have fought for our home. And we lost the fight. That is a bitter pill to swallow. A very bitter pill."

The grandfather clock kept steady time as the room fell silent.

"I understand, or I would like to someday fully understand, how you must feel," Dykes said. "I see strong people in this community, and I feel lucky to have joined it."

"Well, we're glad to have you," Mosby said. "Did I tell you Sol found Pappy when he had wandered off last spring? I feel I still owe him a debt."

Mrs. Russ stood up. "You owe him nothing, Jeb. I have no reason to doubt you are a kind man, Mr. Dykes, but Jeb owes you nothing." She went to a small box on the mantle and opened it. "I'm glad you've come calling, Jeb, as you've been on my mind. You may recall the jacket I was wearing — I believe it was when Tom was missing?"

"I do," said Mosby.

"Well I had four of those buttons made into two pair of cuff-links. A curious thing to have done, perhaps. But I would like you to have these remaining five. I have no use for them, though they remain dear to me. They need a caretaker." She stretched her hand out to him, exposing the cluster of brass buttons, kept polished with care.

"I can't take these. Thank you, though."

"What am I going to do with them?" She jutted her hand further to press the offer. "Please, Jeb. The Lieutenant Colonel would approve of this gesture — he did so love Tom."

Mosby hesitated a moment more and then took them from her hand. "Well I will certainly treasure them. Thank you, Gwen. He was a fine man. A fine man."

"Indeed he was," Mrs. Russ said with an absent gaze at the floor.

"Fannie will count these as precious, as well, I'm sure." He looked to Dykes. "And speaking of Fannie, we should be getting along. I hate to make it such a quick visit, but I did want you to meet Mr. Dykes."

"I'm glad of it," Mrs. Russ said. "Please come visit any time."

"Thank you for the water, Mrs. Russ," Dykes said as he rose somewhat stiffly. The group exchanged a few more pleasantries and then the two men were out the door.

Back on the cart they were mutually reserved, jostling down the hill. "She is forward," Dykes said.

"Yep. I told you."

"We haven't discussed it, the war," Dykes said. "Was it hard for Fannie at home?"

Mosby sighed hard and gazed ahead as they turned back onto the main road. "Our daughter, Maybelle. She helped Fannie keep things running after I left, with Pappy able to spend less time in the field. She was becoming a strong woman." He flicked at the reins and gnawed a bit at the inside of his lip. "Yankee soldiers. They took our food stores. They did unspeakable things to our Maybelle and left her for dead. Yes. Yes, it was hard."

Dykes opened his mouth to offer a condolence but his voice did not come. His face burned at his carelessness — he knew they had lost their daughter during the war.

The pair remained silent for the rest of the ride.

CHAPTER 17

DYKES AND MOSBY did not dig a privy hole that evening, and the pistol remained untested. Dykes had thanked him for the ride at the Mosby property and insisted that he walk the piece of road home. They remained pleasant with each other, but there was a fresh uneasiness between them.

Dykes walked into the stillness of his house and laid his knapsack on the kitchen table. He pulled out his sack of provisions, laid the pistol on the table, and fetched an oil lamp. He was not yet hungry, but the light was fading and he wanted to use a new stationery set he'd bought at Cogg's to pen a few pieces of correspondence. The first, to Cassius Freeman.

Before moving into the Stibbs property, Dykes had taken Freeman up on his offer to come calling in Lincoln. He had enjoyed their brief encounter on the road to Leesburg and felt they had connected in a very positive way. And the town was not far west of Leesburg. Once the matter of the land purchase was in order, he made the walk in a morning.

With the little knowledge he had of the place, he quickly found the school where Freeman worked by asking a passerby just outside of town. The Oakdale School. It was a one-room brick building with a peaked roof and wide, sunny windows.

The Quakers had built it to the south of town in a sparse patch of trees, dedicating it to education. The modest square building held classes for both youths and adults, white and colored.

Dykes rapped on the open door frame, having arrived at the school between classes. An older man, cleanly but simply dressed, was inside collecting woodworking tools from tables at the front. He turned.

"Yes? May I offer thee help?"

"Yes, sir. I am hoping to find a Mr. Cassius Freeman. We spoke last week and he mentioned working here."

"Yes, Cassius Freeman. He has just stepped out on an errand but should be back momentarily. Would thee care to wait?" He spoke in the old way, as Dykes had heard Quakers do, even and slow but purposeful, with a Northern timbre to it.

"Yes, thank you. My name is Solomon Dykes." He approached the man with a handshake.

"Jacob Palmer. It is a pleasure." He shook with a tight grip, despite hands bent from age. A wiry graying neckbeard bushed out from under his clean-shaven jawline. "Thee may place thy bags wherever there is space."

Dykes leaned his bags against the wall near the door. "Can I help?"

"Well certainly. I am just tidying up ahead of our second afternoon class. Today it is both woodworking and metalwork in the afternoon." He paused as if to savor a breath through wispy nostrils. "The children are here mornings."

"Metalwork?" Dykes walked past benches to the front of the room and began wiping wood shavings off a table top into his cupped hand. "I have some skill there."

"Does thee? That's fine." The man continued his work and fell silent, save for the whispers of his nose hair between breaths.

Dykes had only cleaned two of the table tops when Cassius arrived. Jacob looked up as he walked through the doorway.

"Hello to thee, Cassius Freeman. This man has been helping me while he waited on thy return."

Cassius' face lighted with recognition. "Yes, yes — well hello, Mr. Dyke."

"Hello, sir. It's Dykes, but I'm impressed by your memory nonetheless."

"Pardon me, Mr. Dykes," Freeman shook his hand vigorously. "I should say I'm impressed by yours. So you found me?"

"I did indeed. I finished some business in Leesburg and seem to have a bit of time on my hands. Thought about our conversation, your school here. Perhaps I could be of help?"

Freeman looked to Jacob across the room. "I'm sure you could. No doubt you could. Mr. Palmer, is there work to be done? Mr. Dykes here has come from up North to do some good in our part of the world. Connecticut, if my memory serves?" Dykes nodded.

Jacob slid an armload of tools into a chest along the back wall. He finished his task slowly, closed the chest, and walked over to the pair. He eyed Dykes.

"We could always use help. What kind of help is the question. What work does thee do, Solomon Dykes?"

"Well you mentioned metalwork. That has been my profession—tinkering, really. My trade if I were to be pinned with one."

"Britannia ware, correct?" Freeman added.

"Yes, Britannia ware. It's a pewter."

"Fine. Britannia ware. Fine," Jacob continued to study Dykes with his jaw slightly jutting into the air between them. "We have a tinkering class this afternoon. Feel free to stay and observe. If thee sees the opportunity to help, we will be glad to have it."

* * *

DYKES DID STAY for the class. It was taught by Thad Williams, who worked at the tin shop in town. As students — adults and some adolescent children — filed in, Dykes and Freeman took a seat on a bench along a side wall. The room grew quiet and instruction began, the students working at folding and pressing a piece of tin. Dykes leaned over with a whisper: "I'm surprised at the mix."

"Surprised at the what?"

"The mix. The mix of whites and colored folks. It is not what I expected, but a pleasure to see."

"Ah yes, the mix," Cassius said. "There are plenty in need of new skills in these times, regardless of color or creed."

"I suppose so."

After a pause, Cassius added, "These people are something else, the Quakers. You should stay here a spell to soak up some of their nature, if nothing else. In these times, they stand like a balm against the chafe of society."

Dykes considered it as he watched the rest of the class. The group left with some new skills and a simple candleholder to show for it, scraps of tin bent, riveted, and held with a simple weld to keep a candle upright and its wax from spilling. Those bold enough added a finger loop. Dykes spoke a bit with Thad, the instructor, after the class, before finding Freeman outside.

"Thad Williams is open to my assistance for as long as I can offer it. I don't see why I couldn't stay the week through," Dykes said. "I need to stop by his shop to coordinate timing."

"I am pleased to hear it. You won't find a better way to spend your time, especially if you can speak with men like Ben Tyson. He's an elder here in the community. Now what's a shame is that you missed Samuel Janney. He is a fine man. But he moved on. Fairly recent, but he moved on."

"Janney? Where did he go?"

"Left for the west — Nebraska? Sounds like a world away. Doing work with Indian affairs, what we've heard."

"I would imagine we have some things in common," Dykes said. "Finding a cause at a journey's end."

"He's a special breed." Freeman nodded. "But you watch yourself talking like you do. Not many folks around here would consider themselves a cause. And I wouldn't say you're quite at journey's end, either. It's a hard road you're on." He looked up at clouds overhead crossing the sun. "But I like where you're headed. So where will you stay while in Lincoln? Or have you already made acquaintances around town?"

"Ah yes. I haven't thought that far ahead. Where would you recommend?"

"There are a few homes that offer rooms for rent. But I think you're an interesting man, Mr. Dykes."

"What does one have to do with the other?"

"I'd like to see how you spend your time here in Lincoln. There's a blanket and a nice piece of floor in my home if you're so inclined."

"Well, that's a kind offer," Dykes said with a smile. "I'm flattered you'd have me."

* * *

FREEMAN'S HOUSE was a modest one-room clapboard cabin in a cluster of like structures shaded by a stand of cottonwoods. It had a covered porch, and inside was a cast-iron stove on a pad of brick, a tidy sitting area, and a well-made cot. The walls were papered with broadsheets from what seemed to be a variety of newspapers. Without leaning in close, Dykes could only make out a few headlines in the dimly lit room, most from before the war, he guessed.

"You like my wallpapering?" Freeman asked with a slight grin. "I hung all of these. Keeps the drafts out and keeps my mind occupied." He walked over to a corner and smoothed his hand over one piece of tattered paper, *The Memphis Daily Appeal*. "I learned to read with this sheet right here."

Dykes stepped over to take a closer look. The front page held some news about railroad routes and expansions, and several advertisements.

"See these pictures?" Freeman pointed to an illustration of a tiny train, a ship under sail, a fish — all scattered among text in each column. "These were my guide. These words here must be about a train. These, about hats or clothing or what have you."

"You taught yourself to read?"

"I did indeed. I did have some help clarifying a word here and there, of course, but I had this as my tool. I had time, and I had determination. It's amazing what a man can do with time and determination. Me and this paper here, we've been some places together." He took Dykes' bags. "And now you join us. Welcome!"

"You're very kind to invite me in."

"Think nothing of it. I'll leave you to rest a bit and get settled. We all share a necessary house over yonder, and I fetch water from a creek a short walk away. Let's see. We tend to share meals together as a group, me and my neighbors, and you're welcome to join."

"Sounds fine," Dykes said. "Are your neighbors Quakers?"

"We're not all Quakers, per se, but we're all friendly to them. If you really want to get to know some Quakers, you should start by attending a meeting. Their worship service."

"When are meetings?"

"Thursday. And Sunday. Tomorrow. First Day, they call it. I'll join you if you do care to go."

"I should like that, yes," Dykes said. Freeman nodded and turned to reenter the fading sunlight outside. Dykes took another look around the room and moved his bags to a corner. Eyeing the *Daily Appeal*, he walked over to study its headlines, imagining how an illiterate man might come to make words and phrases from what would seem to be jumbled stacks of letters. Not even letters to those eyes, but mere symbols. The disorder of it all would be overwhelming to most in that position.

Time and determination, indeed.

* * *

DYKES SPENT a restful night on the floor, sleeping fully among heavy quilted blankets. Freeman had warned him that raccoons occasionally found their way through the latch to try their luck with tins of food kept on a shelf along one wall, but if they came calling in the night, Dykes slept through it.

When he awoke, Freeman was not present but had left a basin of water on the floor near the pallet. A small towel was folded next to it. Dykes obliged himself to the basin and washed up, still nestled among thick ropes of warm quilt.

He emerged onto the porch to see a group gathered on benches along a table beneath the tallest cottonwood tree in the stand. An open-air structure served as a kitchen for this small colored community, best Dykes could tell, standing off to the side of the tree but still under its shade. It had one wall in the back, lined with shelves, and a large table for food preparation, all sheltered by a simple, slightly pitched A-frame roof. A large, older woman busied herself at a kettle hanging over a nearby fire pit.

The group was talking quietly and eating breakfast, occasionally passing a piece of fruit or a basket of bread among them.

Dykes didn't spot Cassius, but approached the table nonetheless. "Good morning," he said warmly, raising a hand.

Those with their backs to him turned. "Well good morning, sugar," said one of the older ladies. "You hungry?"

"I am, thank you." Dykes was growing accustomed to frequent hospitality from complete strangers, although it still seemed a bit undeserved to him.

"Cassius said you'd be waking shortly. And here you are, risen with the sun."

"I suppose I am." He took a seat at the end of a bench as the group shuffled over to accommodate him. "With the sun."

"Miss Patience don't wait for the sun," a young man with a clean-shaven head joked from the other end of the table. "She work harder than that sun." Everyone laughed.

Dykes smiled and nodded. "I have a lot to learn from Miss Patience, it seems." Who he now assumed was Miss Patience emerged from the kitchen area with a bowl and spoon for him. She ladled in some oatmeal from a common pot and set it before him.

"Here, sugar. Start your day right."

He thanked her and took a few bites of the oatmeal, testing its heat. It was warm but gummy, without much flavor. The table was silent for a moment, so Dykes took advantage of the pause. "Where is Cassius? Has he eaten already?"

"Don't know, but he'll be back shortly, so he said," said the young man. An uneven scar ran from above his ear to the nape of his neck in a hooked U-shape. Dykes wondered how he shaved around it. There was no stray stubble — it was all shaved smooth. Dykes nodded again in response.

After another minute of quiet eating they started a conversation that Dykes assumed he had interrupted.

"I tell you one thing," said a thin, hard-looking lady. She took a pause and chewed some bread. "She ain't gonna wear that dress no more." Everyone laughed heartily at this.

"Maybe just on Sundays," another said. They all laughed again.

"Maybe…" the young man tried to talk but started laughing. He lowered his head to the table and his shoulders shook with a silent merriment. "Maybe she wear it again for Sam Davis."

This got the table. Miss Patience whooped with a surprised laugh and the thin lady leaned back with a broad smile. "You stop that now," another finally said through a laugh. "We gonna get in trouble. You gonna run off this nice man here."

Dykes nodded and smiled. "I can't run off with this oatmeal here," he said.

"Smart man," another replied.

After Dykes had taken a few more bites, Cassius walked up from between some of the small houses. Dykes looked up in relief. He wasn't sure when the Quaker meeting was and had yet to devise a polite exit from the table.

"Good morning, Mr. Dykes. I see Miss Patience is fattening you up a bit with her breakfast."

"She is indeed," Dykes said. "This is a fine way to be treated by new acquaintances."

"Well Cassius said you was a good man, so you're welcome at this table," Miss Patience said.

"He is a good man," Cassius echoed. "And he is due at the Meeting House. You about done with your breakfast, Mr. Dykes?"

"I am indeed." Dykes took a handkerchief from his pocket and wiped his mouth and the spoon he was using. He placed it back on the table next to his empty bowl. "Thank you all for your hospitality."

The group offered a general farewell as the pair left them and the shade of the cottonwood trees.

"They treat you alright?" Freeman asked as they walked.

"Your neighbors there? Yes, of course. That was a fine welcome to start the day."

"Well I apologize for starting out without you this morning. I had a few chores to do ahead of the meeting. And you seemed to be sleeping soundly."

"I appreciate it. And I'm happy to help with chores where I can," Dykes said. "Just say the word."

"Thank you," Freeman said. "I surely will."

* * *

THE TWO-STORY BRICK Meeting House was not far off the road, with a spotty patch of lawn in front where churchgoers — friends, as Dykes learned they called themselves — paused with greetings before stepping inside. A tall, rather gaunt looking man, with a neatly kept dark gray beard along his jawline, stood under the roof of the porch to greet all as they entered. He smiled at the sight of Freeman.

"Good morning, Cassius Freeman. So glad to have you with us today."

"Good morning, Mr. Tyson. I would like to introduce you to a friend of mine, Mr. Solomon Dykes." He turned to address Dykes. "This is Mr. Ben Tyson."

"Hello, Solomon Dykes."

"It's a pleasure to meet you, Mr. Tyson." Dykes shook the man's lean hand.

"Thee is new to our community?"

"I am visiting, but new to Virginia, yes."

"Well, we are pleased to have thee. And thee is in good company with Cassius Freeman."

"It is mutual," Freeman said.

"Very good," Ben said. "I will be glad to see thee inside."

The pair shuffled in among other Quakers and took a seat at the end of a pew along the back wall. The room was simple, with rows of pews facing a narrow podium at the front center of the room. A bare, windowless wall was behind the podium.

Once all had taken their seats, Ben approached the podium and smiled warmly at the group. "In this day, despite all manner of acts and alms given, I beseech ye to remember this one truth: the old covenant was broken for the new, of which Jesus Christ is sole mediator. As also the mediator between God and man, it is through Jesus Christ that man might ultimately be reconciled to God, absolved of sin. It is this state for which we strive."

He then took a seat in a chair at the front of the room and gazed quietly out at the crowd. No one spoke for a long pause. Dykes looked around the room in the growing silence for who might be missing a cue. No one seemed to be at the ready, no one opening a book or shuffling sheet music for the start of a hymn. Ben remained unflapped. Dykes glanced at Cassius, who seemed ready for the questioned look he gave him. He just held a finger up as if to say "wait."

Wait he did. The pause turned to minutes of silence, save for the occasional creak of a pew or the chirp of a bird through an open window along the side walls. After some time, a woman near the front of the room stood.

She cleared her throat lightly. "To not show love is not to show hate, but to show selfishness." She let her words linger for a moment and then sat down.

Dykes pondered the statement as the room settled back into silence. Moments later a young man stood from a seat just ahead of them.

"Behold, I have created the smith that bloweth the coals in the fire, and that bringeth forth an instrument for his work; and I have created the waster to destroy." As he spoke, the man's voice rose up and cascaded down as if he were singing a song with no music. "No weapon that is formed against thee shall prosper; and every tongue that shall rise against thee in judgment thou shalt condemn."

Several around the room nodded their heads as he took his seat.

The silence seemed to grow deeper at that moment, and the crowd fell into the rhythm of it. Dykes resisted the urge to check his watch as the minutes wore on. He studied the floor between his feet. Three nails held the edge of a floorboard down where one should have done the job, two of them bent by an unseen knot in the wood. He wondered if Cassius ever spoke. He wondered if he should speak. It would be just as easy to stand. What would he say? He knew only one Bible verse, which didn't seem an appropriate addition to the orations on record.

A man at the front corner of the room stood. Ben's face turned to gaze at him peacefully.

"I slew a hog on the fifth day last," the man began. "But I stuck him in the gut, and the blood ran slow. He made grunts and squeals could be heard in the house. Mama said to stop it, so I returned to dispatch him with a hammer. But the hammer..." The man stopped and put his head down. He shook it from side to side rapidly before staring hard ahead. "The hammer fell to his skull and drew the grunts out slower and lower."

Two ladies a few pews up exchanged horrified glances.

Ben interrupted, politely. "Friend, please bring thy message to conclusion."

The man looked at Ben as if startled out of a trance. "I left him where he lay and the meat turned." He sat down quickly.

Ben cleared his throat. "Said the Lord to Peter, 'That God hath cleansed, that call not thou common.' Should a hog fall again under shameful blows, friend, seek repentance as thee did. But make its death known to the community, and they shall eat of it."

This seemed to satisfy the room, and the silence returned.

CHAPTER 18

Dykes did not return to the Meeting House during his stay in Lincoln. He found the town and its people refreshing, though, and following the meeting, he committed himself to making good on his offer to help. He began that afternoon with a visit to Thad Williams' tin shop. It stood alone in a cluster of buildings in the central part of town — much quieter than the bustle of Leesburg or even the main thoroughfare through Middleburg.

The shop was small, its ceiling made lower by thick beams encrusted with hanging pots, kettles, and other such wares, affixed to the wood like barnacles. Dykes wondered if any of it was ever sold. When he entered, Williams was cooling a weld in a barrel of water by an open window near the back of the shop. His gray-streaked hair was long and wavy but kept neat, pulled back tightly in a queue. He looked up and gave Dykes a nod, his hands busy with the tongs.

"Good day to thee! I am just finishing up a bit of work on a cup." He brought the piece up for a moment of air to study the weld of its handle. He furrowed his brow at it and plunged the cup back in. "This shop must be familiar to thee. Did thee have a shop in the north? Where is thee from, again?"

"Connecticut. Yes, it is indeed familiar." Dykes took a deep breath. "The smell of metalwork is unmistakable, and still somewhat dear to me." He took a seat and watched as Williams finished with the cup. "I can't say I'd ever have a shop like this again, though."

"Oh?" Williams dried the cup to shine and hung it on a peg near the window.

"My plan is to farm. But I find it fortuitous that I should have met you and found some work at the school. I am always glad to share my former craft."

"As thee has seen, another pair of hands would be of help. How long will thee stay in Lincoln? Yesterday Cassius Freeman spoke as if thy presence was transitory." Williams peered out the window as he spoke, his eyes studying something behind the shop.

"I had planned on a few days, but I could make it a bit longer if I'm needed. I have recently purchased some land near Middleburg, but the deed has not yet transferred."

"Ah. Thee is always welcome during my classes. I hold them five times a week — every day at two o'clock, but for First and Fifth days." Williams scowled, then pointed out the window. "I have unwelcome guests."

Dykes stood and walked over to see what could be back there. There was a pile of timber among the sagging remnants of a derelict structure. A few scrawny cats poked among the boards.

"My shed draws mice, mice draw cats, cats draw dogs." He looked at Dykes with wide eyes. "I do not want to see what dogs draw."

Dykes chuckled and studied the mess. "That's a shed?"

"Was a shed, I should say. The roof leaked and the frame rotted out, so I had it toppled. The clapboards are strong, though."

"I see." Dykes picked a tin plate off a nearby shelf and turned it in his hands. "You do fine work, Thad — this plate is smooth as china."

"I thank thee. It has been my family craft for generations. So, when could thee join me for class?"

"Well, how about this week I just plan to work alongside you at each. If you feel it goes well and I'm not just in the way, perhaps I could stay a bit longer."

Williams smiled broadly. "The class will be better for it. I do certainly appreciate it. Perhaps I can pick up a bit about Brittania ware from thee."

"I'll be happy to share what I know. I'm sure you can teach me a thing or two yourself."

The sound of loose boards clattered outside as a cat darted about in pursuit of unseen prey.

* * *

During his stay on the floor of Freeman's cabin, Dykes took to rising early with his host. The pair would walk down to a lively brook curving wide around the cluster of houses, wash up, and make their way to greet Miss Patience and whoever else might be up at that hour.

At the end of a week the same order was followed, although Dykes took a little extra care in making up his pallet on the floor. There was work for him at the school, although he had become a bit anxious what with all the time between classes. He wanted to check on his land and get to know Middleburg before the transfer was settled. Time lodged at the town's inn would do him good.

The sun broke through the cottonwood trees at a harsh angle as he and Freeman walked up the gentle slope from the brook to the kitchen shelter.

"It just struck me: today is Sunday," Dykes said. "Will you be going to the Meeting House?"

Freeman shook his head. "No, no. Not today. They're fine people, as I've said and as you've now seen, but their Meetings aren't for me. I prefer a bit more jubilation in my worship."

"Yes, I could see why. The silence would take some getting used to."

"It has its purpose, and I can respect that. Sometimes a quiet mind is the best place to hear God speaking. But when I'm gathered in worship, a joyful noise seems more natural," Freeman said.

"So where do you worship, then?"

"Well, funny you should ask."

Miss Patience straightened up as they approached the kitchen and greeted them with a wide smile. "Good morning to you, gentlemen! I have a treat for us today. A Sunday breakfast of ham and eggs with blueberry biscuits."

"My goodness." Freeman gave her a hug. "And to think this morning Mr. Dykes said to me: Cassius, let's just sleep in and breakfast on what you have tinned here on your shelves."

"I said nothing of the sort." Dykes had grown accustomed to their ribbing. "I am no scholar, Miss Patience, but I know well enough to breakfast at your table whenever presented the opportunity."

Freeman laughed. "No tinned meat for you, Solomon? Well I just hope Miss Patience has enough eggs for you."

"You stop teasing this nice man," she said, giving Freeman's arm a pop with a towel. "It's you I don't have the eggs for."

Freeman took a seat on a bench pulled just under the roofline and leaned his back against a support post. "I'll take some eggs off Abraham then."

"That boy needs all the eggs he can get, Mr. Freeman. You're out of luck on that one."

Freeman laughed. "Mr. Dykes was just asking me where I worship on Sundays."

Miss Patience's face lit up. "Was he now? So he don't know?"

"No, last week we went to the Meeting House together. This is his first Sunday otherwise."

"I suppose it is." She walked over to tend the fire pit where several cast-iron skillets were warming on coals.

"Well, you're looking at it," Freeman motioned to the beams above their heads.

"Oh — you worship here, in the open?"

"Indeed we do. It's mighty fine this time of year," Freeman said.

"But you don't want to come around in the winter months," Miss Patience chimed in from her post. "Or the summer. Lord, the summer. Bugs will near eat you up. In the winter, the wind will turn you right back 'round to your cabin."

Dykes studied the shelter around them. "So why does it not have walls, then? It's a fine looking structure otherwise. The post footings seem to be sound. Roof beams straight and well supported."

"We began building this last summer, as our own Meeting House, if you will. A church, a place for community," Cassius said.

"We tired of worship in drafty barns, musty basements, and stuffy cabins," Miss Patience added. "We need a proper house for the Lord."

"The townsfolk were quite helpful in getting us this far," Freeman continued. "But we just ran out of time and materials, plain and simple. We've all got other jobs to keep us busy. And then winter came, and here we are."

"Well that's a shame." Dykes ran his hand along the vertical length of a pillar, feeling its plumb. "Will building start up again now that the weather is in your favor?"

"I like to think so. If we find a good source of lumber, perhaps."

Freeman raised his hand to greet a group coming up from behind Dykes. He turned to see many of the now-familiar faces he had first breakfasted with a week ago.

"I know we have you for breakfast, but what are you doing with the rest of your day, Mr. Dykes?" Miss Patience asked.

"To be honest, I had planned to travel on." Dykes looked at

Freeman as he answered. "I feel I should check on the land I've purchased and become acquainted with its surrounds."

"That makes sense," Freeman said.

"Well before you go and do anything why don't you join us for worship?" Miss Patience said. "We'll clean up after breakfast here for the service and then get you on the road with a lunch packed and your soul full."

"I certainly do appreciate the invite," Dykes said. "Yes, thank you. It would do me good."

* * *

As the last of the blueberry biscuits were finished and cups were filled with second servings of coffee, Dykes looked out from under the cover of the shelter to see a black-clad colored man riding a scrawny horse into the stand of cottonwoods. He wore a flat-topped hat, similar to a Hardee hat but with a wider brim, and a long riding mac over a white shirt and tie. He slowed the horse to a stop and grinned broadly at the group.

"My flock has assembled! And a blessed morning to you all." His voice was deep and rich. He dismounted as Abraham, the young man with the hook scar, took the horse by the bridle. "Brother Abraham, you're looking well." The pair clasped hands and pulled into a hug. He unbuckled a strap on his saddle bag and reached in to take out a thick black book — a Bible, Dykes presumed.

Freeman walked over to Dykes and poured a coffee from the kettle nearby. "The Reverend Ainsley. A circuit rider of the Methodist Episcopal church."

"An itinerant preacher?"

"Indeed, and a fine one at that."

The Reverend made his rounds through the crowd, shaking hands, sharing hugs, and catching up with the group. He eyed Dykes twice as he did so, clearly making his way to the newcomer. Miss Patience offered him a mug of coffee as he stepped under the shade of the roofline. Dykes rose to greet him with a handshake. His grip was strong, his meaty palm calloused.

"Good morning to you, Reverend. I'm Solomon Dykes, a guest of Mr. Freeman's."

"A blessed morning to you, Mr. Dykes. Jon Ainsley, but you can call me Preacher Jon."

Miss Patience stood to the side, between the two, smiling as a witness to the introduction. "He say you can call him that, but we call him Reverend Ainsley."

"Ms. Ulbright is too formal," the Reverend said, giving her arm a squeeze. "So where are you visiting from, Mr. Dykes?"

"I'm in a bit of a transition, to be honest. I traveled down from Connecticut last month, now planning to make a home near Middleburg. In the interim I have found most wonderful hosts here in your congregation."

"Well I am not surprised to hear that at all. You are staying for worship?"

"Indeed I am," Dykes said. "And where are you traveling from?"

"My home is north, in Waterford. I stayed last night in a community between here and there and gave a sunrise service this morning. Before riding here on old Samson. For my second cup of coffee!" He raised the mug and grinned at Miss Patience. "The better cup, if I must say."

He had a bite to eat and finished his coffee as the group moved a table and lined benches up in rows. Dykes took a seat in the back, apart from Cassius, in an old chair with two missing spindles.

In time, Rev. Ainsley stood and walked to the front of the benches, a sign for the group to quiet and take seats. He opened in a short prayer, his big voice filling the shelter and spilling out into the cottonwood grove. All heads were bowed, a few arms were raised with hands outstretched. Almost seamlessly, the prayer ended and his voice shifted into song. He alone sung at first:

"O, for a closer walk with God,
A calm and heavenly frame;
A light to shine upon the road
That leads me to the Lamb."

He raised a hand and the group echoed his last lines, booming out in a chorus of mixed sopranos, tenors, baritones, and bass — all different, none perfect, but wholly joyful:

"A light to shine upon the road
That leads me to the Lamb."

As Rev. Ainsley led into the next verse, Dykes looked over the assembly with a slight smile on his face, watching with the self-aware satisfaction of someone appreciating a thing foreign to him, knowing it will never be his own.

CHAPTER 19

THE PEN SCRATCHED a signature onto the stationery in the lamp-light. The light outside was the deep rust-orange that comes before some summer nights. Dykes blotted the letter to Cassius, folded it, and put it aside. He took a breath and creaked back in his desk chair, stretching his arms and shaking his right hand, out of practice in writing.

He reached furtively for the next piece of stationery. A letter had formed in his mind, but to put it to paper made him nervous. He leaned forward and dipped his pen.

Dear Ms. Tompkins,

I shall like to think that you recognize the name on this correspondence, but I cannot presume my acquaintance would hold in your memory. You were kind to me one night in the spring as I traveled through to Virginia. My mind's eye turns often to your warm home and the hospitality you showed me. I remain a stranger now as I was then

He stopped. Studied the letter. And crumpled it in his fist. He sighed and took another piece of stationery from the set. He wiped his hand on his shirtfront to dry sweat from the meat of his palm and dipped the pen once more.

Dear Beth,

Some time has passed since we met, and true to our conversation in the cool of a spring evening, I have traveled to Virginia to make a home. It is beautiful here, much more beautiful than I remembered, perhaps due to a peace that has settled over the land. Gone is the canon fire, gone are the marches and thundering hoof beats of armies on the move.

Your map proved invaluable in my journeys, as it remains to this day. Through it I have the advantage of geographic details that many locals may not even enjoy. Through it I have met friends, found my home, gathered provisions, and made plans for future travels. How fortuitous to come by such a cherished thing through our chance meeting.

In my experience thus far since leaving the boundaries of Connecticut, I remain most impressed by your hospitality and the kindness you showed a stranger in need.

I should like to think that, should you find yourself in Loudoun County, you would come calling so that I might return your hospitality and treat you as a guest in my new home. It is a simple farmhouse, but it stands on a piece of fertile land nestled among woodlands, neat-stacked stone walls, and creeks flowing freely from the mountains yonder.

You had mused that you could not imagine a reason to venture south to Virginia. I only hope that this correspondence and my invitation provides you some shred of reason. Until then, I remain.

Most sincerely,

1st Lt. S. Dykes

Dykes sat back and considered the words on the page. Satisfied, he blotted it before carefully penning directions to his property on another sheet of stationery. He blotted that, laid it behind the other and married the two with a crisp fold.

He snuffed the oil lamp and went to the kitchen for some dinner.

CHAPTER 20

JOURNAL *of 2nd Lt. Solomon Dykes*

Wednesday, January 14, 1863

Another eventful day has passed along the Bayou Teche. After yesterday's encounter with hardscrabble rebels firing upon us from their lightly armored steamer, I had hopes to return to our unit and prepare for any ground troops that may be accompanying the vessel along its route. The loss of our ferry crossing proved that more of a task than initially thought, however.

Soon after daybreak we were met by a troop transport, the Drummond, which is a rear-paddlewheel steamer commandeered from a cotton company in Mississippi. She's a lovely craft, with a flat, broad main deck and tiers of open decks above, some with cabins on the interior. Ironwork flourishes ring her railings and columns between decks. One can walk all the way around the vessel on any upper deck, save for the top pilot house, flanked by two rather stately smokestacks. It is lightly manned, having recently deposited a company of men some miles upriver.

Although I would have liked it to maneuver to the opposite bank once accepting us on board, serving as the mere ferry vessel we desired, it seems our cohort's intentions did not reach so far as the captain or the pilot. For once we cleared the gangway, she steamed full on down river. My companions and I exchanged baffled glances as the opposite side of the river crossing — and the road back to our regimental camp — quickly disappeared behind us.

We soon surmised that the transport had orders to tail the Confederate craft we had caught a glimpse of yesterday, and remain just within view from behind until our fleet of gunboats could arrive and engage it. The plan seemed well enough, and my companions and I situated ourselves behind a portion of bulwark near the bow, rifles at the ready.

The Drummond steamed on without incident for an hour or so, until an island came into view, cleaving the main tributary of the bayou in two. The left passage was wider than the right and an obvious preferred means of transport, although as we neared it became clear the passage had been blocked. The water was relatively shallow here, and all manner of limbs and debris were locked together creating a fairly formidable obstacle. Even portions of what seemed to be an old barn were visible among the mess, presumably dragged and placed by the crew of the cottonclad steamer, of which there was no other sign.

Our vessel was quickly pivoted and turned for the narrow, seemingly clear passage south. Within minutes, however, the banks hemmed us in and the water became clogged with looming cypress trees, waterlogged hardwoods and interlocking limbs and debris amongst them all. The transport pushed as far in as she could before wheeling to a halt. The captain ordered her crew to the bow, to take up poles, axes, and whatever other tools could be found to help clear the mess. It seemed one could almost step out and walk across the litter floating amongst the swampy forest, and some proved it possible in an effort to clear the debris. My mind instinctively fixed on our vulnerable position — the woods were dark and crowded, and our being here by rebel design made me most uncomfortable.

After the better part of an hour was spent tossing limbs aside in an exhausting act of futility, our crew heard movement in the woods on shore. Peering among the trees, one could make out the comforting deep blue of Union uniforms fanning out through the forest on patrol. We hailed them, and after an exchange with the captain of the Drummond it was settled that our group could join them, eventually to make our way back to our regiment by land. At least we were on the right side of the river.

The troops were a mix of several batteries sent north from a flotilla of four of our gunboats — men from Massachusetts, Maine, and New York. From their telling, the Confederate steamer, appropriately named the Cotton, had churned south, blocking passage behind as we'd discovered. Sometime in the early morning she hit the remains of an old bridge spanning the bayou and sat idle. The calm was not to remain, however, for our ships arrived and gave her a pounding from over the bridge, sending her back north. The Cotton was hemmed in by her crew's own making, leaving it only a matter of time before we could get at them.

Our group ventured back south along the river, staying a safe distance inland and occasionally engaging shoreline rebel rifle pits from behind. My regimental companions and I did not have the opportunity to fire our rifles, for most of the action was taken on by sharpshooters from the New York battery.

At one point in the early afternoon, our group halted at the sound of maneuvers on the river. We laid low and moved slowly for a better view, only to see the Cotton, visibly damaged, engaged in a slow turn. The vessel was shifting its paddles from forward to reverse and back again to make the turn in the narrow channel. Some of her cotton bales had been toppled, many had blown out of their banded burlap and were shedding contents into the breeze, like snow flurries stark against the murky river below. As close as I was to her, I could see bands of iron had been fastened to her hull, at some points bent into and splintering the wood beneath. A group of men peered down over the bow, another over the stern, calling directions to the pilot.

We scrambled to take shelter behind trees along the bank and began giving the ship volleys of fire, sending the men onboard ducking for cover behind the remaining bales. They pivoted a deck gun our way and fired into the trees above, raining a hail of moss-tangled limbs down onto us. This went on for minutes as the ship continued making the turn. Once her bow was pointed southward enough to avoid the bank, *the paddles were thrown full forward and churned away from the hell we were giving her. Our cheers from the forest were returned with taunts and vulgarities from the deck of the departing steamer, a few of the rebels firing back at us from the stern. The Cotton's flag was hanging limp from its pole, in tatters.*

CHAPTER 21

A ROOSTER CALLED WEAKLY in the strong light of day. Mosby tore at a piece of buttered bread and stared at Pappy across the kitchen table.

"Lands sakes, Pappy. That rooster is broke."

Pappy didn't respond but sipped coffee with his gaze fixed toward the window.

"He's been rising later each day," Mosby added. "Must be the laughing stock of the henhouse by now."

Pappy took a sip of coffee. "Well. Robert will dispatch him rightly as part of his morning chores."

"Robert Welch?" Mosby stirred his eggs with the bread. "Robert. He died, Pappy. He died years ago. You remember? He moved up to Goresville and spent many a good year there before the war."

Fannie came in from the yard shaking out a blanket. "I had this out there all night and it's as damp as when I first wrung it."

"Damned wet heat, Fannie. Try working in it."

"I do work in it, thank you very much. Stand and stir a boiling cauldron of your old shirts for ten minutes and we'll see who complains about the wet heat." She poked at the coals in the fireplace and draped the blanket over the mantel.

"So Pappy is remembering ol' Robert. Did you ever meet him? I forget."

"No, I did not have the pleasure. But I have heard plenty of stories about him. I know mama loved having him around as a balance to you, Pappy."

Pappy took another sip of coffee and sat quiet.

"Are you going to take that Pappy? Sounds to me she's calling you useless." Mosby gently swatted Pappy's shirt at the elbow to stress the joke of it. Pappy drew a slow breath and looked out the window.

"Okay. Well. I need to go into town today, Butternut. My hoe broke and I just as soon replace it as try to mend it again."

"I saw it out there on the porch and figured as much. Stop by the ordinary and try to catch up on some news. I feel like I'm so out of touch lately," Fannie said.

"I could take lunch there. It's been awhile. I might need a pint, though."

"Well if you're asking my permission, you don't need it," Fannie said. "I'd like to sit in there and have a pint someday."

Mosby laughed. "I'd like to see that! You'd put all those asses in their place in a hurry. We'll see how today goes. Maybe next time you go and chat up Harlan Kirkbride."

"I'll do it," Fannie said with a grin.

"I know it. And all the problems of their world would be solved."

* * *

Mosby was smiling to himself as he entered Beveridge House, imagining Fannie sauntering in and taking a seat in the tavern. He would have preferred her company to the current lunch crowd. Jim Duncan was there, along with the typical crew that surrounded Kirkbride. Harlan, interestingly, was not to be seen.

Bob Spence was tending bar today. Mosby liked Bob,

although he was off-putting to some. His intentions were good, though he was not a man that bar service came to naturally.

"A hello to you, Bob," Mosby said, giving his palm a double smack on the oak counter. "How are things?"

"Things are good, Jeb. What can I get you?"

"That depends. What should I get?"

"For lunch? To drink?"

"Both."

"Well, we've got a ham that's nicely seasoned, served with potatoes. I'd recommend a cut of that before it's gone. And ale is ale, but I assume you'll need a pint?"

"You are correct, and the ham sounds fine. I'll take a seat with that lot." He gestured toward the small crowd seated around empty plates and half-drank beers. Bob nodded and Mosby walked over to the group. He took an empty seat at a table with two other farmers and joined a discussion about summer work and progress on this year's crop.

In time Bob came around with a pewter plate of ham and steaming potatoes, and half-tossed it onto the space before Mosby. He set a pint glass down somewhat carelessly, tilting its head over the rim.

"Thank you, Bob. My compliments. It looks fine." Bob nodded and shuffled back to take his place behind the bar.

Mosby took a cut of potato and rolled it around with his tongue to avoid burning any one part of his mouth. Out of habit he always ate a vegetable first when presented with a plate. Some part of him thought it crude to tuck into the meat straightaway. He took a sip of the warm ale to cool the potato a bit more, and placed it back square on the dark wet ring it had already made on the table. The ham was good. Just the right amount of brine to it.

"Good ham, Bob," Mosby called across the room. Bob glanced up and gave a nod.

Jim Duncan was seated at the opposite side of a long table

next to Mosby's, and their eyes met as Mosby speared another bit of potato with his fork.

"Afternoon, Jeb. I haven't seen much of you lately."

"Oh, I've been around. Working hard though to keep things in line back at home. You round up any trouble lately?"

"All quiet. Usually the heat gets to folks, but we haven't had much more than run-ins with varmints. A few strangers pass through to keep an eye on, but they never do no harm."

"Good to hear. I'll pass that on to Fannie and I'm sure she'll rest easier."

Duncan took a sip of his beer and sat back in his chair. "How's that neighbor of yours getting along?"

Mosby chuckled a bit. "That's something, isn't it? I was about ready to call you when I saw someone down on the Stibbs' land, and come to learn it's that Yankee fellow."

"Sol Dykes."

"Yes, Sol. Solomon. That was a surprise. Quite a surprise." Mosby stuffed a cut of ham in his cheek. He let a silence settle between him and Duncan and turned his attention back to his table. "Alright, so are either of you seeing as many cicadas this year as I am? Is it me or are there more of those damn things than ever?"

Within a few minutes the inevitable happened. Right in line with Mosby's expectations, Kirkbride ducked in through the entrance and knocked his boots loudly at the door frame. He stopped and spoke to Bob at the bar before strutting over to his usual table, already circled with his cronies. He sat without a word to anyone and slipped a flat, rectangular tin can out of his vest pocket. Its label was intricate and covered in scrollwork, best Mosby could see. On one side it had a little key, which he slowly cranked to roll back the top of the can.

"The hell is that?" Duncan asked, taking the bait. "That an opener on the can?"

"It is," Kirkbride said, focused on his task.

"And I thought I was something with my Bully beef opener."

"Well, this makes it easy. Efficient," Kirkbride said.

"Where'd you come by that?" another asked.

"The sardine tin? Me and that redbone from Louisiana who passed through some weeks back fell into conversation one evening. As it happened he was quite laden with wares from the Gulf port down there." He slipped a small bottle from his other coat pocket. "For instance…"

He placed the dark bottle on the table. It had a white diamond label on its side.

"That a bitters?" someone asked confidently.

"No, sir. It's a sauce. Tabas-co. A pepper sauce. Liquid pepper." From the can he forked out a dull silver piece of fish the size of his thumb, and flaked half its side from the bone beneath. He dashed on some of the watery sauce and popped the sardine in his mouth, chewing quickly and vigorously. His eyebrows lifted, making a show of it. "That's fine. That's just fine," he said, still chewing.

"Well, that's something else, Harlan," Duncan said. "I didn't know that redbone would've been worth a damn thing, let alone all these delicacies. I suppose you never know these days, what folks are up to."

"You never can tell, Jim," Kirkbride said. "Redbones, Indians, Gypsies, negroes, Melungeons — hell, the Irish." A few chuckled. "You just never know what someone may be worth, who someone may know these days. Not as simple as it used to be. That's why I welcome all, at least to a table for conversation. My next business venture may be with a negro."

Someone scoffed loudly.

"I'm serious," Kirkbride said. He worked out another stub of fish. "Maybe we should learn something from our Northern neighbors. They sold their souls to the dollar, putting industry ahead of all regard for family, tradition, cultural pride. They take all walks of life and turn a profit off them. Work side by side with them. Take orders from them. Could you take orders from a negro, Sly?" He cut his eyes toward a lean young man at the next table over.

"Hell no I couldn't," Sly said.

"Well you best get used to the idea. Mr. Mosby here will tell you about it. You take orders from a Yankee poltroon, don't you, Jeb? Dykes. That must be Irish." The group laughed. "I saw you playing coachman to him the other day, trotting him out of town. He pay you well for that?"

Mosby sighed and put his fork down. "Come on now, Harlan. You know it's not like that. He's a neighbor."

"He's a threat. You told me to rest easy, Mosby. You remember that? You think I've been resting easy now that he's settled into the Stibbs place? Doing God knows what on that land, coming into town and leering at the Cogg girls?"

"You and I both know it's nothing like that. He's a decent man."

"I'm keeping an eye on him, Jeb," Duncan chimed in. "You just can't trust people these days. It's like Harlan said, folks can be up to all manner of things. He thinks he's found a bunch of rubes in us, I'm sure. You've got to think about Fannie. About your Pappy."

"Look," Mosby said, scanning the group to meet eyes with each. "He's my neighbor, I treat him neighborly. I'd do the same to any of you. It doesn't mean I'm going to let him — or any of you, for that goddamned matter — take advantage of my family."

"Okay, okay," Kirkbride said. "You've made your point, Jeb. We all know you're soft."

"Goddamnit, Harlan…"

"No, I'm serious. Let's not waste any more breath on that Yankee interloper. He doesn't deserve as much." Harlan raised a finger and circled it above his head. "Bob, bring Jeb his next beer, on me." The group fell silent. Harlan worked at the last piece of fish in his tin. "Jim, you hear anything from John Stibbs and his, speaking of them?"

"Well, yes, as a matter of fact I heard a few days back from the constable down in Sperryville. They're settled down there for the moment. On a cousin's property, I believe."

"He find work down there, that you know of?" someone asked.

"There's a new tannery down there, drawing a lot of folks," Duncan said. "He's likely found work there. If not, they've got their hogs."

The group seemed satisfied with his answer.

* * *

MOSBY STAYED RELATIVELY quiet once he obtained the Stibbs family news he was after, uneasy with the attention cast on him by Duncan and Kirkbride. He finished his plate and drank both pints of beer, taking in deep drafts of the second while listening to speculation about crop prices. While Kirkbride was engaged in conversation, Mosby stood and made for the door, giving him a touch on the back and a word of thanks for the beer on his way.

He emerged into the heat of the day ready to bolt for Presh to put the company of the tavern behind him, but he remembered his errand and turned to Cogg's General. He had not yet cleared the planks of the Beveridge House before he heard the door open again behind him.

"Jeb! Come on now, you can't have needed to get off that quickly," Kirkbride said. "I thought we might enjoy a beer together."

Mosby closed his eyes and took a breath before turning. "Well, I do appreciate that drink, but unfortunately I have to finish an errand and get back on home. I need to mend some fence before dark."

"Our work is never done, friend." Kirkbride planted his

meaty hand on Mosby's shoulder and held it there, with a slight press of his fingers into the muscle of it. "But we have to take time to converse with our fellow countrymen. Ruminate. Build community. That sort of thing."

"Rumination doesn't keep raccoons from my chickens. That fence can't wait."

Kirkbride laughed and gave him two swift claps on the shoulder before settling his hand to rest there once more.

"Just the same. Say, Jeb. I have a favor to ask of you. We all do, really — Jim would be out here himself, but he's presently engaged."

Mosby held his expression flat. "What might you fellas have in mind, Harlan?"

"It's a small thing, really. Nothing more than what you do anyway in looking after your family, I'm sure. We just need a good, trustworthy pair of eyes on that... on Mr. Dykes. You seem in a good position to do so, what with your proximity to him and all. Just a pair of eyes on him to make note of any indiscretions and report them to the township authorities here. Again — something you'd do without asking, no doubt."

"Harlan, you know me to be an honest man who cares for what we have here. I wouldn't stand for any threat to that, from outside or otherwise."

"Of course, Jeb. It's just... this is a special case. We know Mr. Dykes doesn't have our best interests at heart. Constable Duncan, myself, others — we'd like to see him held accountable. It's simply a matter of finding some proof of it. Proof can be in small things. Things that may not otherwise be made known to us. He sees a confidant in you, Jeb. I know it. Just keep your ears pricked, that's all." He gave Mosby's shoulder a final clap and released his hold of it.

"Have a good afternoon, Harlan. Do apologize to the others for my leaving in haste."

"Thank you, Jeb. I thank you for your help in this matter. Good afternoon to you and my best to your family." Kirkbride opened the heavy door and returned to the dimness of the tavern.

Mosby sighed and walked on toward Cogg's, feeling the dampness from Kirkbride's grip. His boot steps fell heavy on the boardwalk, the only sound on a street otherwise muffled by the heavy heat.

CHAPTER 22

THE SUN WAS NOT YET up when Dykes entered the barn, breaking its stillness with the throw of the latch. The old hinges creaked as he heaved open the tall door. He heard the horse shuffle a bit, but it was otherwise quiet. He had a mistrust of stillness like this, made more acute during the war. He thought of the lantern and returned to retrieve it from outside the barn.

Shadows from the stall's pickets shifted across the horse's side as he walked to greet her. "Good morning, girl." He held his hand to her nose and felt the moist warmth of her breath. He scooped oats out of a bin he'd fashioned near the door and dumped them in a low bucket before the mare. "What's your name?"

He couldn't settle on a name that felt right, though he'd given it some thought. For once in his life, he felt no rush.

Dykes let several minutes pass as he stood there in the dark, listening to the horse grind her oats. He had formed only a loose idea of what he wanted to accomplish with his day. He needed chickens, and thought to start enclosing a coop that was somewhat off-kilter, leaning from neglect. The coop should probably be righted, as well, while making a proper home for a future flock. Perhaps that's what the day would hold. He hadn't any fencing, and he didn't want to go into town to fetch any. The road was hot, and the townsfolk seemed more ornery to him under the swelter of summer. Perhaps good company in town would come with cooler weather. He imagined a street bustling with activity, harvest workers, millers, and merchants brought alive by the profits of a good harvest.

He sighed and pushed off from the stall, making a trip to the spring house to fetch fresh water for the horse before returning to the house.

A few lamps were lit in the kitchen, giving it a comforting glow as the sky grew light outside. The crickets were tapering off. Soon they'd be replaced by the low pulse of cicadas, scrambling to mate in the midday heat.

Breakfast was a thick portion of bread, buttered and pan-fried, and a sliced tomato Dykes warmed a bit in the skillet, still greased from the bread. Both were satisfying with the coffee he'd brewed. He savored the flavors together, the coffee seeming to bring out a full but pleasing acidity in the tomato. The remaining coffee was set aside for lunch.

Though early, it was already quite warm. Dykes relished the heat. Every bit of this climate suited him, following his experiences with summers in the Deep South and winters in the North. Even summers in the North were displeasing — he would take mosquitos over swarming black flies any day.

The kitchen window's thick panes provided a hazy view of tall hardwoods made soft by the morning light, yielding to the expanse of open property rolling on to the west. The land's potential was great, but progress was slow. Perhaps he could hire some hands when cooler weather came, to speed along the land's reconstitution. He finished the last swallows of coffee and studied the dented bottom of the tin mug. The same pattern of dents he had studied so many times before. Need to get to work on that chicken house, he told himself. First, a quick wash-up and a change out of nightclothes.

He was upstairs cinching his pants when he heard a few light raps at the door. His eyes grew wide for a moment at the prospect of company. His acquaintances were limited, and he kept little on hand to offer. But he finished up as quickly as he could and tramped down the stairs.

One of the few it could be greeted him as the door swung in. Jeb Mosby stood, hat in hand.

"Why, good morning, Jeb. What brings you down this way?"

"Solomon! Good morning to you. I apologize for my early visit, but Fannie wanted me out of the house."

Dykes studied him for a moment, searching for a joke. The brief silence was a prompt to Mosby.

"Actually, she recommended I come by and make good on my offer to set you up with a functioning privy. Thought I'd pay a visit before you set to other tasks today. And before it gets too damned hot. Privy work is best done in the morning. For various reasons."

"Well, that's very kind, but unexpected," Dykes said. "Still. I'll take you up on it. Come on in. I've some fresh coffee to get us started."

Mosby tamped his bootheels on the doorframe and made his way in through the bare, yet cozy, parlor. Dykes had outfitted it with an oval knit rug and two chairs before the fireplace, one a rocker. A modestly ornate smoking table stood between them. A book rested on its dark, worn surface. Its spine faced away from Mosby, but gold-embossed figures stood before a doorway on the maroon cover.

"You've cleaned this place up fine, Sol. I must admit this is a new experience for me: a desire to sit and stay a spell at the Stibbs place!"

"Well, it's taking some work, but I feel it's paying off in measures," Dykes said. "I'll admit to feeling overwhelmed from time to time. There was the attic space."

"The attic? Good Lord in heaven, do I want to ask?"

Dykes grinned. "I had quite a burn in the Front Field that night."

Mosby laughed and accepted a mug of coffee from his host. "I do not envy you. Lord Almighty." He savored a sip and squinted through the kitchen window. "So what's your plan here, Sol? We've talked it over some, but do you have a clear idea of what you want to make of this place?"

Dykes poured a measure of coffee into his own tin mug. "I've been thinking hard on that as of late, Jeb. There's much to do and I feel time is slipping past. I'll likely hire some hands in the fall and make this place right."

"Plant a winter crop?"

"Maybe. What do you recommend?"

"You could start with a big garden, a piece larger than a kitchen garden, to get an income stream. I've had luck with winter root vegetables, greens and such. Just so the land isn't sitting idle. But hell, I don't know. I can't tell a man what to do with his land. I've never put a pen to another man's ledger, if you know what I mean."

"I don't follow," Dykes said, taking a sip.

"Your ledger. I don't want to tell you what to do to ill effect on your livelihood."

"I can't say I keep a ledger."

Mosby's face lit with surprise as if he would spit out the coffee he'd just taken in. "Can't say you keep a... well that's a fine project to start in on if you find time on your hands. If you can't account for what's going into your land, you can't rightly take much solace in what's going out. Next time you're in town, get a ledger. And mark its cost down on page one."

"Noted," Dykes said. He sighed and stood. "Shall we get to the privy work?"

"Fine," Mosby said. "As I said, don't want too much heat on us out there."

* * *

THE MAIN TASK of moving a privy involved digging a hole, the deeper the better, for it would put off repetition of the job by that much more time. Ideally the hole would be a few feet off from where the outhouse presently stood, and what dirt could fill the old hole would come from the new. The structure would then be slid into place over the newly vacant space.

Dykes and Mosby had made good work of digging, and Jeb had taken it upon himself to jump in and make deeper headway by scraping away at the bottom and sides with a metal pail. When he stood, the ground was at his shoulders. While his excavation work was taking place, Dykes carted off top layers of filth from the old privy. In that the Stibbs family had filled it to overflowing, it needed to be worked down a bit before it could be properly covered with earth.

Dykes was returning from dumping his final cartload when he saw the pail sail out from the hole and land with a dull clang some feet from the worksite. Mosby's head popped up as a groundhog might. He turned until his eyes found Dykes.

"She's done, that'll do. It's plenty deep." He was slightly out of breath and dusted with earth, muddy where the sweat came down.

Dykes dropped the cart and went over to offer him a hand up.

"I surely appreciate your assistance here, Jeb. This would have taken me nearly a week of mornings to get done."

"That's why I'm here. Can't leave a man to dig a privy hole on his own. I trust you'll remember my pail work when our own outhouse needs tending to."

"I certainly will."

Mosby clasped his outstretched hand and pulled on it to aid in his scramble upwards. "Whoo! It's hotter up here. How's your end of things coming along?"

"It's done. And glad to be rid of it," Dykes said. "First the springhouse, now this. That's the last cart of refuse I hope I ever load."

Mosby gave him a sympathetic look and walked over to

study the privy structure. "Odd, this." He eyed both sides of the door. "Latches on the outside. What do you suppose that's all about?"

Dykes walked over to inspect the door. Sure enough, the metal latch was fixed to the outside, with a nothing but a pull-rope hanging down on the interior side of the door. "Well that is odd. I can't say I've noticed it, given its unusable state up to now."

"You want to flip it so it latches proper, instead of whatever unseemly intentions Stibbs had with it?"

Dykes studied it a bit more. "No. No, it's fine. I won't need the latch either way, it being just me."

"It's that kind of bold talk that gets a man married. But suit yourself."

Before moving the structure over, the pair agreed to sit and break over a canteen of water. Dykes had continued to use his army canteen, but if Mosby noticed its emblem as he took drafts from it between passes, he chose to consider the limbs of the trees above instead.

Mosby couldn't help but break the silence between them.

"I kid about marriage, but what of it? You plan to settle down here proper, with a family? Change that latch around before too long?"

Dykes took a sip and shifted his gaze toward some spot near the barn. "I really can't say, Jeb."

"You'll focus on your farming, then," Mosby said decidedly.

"I can't say that, either."

Mosby ceased his study of the oaks above and stared sincerely at Dykes. "Well now I'm confused. What's this all about, then?"

Dykes paused for a moment to find the right words. "I wish I could say. My mind has been elsewhere, lately. Maybe it's the loneliness of the summer. I can't say."

"Do you not like this place?"

"I love this place. This is what I'd dreamed of. But there's something more that I need. And it may not be here. Right here, that is. It may be close, but not here." Dykes took another sip from the canteen. "That won't make sense to you."

"No, I can't say it does, but I'm not one to judge." He took the offered canteen from Dykes and finished its contents. "Empty. Thank you." He passed it back. "Does this have anything to do with what came up at Mrs. Russ' house? That stuck with me, and I feel we never cleared it, you and me."

"No. But that did put this place a bit further from home for me, to be honest. I told you about the time I spent in Lincoln, correct?"

Mosby stared at him blankly before sparking with a recognition. "Goose Creek. Yes, you mentioned you stayed a spell there. With the Quakers."

"Yes, with the Quakers. Though most of my time was spent with a colored community just on the outskirts of town. Such a hospitable group. It was for them I stayed on longer than I would have guessed, as a matter of fact."

"How so?" Mosby had picked up a stick and was breaking it into inch-long pieces.

"We built a church."

Mosby looked up in surprise. "You built a church?"

"Well, finished a church. They needed a place of worship and had raised as much as a roof and frame. I came by some lumber through a connection I made in town, and stayed on for a few extra weeks building up some walls. Some Quakers joined in to help finish the job — it's lovely. A pretty little whitewashed church under an old cottonwood tree."

"Well I'll be damned. I didn't know you had any skill in carpentry."

"What, from my lack of skill with a crosscut saw?" Dykes grinned.

"Now I didn't say that. Just thought you were more the metalworking type."

"I am, though I picked up carpentry over the years as a

necessity," Dykes said. "Regardless, that church seemed to make a real mark on that place. It was the kind of work I imagined doing when I bought a train ticket down here. Being helpful, directly, if that makes sense. I don't know if farming, for me, fits that bill."

Mosby nodded. "Okay. I can see that. But farming does make a mark. Beyond just support for a man and his family, farming is sustenance. It's feeding the masses. It underpins ... well, everything."

"And that's what's drawn me to it. It is certainly a noble path. I just don't know if I'll be any good at it, or if I even possess the desire to find out." Dykes looked at the empty canteen. "I'm going to refill this so it's on hand after we move this abomination." He stood and walked to the spring house.

Mosby considered what he might say next. He felt he should warn Dykes of the talk of him in town. This conversation alone, if discussed in the wrong company, could make quick enemies in certain circles. A church was a powerful thing to a community, and a negro church — to some that would represent an unwanted foothold in society.

He considered telling Dykes more about his own plight. About how, regardless of time or place, he couldn't shake a gnawing guilt of leaving his family to fight for towns and fields foreign to him, only to have his one, precious child fall prey to the very enemy he was trying to protect her from. About how, despite finding a friendship that he would like to take hold, he could never quite overcome a lingering mistrust of those who he had once faced off against on the battlefield. About how he has witnessed the strength of his father wane slowly over time, leaving him a mere shadow of the man he was. He considered dropping his planned afternoon chores to sit down and just start a damned ledger with him, to at least put some fraction of order to the place beyond a clean privy.

But he said none of these things. He said nothing. Dykes returned, and with a motion to the outhouse, they each heaved away with only coordinated instructional remarks made between them.

* * *

THE SUN WAS HALFWAY to its midpoint in the sky when the pair finished the task. Mosby studied the work.

"Well that looks just fine," he said. "Don't be surprised to find me here if my own accommodations are occupied. Looks like a man could do some good thinking in there."

"I would be quite surprised, but you are always welcome. You know how the latch works."

Mosby smiled and gave him a half-clap on the shoulder. "Alright, Sol. It did me good to see you. Don't let the summer heat get you down — we're almost out of it. And don't get too down about your farming. It takes time. Your skills will come."

"Thank you, Jeb. And I thank you again for your help here. I mean to have you and Mrs. Mosby over for dinner once I get my feet under me. I owe you that and more."

"There's certainly nothing owed, but we'd take you up on the supper invite. And your feet will be under you before you know it."

"You are kind and inspiring, as always," Dykes said.

The pair parted with a handshake, and Mosby strode out to the road. Dykes remembered he'd wanted a bit of advice on the chicken coop, but his voice never rose to speak.

Instead he stood silently, covered in filth, and watched as Mosby's lean frame bobbed out of view.

CHAPTER 23

THE CORN WAS GROWING TALL, and with rains coming steady in the afternoons, Mosby aimed to just let it grow. He turned his attention to upkeep around the property and the vegetable garden near the house. He liked the break from days spent far afield, and the chance it provided to see more of Fannie. His hands were making quick work of bunches of weeds that had crept up through the squash vines when he saw her drop a basket of wet laundry on the ground near the clotheslines.

He pulled at another bunch and ripped the roots from the ground, trailing a spray of earth with them. A fat white grub lay in the disturbed patch of soil.

"Why, you son of a bitch." Mosby leaned in to study the curled creature, pale and disoriented in the late afternoon sun. "You been eating on my garden?" He took a folding knife from his pocket and deftly thumbed it open. He took care in centering it over the grub and pressed down through it, deep into the ground beneath. Its two halves curled tighter. He stood and crushed it under his boot, grinding it into the ground and out of sight. He wiped his blade on his pants leg and closed it, returning it to his pocket.

Fannie had pinned up two sheets in the time it took him to

dispatch the grub and walk over. "Well hello, Butternut. Fancy seeing you here."

"Good afternoon to you, sir. How's the garden work going?"

"We still have some butterbeans. Tomatoes are going strong. Cabbage, collards all coming in. I'd say we're going to have some good looking squash this fall. And I'm hopeful the cucumbers will return."

"That's a fine garden report — as if from the Almanac itself," Fannie said.

"Those pumpkins are coming along, too."

"Even better. I shall keep my pie tins at the ready."

"Yes, please."

Fannie shook out a pair of trousers and pinned them to the line, folding over a corner of fabric under each pin to keep it tight. She had a row of pins at the ready along her apron pocket. "How did it go down at Mr. Dykes' place this morning? Did you get that outhouse moved?"

"We did, indeed. I did most of the digging, but I suppose I asked for it."

"How does the place look?"

"It's coming along nice enough. A lot of work, though. I wouldn't wish that on anyone. I feel as if he's drifting a bit, too. In purpose. He's new to farm work, you know."

"So he's said," Fannie said.

The sound of hounds drifted in from the back of the property, wild at a scent they had caught. Their voices were desperate but focused. Jeb and Fannie both looked toward the ruckus but saw no signs of the pack otherwise.

"He's running fox now? A little early, isn't it?" Mosby asked, not expecting an answer. "That Harlan Kirkbride is becoming a bit of a nuisance."

"What, with his hunting? You've never minded it in the past."

"No, I don't mind that. He's becoming more aggressive in a quest to... keep the county unadulterated."

"Why whatever does that mean?"

"He's all worked up about our new neighbor, him having been on the other side of the fight. Harlan thinks he means to take advantage of our unstable political situation down here," Mosby said. He squinted at the horizon, still looking for some sign of the hunt. "He's mentioned violence against Sol on more than one occasion."

"Oh horrors, Jeb. He can't honestly believe Solomon Dykes would be up to no good? Has he met the man?"

"Yes, but you know that doesn't make any difference to Harlan. Once he's made up his mind, that's it. I'm sure he's read up plenty on the pillaging of the land by Yankee opportunists, and he's chomping at the bit to root out the enemy here at home."

Fannie finished one line and motioned to the basket on the ground. "Move that over here, if you will." She began pinning shirts on a new stretch of line. "Well, let me ask you this: Knowing what you know about Mr. Dykes, would you say he's looking to take advantage in some way?"

Mosby watched as she pinned. "I like that shirt, by the way." A blue calico shirt hung wet and heavy on the line. "Mrs. Russ made good work of it."

"Of course she did. It fits you well, too."

"Of course it does." He puffed up with mock swagger but she didn't notice. He held the stance for a moment before deflating. "Sol, though. Would he have any malicious intent in his heart?" He paused and thought, earnestly. "I think not. I honestly think not. But it doesn't mean he won't find trouble, or trouble won't find him. And I don't want to be around when it does."

"That's wise. But I wouldn't let that color your relationship with him. He seems a good man. And a good neighbor."

"He is, that. He offered us a dinner, once the place is shaped up a bit more."

"That's very kind. I should like that," Fannie said.

"Still." Mosby idly picked at a thread on a quilt hanging on the line. "I think I best put some distance between us. Just for now. Perhaps I'll check in on him once the harvest is in. Otherwise, I needn't go poking my nose in his business, so don't go sending me on any errands his way."

"Whatever errands would I send you on?" Fannie stopped pinning and stared at him, sticking a hand to one cocked hip.

"Well, you sent me down to dig that privy!"

"I just asked you make good on an offer that you yourself wouldn't stop talking about. Don't fault me for that."

"Fair enough, but still. I'll just put some distance between us."

"Whatever you think is best, Jeb."

"Alright, Butternut." He gave her a peck on the cheek. "Is supper on?"

"It is. You going to wash up?"

"I shall. Let me feed Presh and I'll be in shortly."

She put two pins in her mouth, holding them with her teeth, and continued her work.

Jeb made his way to the barn, but paused midway and gazed up the road cresting the hill to the High Field. He turned and trudged up it a bit, just until the elevation started to break off and he could get a better view of the back property. There was no sight of Harlan Kirkbride, his hounds or his hunters. The otherwise still of the afternoon was interrupted by a gentle gust of wind, bringing with it air cooled by the creek yonder. The first sign of fall.

Mosby breathed deep, relishing the promise of a new season, before turning back to tend to his final chores before dinner.

PART III

THE FALL

CHAPTER 24

THE CHANGE in seasons did not fail to meet Dykes' expectations, and with cooler weather came a bustle of activity. The turnpike grew busy with carts hauling grain to be milled, wheat sat sheaved and stooked in the fields, and corn shocks dotted the landscape, left to dry in the autumn sun. All this work took field hands, and for those who could afford it, they appeared as if from thin air. There was money to be made, and money to be spent.

It was a clear day in early October when Dykes took it upon himself to venture into town for a few small provisions, though it was largely an excuse to get about and see something outside of his property. He felt a faint giddiness in the old familiarity of packing his rucksack for the trip, short as it may be. He planned to walk it. In went some wrapped cheese and bread, a folded poncho in case of rain, his pocket knife, and, slipped down one side out of habit, his Navy Colt revolver. He filled his canteen and slung it over his chest before donning the rucksack. It felt good on his back.

On his way to the road he took a moment to scatter some crushed corn over the fence for the chickens, already pecking about in the morning sun. He also stooped to examine the fresh young leaves of collards and cabbage that had sprouted up out of his winter garden. The greens stood a few inches above ground now, and he threaded his fingers around the base of one to study it more closely. No sign of pests, that he could see.

The horse had been fed and watered before breakfast, so all was well with the property. He gave it a final once over before turning to the road. He grinned slightly as he took a deep breath of the crisp air and fell into the rhythm of his walk.

He passed the Mosby place and was prepared to give a wave, but saw no sign of movement from within or without the house. Perhaps they were back in a field doing harvest work. He hadn't seen any hired help come their way, and imagined Jeb and Fannie must be doing most of it themselves, with the help of Pappy where he could. Perhaps he should offer a hand. He could stop in and see how they were making out before returning home.

A large black crow startled him as it flushed out of the woods to his right and lighted across the road, on a portion of the Mosby's fence. It joined a few others in creating a relative ruckus of syncopated cawing. Dykes couldn't readily tell what might have drawn them — their organization seemed aimless aside from their proximity to one another.

Once he reached the hardened surface of the turnpike, his pace quickened. Stone walls spanned both sides of the road along this portion, which he found quite idyllic. They were well-kept by their owners; Bob Jenkins on the north side of the road, and another he did not know by name on the south. The south-siders had built their house as if up from a portion of the wall. Quite close to the road, Dykes thought, but otherwise seamlessly integrated into the stonework circling the property.

He noticed the Jenkins field had been cleared beautifully. No crops stood after harvest, but even-shorn stubble gave sign of some earnest productivity following a summer of neglect and dense weed growth.

As he neared the stone house along the road he could smell a mix of wood smoke and the sweetness of apples. A light plume rose into the sky from the far side of the house. He peered into the yard as he passed.

Three old women stood around a large copper kettle on the boil. One stirred slowly but constantly with a wooden paddle. He would have figured it laundry, but for the sweet smell.

He stopped and stood in a manner to make his presence known. "Good morning to you!" he called.

The three turned their heads to him in unison. Only one, in a checkered blue apron, responded. "Morning."

"Are you brewing something?" Dykes asked.

The woman stirring returned her gaze to the contents of the pot. Her fingers bent in such odd angles Dykes thought it a wonder she could maintain a grip on the paddle.

"Aye. Apple butter," said the woman in the apron.

"Well it smells lovely," Dykes said. "Does it take a long time?"

"Aye," the only talkative one said. "Much stirring. Must keep stirring."

He noticed then a long table they had set up along the side of the house, where the contents of a bushel of apples were being peeled and sliced by a fourth, similarly bent old lady. A mound of shaved skins sat on one end of the table.

"Alright then," Dykes said, sensing it unproductive to engage them further. "Best of luck to you. Enjoy the day."

"Aye," the one repeated. The three resumed their gaze into the kettle.

* * *

DYKES MARKED the walk between home and town by three landmarks, the first being the stone wall house. The second was a toll gate, the third a spur road to the south that, the one time he took it out of curiosity, afforded a grand view of the western mountains due to its rise in elevation and the cleared, open grazing fields flanking it.

The toll gate generally puzzled him, in that he received conflicting instructions on payment based on who happened to be manning it on a given day. Typically, if he was on horseback he could expect to be asked to pay, but not always. On a few occasions, he offered the toll only to be shooed away by the older of the two gentlemen who stood or sat near the gate. Dykes assumed both lived in the house just off the road at the gate, but again, he never got a clear sense either way. Perhaps neither lived there.

But never had he been asked to pay while on foot. He would usually give a nod and step around the end of the long wooden pole that reached across the road from the gate operator's seat. Today was a first, though. Today his nod was met with a frown.

"Toll," the man called from the other side of the road. Dykes didn't recognize this man. He was middle-aged but weather-worn. He wore a red kerchief tied around his throat.

Dykes stopped and did his best to sound helpful. "Good morning. Yes, I live just up the road a piece, actually. On my way into to town for a bit."

"Toll due," the man said. "You're on a toll road, here."

"Yes, I realize." Dykes sighed and slung his pack off, walking the length of the pole to meet the man. He fished a coin purse from the pack's front pocket and sorted through it. The man extended his hand while maintaining a blank, yet fixed, gaze on him. Dykes put one coin in the ruddy, outstretched palm.

"Thank you, sir," Dykes said. "Nice day."

"It is, that."

To Dykes' surprise, the man turned and began pulling at the rope to raise the gate. Dykes stood obediently as it slowly inched into the air. Only once it was fully vertical, as a flag pole, did he feel it proper to continue on his path. The gate was slowly lowered behind him as he walked on.

He had walked twenty yards or so further when he heard the

brisk sound of hooves and cart wheels approaching the gate behind him. He turned out of curiosity and watched as it neared, taking a few steps backward as he did so. The buckboard stopped at the gate, and its driver squinted through glasses in Dykes' direction. He raised a familiar hand in greeting.

The driver cupped his hands and called out, "Solomon Dykes!" It was Cassius Freeman.

* * *

DYKES FELT fortuitous to be able to share a ride into town with such welcome company. He gladly abandoned his walk and climbed onto the bench beside Cassius.

"How you been getting along, Mr. Dykes?" he asked as the horse returned to a comfortable clip.

"I've been well, thank you. I'm making progress on the farm. So there's some end in sight for me, though I still feel more a tinker than a planter."

"I applaud you for putting yourself outside of what you know," Freeman said. "We could all stand to view the world from a different perspective." Cassius gazed ahead in the way Dykes had grown accustomed to, peering out of spectacles perched on the tip of his nose. "Have you heard news of the vote?"

"The vote? I apologize, but one goal of my trip into town is to come by some news of the world outside chicken houses and winter planting. And laundry. By God, do I have a distaste for boiling clothes."

Freeman cast an eye his way. "Well, it's a pretty big vote. You picked a good day to come in for news. I'm doing the same myself."

"So what was voted upon?"

"Constitutional amendments. Virginia has to accept them to rejoin the Union. There are two in question — one gives me and mine protection under the law, the other gives me and mine the right to cast a vote unmolested."

"You and yours? Colored people?"

"All men, but it's really all about us, isn't it?"

"I suppose so." Dykes put a hand on Freeman's shoulder. "This is good. This is progress."

"We haven't heard news of the vote, yet. But the fact it's even being considered is progress." Freeman sighed and squinted to follow the path of the road. The trees had parted to let the morning sun cut through. "We have come so far in so short a time. Two years ago this month I cast my first vote. I was so proud. Couldn't believe it. Put on my suit and hat and waited in line for a morning just to put my paper in that little jar."

"What was it like? I would have been in Connecticut then, where I'm sure the mood was a good deal more celebratory than it would have been down here."

"Yes, well 'celebratory' definitely isn't the word I would use. But my, was there an energy in the air. More defiance than anything. Especially given the likes who showed up at the polling place." Freeman paused. "You cross paths with a Mr. Harlan Kirkbride yet?"

Dykes chuckled lightly. "Crossed paths? Yes, I'd say so. He's not taken so kindly to my settling here."

"Ha! Well he doesn't take kindly to much of anything doesn't involve his hounds or folks nodding in agreement with him. So you know Mr. Kirkbride. Well he was there at the day of the vote. Him and his crowd."

"They gave you trouble?"

"Oh, did they. They went all out. Wearing dark robes and white sacks on their heads, with the eyes cut out. Something like a grimace painted on where their mouths would be. Supposed to scare us away, I suppose, but they don't know what all we'd been through to be there at that polling place," Freeman said. "It was spooky, but we walked on by, eyes fixed ahead, and cast those ballots."

"How did you know it was him?"

"You must not have spent much time around Mr. Kirkbride. All of his business is public knowledge, whether we want to know it or not."

"Yes, I could see that. Well let's hope there are no robes being worn in town today."

"No, they've been beat by progress now. The times are against them." Freeman popped the reigns lightly and clicked his tongue at the horse. "Unless that vote didn't pass. I don't know what we'll do if that vote didn't pass."

CHAPTER 25

MIDDLEBURG WAS BUSY, so Freeman found a place to hitch his cart just outside of town. Wagons loaded with wheat and feed hay jostled by as they walked, powdering the otherwise clear October air with fine swirls of dust. Down a slope south from the road bed, in a field of clover, a group of children were swinging about in a fierce game of snap the whip. A little one in a stocking cap went soaring from the end of the line as the others squealed with delight.

The sky was a striking and absolute blue, but for a few wisps of white tracing high in the heavens above.

They passed the ordinary on the left side of the road but stayed to the right. Dykes had planned to avoid it anyway, and assumed Freeman was doing the same.

"What's the best spot to get news?"

"McVeigh's barber shop. Best place for news and a shave," Freeman said. He studied Dykes' face. "Looks like you could use both."

Dykes rubbed his jaw where his beard and mustache had blended into broader facial hair. "Fair enough."

McVeigh's was another block down from the Beveridge House, on the opposite side of the road and positioned between two shops where many a wife bided time while her husband had his whiskers trimmed. To the left of the barber was a millinery shop, offering Sunday hats, bonnets and such, as well as basic sewing needs. To the right was Tabitha McVeigh's Fancy Store, filled with all manner of trinkets, many from as far away as England and France. It shared a door in the back with the barber shop, it being run by her husband, Patrick.

A little set of bells rang lightly above them when they opened the front door of the barbershop, but Patrick McVeigh kept his eyes on the straight razor before him as he scraped it deftly across the throat of a patron leaned far back in the chair. It was one of two matching chairs along the wall — the other stood unoccupied. Each was padded with leather and fairly tall, with equally tall footstools before them. Freeman had hoped McVeigh's assistant would be working, a colored man, but it appeared he was not in the shop at the moment.

Two other men sat waiting, one a soldier and one who Dykes presumed was a farmer, dressed in dingy work clothes, a wide-brimmed straw hat on his lap. The farmer's left arm stopped short above the wrist, the nub of which he clasped with his right hand.

A pile of books and newspaper pages littered a table at the front of the shop, and Freeman went to it straightaway. He sifted through the pages and lit on the latest newspaper. His eyes sparked behind his spectacles.

"Ha!" He held the page up and smacked it with the back of his hand. "I'll be damned if it didn't pass!" He quieted himself and read past the headline. "Both votes." He held it for Dykes to see when he joined his side.

"Yep," the barber said dryly. "We're quite the prize, if the Union'll take us. Railroad debt up to here with nothing to show for it now that they tore it all up."

The farmer perked up a bit. "No. No, they'll have us just the same. Got eyes on that tobacco down south. Timber. Coal. Bay oysters. Plenty to fatten their pocketbooks with."

McVeigh was a tall, redheaded man with a barrel chest, his white apron stretched tight across it. His sleeves were rolled to above the elbow. He scraped the last bit of lather from the chair occupant's neck and took a kettle from a tall stove between the chairs. He poured steaming water over a tightly rolled towel, letting it cool for a moment before draping it over the man's face. He rubbed off any remaining soap and gave the man a pat on the shoulder to indicate the end of the shave.

The man stood and studied his face for a moment in the wall mirror. "Thank you, Pat. Feels great." Satisfied, he shook the barber's hand and collected a hat from a peg under the mirror.

Freeman and Dykes took the two remaining seats across from the pair waiting. They both nodded to the soldier. The farmer ignored them.

"You're up, Abel," McVeigh called to the farmer. The man stood up stiffly and hobbled to the tall chair, hanging his hat on the peg before shimmying up to sit heavily. He ran his hand through a thick tuft of white hair standing up on his head.

"Got long," he said. "Lower my ears a bit and clean these whiskers up."

The barber strode around the chair and shook out a cape before pinning it under the farmer's neck. He studied the head for a moment and selected a comb and a pair of shears from a small collection. McVeigh combed and snipped a bit in silence before breaking it.

"This day was bound to come. Still hard to believe, though, wouldn't you say?"

Abel sighed and looked toward the group seated by the door. "Don't want to discuss such matters," he said. He turned his gaze forward again and closed his eyes. His hand fidgeted beneath the cover of the cape.

"No, I understand." McVeigh combed out the greasy hair between two fingers and snipped at its protruding ends. "So, what news from out your way, then?"

"Eh. None good." His eyes remained closed. "You hear about the Stibbs family?"

Dykes glanced up. He often wondered what had become of them. He'd hoped John was settled and gainfully employed, though a part of him always half expected to look out the window one day to see the family walking up the road to their old home. Bedraggled and desperate with nowhere else to turn.

"Let's see. Moved down south, correct? John working for a tanner?"

"Yes, Sperryville. And he was. Not sure what he plans now, after what happened to the missus."

The barber stopped cutting and stood up straight, facing the back of the man seated before him. Abel opened his eyes but did not turn. "And what happened to Mrs. Stibbs?"

"Sad. I thought for sure you would've known."

"Clearly not," McVeigh said. He put his hands on his hips, the shears and comb cocked out from the same hand.

"Well, it's sad news, like I say." The farmer finally turned a bit in his chair, sensing the inactivity from the barber. "From what I hear the hogs got her. John was working the tannery, leaving the missus home to tend to them hogs, and she must have slipped or something. One of them rooted at her, I guess, and the others followed suit." He closed his eyes again and his hand fidgeted. "Ate on her pretty good."

"Jesus Lord," McVeigh said, his jaw agape. "I had not heard that news. Sad, indeed."

Dykes stood abruptly and excused himself from the shop, a hand to his mouth. He needed a breath of air.

The bells jingled weakly to mark his exit.

CHAPTER 26

MOSBY WOKE GROGGILY and squinted at the unusual amount of light bleeding in from around the curtains. He sat up with a start and turned to see an empty spot where he'd usually find Fannie.

"What in the … Fannie?"

He threw the quilt off his legs and spun them over the side to rest on the cold floor. "Fannie?" He listened for a moment. There was the muted sound of activity coming from the kitchen.

Mosby entered the kitchen, tucking his shirt in as he walked, to find Fannie busy at the stove and Pappy at the table sipping coffee over a plate of biscuit crumbs and a bit of remaining egg yolk.

"What's this? You forgot me?"

"Forgot you? Heavens no, Jeb, we just let you rest. Last day of harvest — thought we'd let you start it right," Fannie said as she poured him a cup of coffee.

"Start it right? Hardly! I'm all out of sorts! What of the chickens? Who fed Presh and Soupy? I need them in top form today!"

"It's all taken care of, Jeb, relax. I fed the livestock and Pappy fed the chickens."

"I fed the what?" Pappy asked, hearing his name.

"The chickens, Pappy. It's taken care of, Jeb. You need your rest for the harvest."

"Good Lord, Fannie, leave the resting for tomorrow. I've got a whole field to clear of hay today." He sat down at the table, exasperated.

"Hardly a field, Jeb," Fannie said. She placed the coffee and a plate of fried eggs and cured ham in front of him. "What is it, a half-acre left?"

"More than that. Nearly an acre." He tore at the ham and chewed with a vacant look in his eyes. "I know you meant well, Fannie." He sipped his coffee and continued quietly, "damnit if I'm not all out of sorts."

She patted his back and gave it a swift rub. "You'll make out just fine. I know you'll be glad to have this harvest behind you."

"Indeed I will. Did you make biscuits?" She took one from a pan on the stovetop and nestled it by his eggs. "Thank you. You know — I was thinking." He took a bite of biscuit. "Damn good biscuit, Fannie."

She smiled. "You were thinking?"

"I was thinking. Maybe end of this week we owe ourselves a trip up to Leesburg. Do some proper shopping. See some of the county."

Fannie's face brightened. "That sounds fine by me. I have been keeping a list that Middleburg won't satisfy. Pappy, does that sound good to you?"

"What's that?" Pappy turned his gaze from the window to her. "Middleburg?"

"No, a trip to Leesburg, Pappy," Mosby said, loudly. "The three of us."

"That's fine." He turned his far stare back to the outside. He squinted his eyes. "We expecting company today?"

"No, Pappy. Just us." Mosby forked an egg in his mouth. "I could use some help, though. Even on this last push."

"I don't know why you never reached out to Mr. Dykes about

some help with field work. You could have used the help, and he could have benefited from studying you at work, I'm sure."

"Ah hell, Fannie. I've told you — he's the one who mentioned an invite to me. I haven't heard from him since, and I'm damn sure not going to fall over myself trying to be all neighborly."

"Well he's a nice man," Fannie said. "Helpful, too."

"All may be true, but it's the principle of the matter. I'm sure I'll cross paths with him soon enough." He pushed back from the table, his plate cleaned of its contents. "Alright then. That was as fine a breakfast as there is, Fannie, and look at me ..." he spread his arms and opened his eyes wide. "Fit and rested. Thank you, my bride." He kissed her on the cheek and grabbed his hat to go outside.

"Hold on, Jeb," she said. "Don't run off yet. It's cold out there today."

"Oh, I'll warm up in a second once I start swinging that scythe."

"You still have the walk to the barn and to the field and back. Hold right there." Fannie disappeared into the sitting room and returned with his waxed canvas barn coat.

"That thing won't close, Butternut."

"It will now." She handed it over confidently. "I added those buttons you were so kindly bequeathed by Mrs. Russ."

He traced his fingers over the insignia on one of the brass buttons. "I can't wear this, Fannie. It's outlawed. The very reason I have these buttons is on account of Mrs. Russ getting into hot water over them."

"Are there any soldiers in the Lawrence Field who would get you into hot water?"

"No. Alright, fine." He put the coat on. "Thank you. I'll be back for lunch." He kissed her again and walked out the back door. "Stay good, Pappy."

* * *

MOSBY STOPPED by the barn for gloves, the scythe, and some rope. He would cut and bundle the hay in the morning, and work with Soupy to haul it to the barn loft in the afternoon. Some let the hay dry for a few days, but Mosby found that, with his luck, a field of drying hay conjured days of steady rain.

The mule was contentedly chewing a mouthful of hay while the horse dozed lightly, leaning ever so slightly to her left. Mosby gave Soupy's front mane a tousle, gathered his things, and left quietly.

He shouldered the loop of rope, stuffed the gloves in a coat pocket, and balanced the long shaft of the scythe on the top curve of rope. It was a ten-minute walk or so to the Lawrence Field, which got its name years ago after a scarecrow Pappy had taken to calling Lawrence. He never shared the origins of that name, but the scarecrow was always kept dressed to the nines.

Mosby enjoyed the walk. It followed what had become a nicely worn cart path along the edges of the fields closer to the house, cutting through a few stands of woods between them. It was a clear day, with a crisp chill in the air that would likely burn off by early afternoon, despite Fannie's insistence of the necessity of his coat. The sky was a high blue, as it had been all week. Perfect harvest weather.

A split-rail fence once marked the eastern edge of the Lawrence Field, with an opening where the cart path came in. Mosby hadn't seen a need for it and didn't keep it up, but its remnants served as a good spot to stow his things while he worked. He leaned the scythe against the fence and looped the rope around the end of an angled cross-post. He shrugged off the coat and hung it over the rope. Shouldering the scythe again, he walked to the center of the field.

When Pappy had cleared hay, he would start at the edge of a field and work in. Mosby grew up doing the same. But as years passed and Mosby took more authority over the farm, he found greater pleasure in walking through to the center of a field and clearing outward. He liked to start surrounded by the crop, mowing it down to clear a path back out to the edge.

And so he stood, in the approximated center of the field, and looked around at the mature hay between him and the edge of the woods surrounding the field. He took a slow, satisfying breath, grasped the two handles on the scythe shaft, and got to swinging. It breezed through the thin stalks, leaving them toppled behind its long, curved blade.

He had cleared enough to work up a light sweat when the blade swung low through a cluster of stalks and chimed against a rock. The shaft swung forward through its arc erratically, leaving the blade behind.

"Damnit! A damn rock? What's that doing in here? Son of a bitch." Mosby tossed the handle to the side and retrieved the blade. A pin which served to hold it to the shaft was shorn off. He ran his gloved thumb over the rough nub of metal. "Son of a bitch. Okay. Well, back to the barn then."

He picked up the handle but absent-mindedly tossed the blade aside. He had walked a few good paces into the hay when he looked up and saw a large figure, a man, standing beside the fence post. Mosby's heart skipped a beat and he stopped mid-stride. How long had he been standing there? Mosby swore he had just looked in that direction and seen nothing but the open path through the woods.

The figure stood with arms hanging heavily, broad-shouldered, a full dark beard. John Stibbs?

Mosby raised his hand to acknowledge the man's presence and resumed his walk. It only took another moment of study to confirm it was him.

He broke through the edge of the hay and came to stand a few yards in front of Stibbs.

"John?" Mosby said. "This is a surprise."

Stibbs didn't speak but was breathing rapidly. His eyes were wide and fixed on Mosby.

Mosby scanned the woods behind Stibbs for a sign of any

other — the Stibbs boy, or Fannie or Pappy — but they seemed to be alone. "John. You alright? Why don't you come on down to the house with me."

Stibbs' eyes remained fixed and unblinking on Mosby as he reached behind his back and pulled a curved-handled pistol from his belt. Brass ornamentation glinted in the light. His voice broke as if he hadn't spoken in some time. "This is on you, Jeb."

It was almost poetic in its imagery, were an onlooker to view the pair from across the field. The morning sun cast them in profile, one lean and strong, the other hulking but paunchy. An arm outstretched with a gun cocked to bridge the distance between them completely.

But Mosby did not see such a scene. He saw a desperate man, once familiar, with a glint of fear in his eyes. He saw a loaded barrel leveled at his chest. He saw a songbird flit up to the top of a sweetgum tree. And then he saw nothing.

The height of Mosby's lean frame crumpled to the ground unceremoniously. Stibbs grabbed his forearm, burned with powder, and threw the smoking pistol toward the fallen man at his feet. Then he turned, and trotted off down the path whence he came.

CHAPTER 27

Jim Duncan tucked his handkerchief back into a breast pocket as he crunched down the dirt drive of the Mosby property. Fannie was still on the porch behind him, clutching a post and watching as he walked back out to the road. He hated this part of his job. He looked back over their property as he gave his horse's flank a pat and tugged at the girth, making sure it was still snug. The horse nickered a bit and tossed its head.

"I don't know, boy." He stuffed a wooden box that had been tucked under his arm into a saddle bag, cinching a strap to secure it. "I just don't know why some things are the way they are." He mounted the brown horse, Jubilee, and rode back out to the turnpike.

Murder was blessedly rare in his district, which stretched as far east as Aldie and as far north as the outskirts of Philomont. He gave some thought to the last he'd seen as he trotted Jubilee out onto the toll road. Since the war, the only killing on record had been in a negro community, which remained unsolved. There was little evidence to point to a perpetrator or motive — it had likely been a drunken brawl taken too far. Mosby's was the first life taken in cold blood since the war, and Duncan felt duty bound to make sure this crime didn't go unanswered.

A watchman had summoned him to the Mosby property around noon, and the scene he found was unsettlingly familiar, an echo of wartime. A body spread supine in the sun, drawing the first few flies. The field and woods around him heavy and still. There were few clues to go by, save for one whopper: the murder weapon, or what one could safely presume to be the murder weapon. Duncan thought it might have been Mosby's, drawn in defense, but Fannie showed no recognition of it when he presented it to her. It was unique, an old cavalry model — custom at that — which offered him some hope in finding an owner.

Duncan and his watchman had assessed the scene in hushed tones before wrapping the corpse in a sheet of canvas and moving it to the barn at Fannie's request. He'd sent his watchman west, to Atoka, to summon the nearest undertaker. Duncan just hoped the man could arrive to retrieve the body before dogs or other varmints got to it first. They always seemed to find a way, if given the chance.

THERE WAS no shortage of jails in the county, but Middleburg remained without. When Duncan wasn't at the Beveridge House, he worked out of a small office across from the butcher's, two blocks down from the inn. It was two rooms. The front held the desk and two chairs facing it, as well as a rifle case and cabinet where a small collection of town records were kept; the back held a safe where he stored evidence, and a small cot where he could retire after a long night.

Duncan rode past the inn and hitched his horse off the sidewalk in front of the office. He took the box out of the saddlebag and fumbled for a key to the door. Finding it, he pushed through and placed the box on his desk before hanging his coat and hat on the rack near the front plate window. He sighed and turned to face the box.

SCOTT GATES

"Let's see what we've got here," he muttered to himself.

He opened the box and carefully threw back corners of cloth. He lifted out the pistol, turning it over in his hands. It was not loaded, as he'd verified before packing it. There were no markings of ownership, such as an etched name or initials. But it was relatively well cared for, save for tarnish on the brass flourishes and a bit of rust on the firing mechanisms. He felt its weight in his hands for a moment before putting it back in the box, tossing a fold of cloth over it.

The door opened.

"What in the hell is this I hear about Jeb Mosby?" Kirkbride said as he strode in. "Tell me I heard wrong."

Duncan looked up from the pistol. "How did you hear anything? I've only just come from there."

"Small county, Jim. Even smaller township. So it's true?"

Duncan nodded his head solemnly. "I'm afraid so. Happened sometime this morning, so says Fannie Mosby. He was out working a field and trouble found him."

Kirkbride helped himself to a seat in front of the desk. "Isn't that a damn shame?" He laced his fingers together and braced them against the back of his head. "I'm telling you, Jim, we're going to hell in a handbasket here — a man gunned down on his own damned land. Dodges hornets on the battlefield for years and can't be kept safe on his own property." He put his boot heels up on the desk. "What do you intend to do about it?"

Duncan thought a moment. "I aim to catch the bastard who done it, make an example of him. We can't let this stand. I also intend to make sure Ms. Fannie is properly cared for. You know old Tom isn't up to looking after that place, and they don't have any children."

"You don't have to remind me of that."

"That's not meant as a dig, Harlan, you know it. Home guard was stretched thin during that time. You had your hands full."

"You don't have to remind me of that, either. Goddamn Yankees were trying to pick us clean." He sucked at his teeth.

"Say, you got a toothpick? I had mutton for lunch and I'll be damned if I'm not going to be tasting it all afternoon." His cheeks puffed at a restrained belch.

"They've got mutton down at the Bev?" Duncan rifled through a bottom drawer and tossed a sliver to Kirkbride. "I didn't even have lunch. Now you got me hungry."

There was a knock at the door, but it was opened without waiting for a response. John Garrick, one of the younger watchmen, stepped in. He was fairly tall and solidly built, and Duncan had been happy to add him to his payroll.

"You hear word from Caldwell?" he asked Duncan.

"Now how would I have heard from Caldwell? He's out in Atoka, probably stayed for lunch and will stay into the evening."

The man looked down at the floor. "Just thought he might have ridden out with the undertaker is all."

"Again, he wouldn't be here." Duncan motioned for him to take the seat next to Kirkbride. "You find anything out?"

The man sat and removed his hat. "No, sir. Not a thing. Nobody at the toll booth saw anyone out of sorts this morning. No one in in town seen anything. The road is quiet."

Kirkbride chimed in as he studied a soft mass on the end of his toothpick. "No one from out of town at the inn last night but some hired hands. You think one of them could have done it?"

"Not likely." Duncan lifted the pistol out from the box and placed it on the table. "But we do have this."

Both men sat up and leaned in to look at the weapon. Garrick reached for it and paused with a hand hovered over the butt. "May I?"

"Go right ahead." Duncan motioned for him to take it.

He took the pistol and leveled it at a wall, closing an eye to peer down its sight. He pantomimed a recoil after shooting at an imagined target before turning it over in study. "It's old."

"It is that," Duncan said. "Not too old to kill a man, though."

Kirkbride's mouth was agape during the exchange, eyes fixed on the pistol. "Let me see that, boy." He took it from the watchman and turned it over in his hands. "You have got to be shittin' me." He looked up at Duncan. "I know this gun."

"And what do you mean by that?" Duncan asked. "You know the model or you know *that gun*?"

"I know *this* damned gun. Jim Cogg will corroborate, and it's a testament to every damned thing I've been saying about our Commonwealth since we lowered the Stainless Banner down from Richmond. This here gun belongs to none other than that blackleg yamacraw Solomon Dykes, come down from Yankeedom to claim his spoils." He stood up and held the gun above his head. "He was at Cogg's General with this very damned gun not two months ago, I swear it. Ask Jim — he serviced it, he'll know it better than anyone."

Duncan stood up as well, and the watchman followed suit. Duncan thought a moment. "Now that does make some sense, Harlan. That's what I would call a break. If Jim can attest to what you say, well that's quite a break." He motioned for the pistol and returned it to the box. "It would explain why there was no activity on the road or in town — just as easy as a man crossing a fence line. I wonder if he's so bold as to be back at home ..."

"Only one way to find out," Kirkbride said. "I say we show this to Jim Cogg, and if he says what I know he will, the three of us ride on out to pay Mr. Dykes a visit. I'll love to see the look on his face when we show up at that door."

"Let's do this before dark," Duncan said. "Garrick, load up a couple of rifles and pack some extra ammunition. Mr. Kirkbride and I will return after a visit to Cogg's General."

The watchman nodded and wasted no time, turning to open the gun case.

"I saw this coming a mile away," Kirkbride said as Duncan grabbed his coat and hat off the rack. "Now let's go get that sonofabitch."

CHAPTER 28

THE LOW AFTERNOON sun sliced through the spaces in the barn wall and set bits of dust aglow. Dykes scraped at a remaining patch of caked hay on the loft floor, inspired by the season to clear the space of the rotting neglect from a harvest long past. Perhaps next year he would fill it afresh.

He put his spade aside for a moment and wiped sweat from his brow with the back of a sleeve. Though it was cool outside, he warmed quickly while working. He had set the horse out in a field to graze, so the barn below was still.

He was about to take up the spade again when a rustle from outside caught his ear. The impatient tamp of a hoof and the bluster of a waiting horse. He approached the wall facing the house and crouched to peer out from between two slats. He froze. Then hit the floor in a sprawl.

Cautiously, he raised his head again for a view of the house. Two men were at his doorstep, one on horseback and one dismounted. They both carried rifles. The man on foot rapped at the door aggressively. He waited a moment and rapped again. The pair exchanged words before the one on foot strode around to the side of the house nearest the barn. The man stopped and panned his gaze toward the chicken coop. The spring house. The barn.

Dykes laid flat again and looked to the ladder going down from the loft. A matted pile of old hay lay between him and it. He considered scaling the ladder down to confront the men. But as he heard the crunch of boot on gravel nearing the barn, he crawled over to the hay and nestled under it.

He could hear the man at the entrance to the barn. The man cleared his throat and half-shouted, "Solomon Dykes. Dykes? Come on out of there."

Dykes stayed still and his breath froze. The side of his face was pressed against the gritty floorboards. Dry hay pricked his ear and neck.

The man moved through the barn, slowly, and took cautious steps up the ladder to the loft. Dykes closed his eyes. There was no sound, and then more hoof-falls outside.

A vaguely familiar voice called from the yard. "Any sign of him?" Dykes concentrated to place the voice. Harlan Kirkbride.

There was a shuffle on the ladder as the man descended to the barn below and back into the yard. He shouted back to Kirkbride, "Not here. Maybe holed up in the house?"

Dykes followed the muffled sounds to piece together the scene: the man walked back over to join Kirkbride and the other at the front of the house. The three conversed quietly for some time. After minutes had passed, two horses rode back out to the road and all was still once more. Dykes stayed quiet underneath the cover of hay until the light in the barn softened. Slowly, he crawled out from under the hay to the wall of the barn and raised himself up.

One man remained, standing by the front door of the house. His horse was hitched to a tree out front and idly tore at a clump of grass in the patchy yard. Dykes' mind raced through options. His firearms were in the house, but there were a few tools in the barn below. He studied the man and his shouldered rifle. He was heavyset but not paunchy. Taller than Dykes. He'd need more than a barn tool. If he remained in the loft he was sure to be found, eventually. It might not be until morning, but their search of the property would intensify. What did they want from him, anyway? With Kirkbride a party to it, it couldn't be good. Better to elude them for now and approach the situation on his own terms.

The sentry shifted his weight, bored or uncomfortable. He looked to the sky. Down at the ground. After a moment, he repositioned his rifle sling and slowly moved away from the front door. He walked back around to the side of the house and stopped to scan his surroundings once more. The light was low but not yet to the point of blurring details.

After a moment, the sentry walked purposefully toward the privy. He paused before swinging the door open aggressively. Finding it vacant, he turned, backed in and closed the door behind him.

Dykes stood up, his mind fixed on a logical next step. There was little time to enact it.

He moved swiftly but as silently as possible to the ladder, backing down and skipping rungs to hasten his descent. He moved over the barn floor in a half-crouch which he cautiously continued to the door. Seeing the privy door still closed, he paused for a moment and fixed his eyes on its latch. That peculiar, outside-facing latch.

Focused on it, he continued his crouch and raced to close the open space between him and the privy. He near lunged at the latch — felt the cool of its iron — and deftly turned it through to its locked position.

"Hey!" the man inside shouted. He kicked at the door only to find it hold fast. "Who the hell is that?! Dykes? You stop right there, Solomon Dykes!"

Dykes stood and ran to the back door, mapping his route through the house as he approached it. His knapsack and Navy

Colt were upstairs in the bedroom. He tore through the kitchen and bolted up the stairs. The sounds of the sentry swearing and pounding on the privy door could be heard from inside the house. He opened the pack and stuffed in a shirt and pants that were on the floor. On the nightstand were his revolver, the heavy cavalry pistol he'd found in the house, and his pocket watch. He tossed the watch in the knapsack and palmed the revolver. A box of cartridges was in a hall closet, which he grabbed and crammed in the pack as he descended the stairs. He took his canteen and some tins of meat from the kitchen. Scanning the room quickly, he also took a short paring knife from the counter. He thought first to go out the front door, but upon entering the parlor he spied the horse out front, still tied to the tree, and thought better of it. His county map was rolled and leaning in a corner, which he added to his knapsack before dashing out through the kitchen again and into the yard.

The pounds on the privy door had become heavier and rhythmic — Dykes assumed the man was ramming it with the butt of his rifle. The latch was rattling but held for now. He considered running to the Front Field where his horse was likely still grazing, but its proximity to the road made him uncomfortable. Instead he turned to run due west, toward the back of his property and the creek.

DYKES HAD PUT good distance between himself and the house, and hugged the tree line as he ran the length of the field. The sounds from the privy had long faded. As he neared the back stand of trees marking the edge of the field, through which Goose Creek ran its course, he stopped and turned to look toward the house. The evening light was dim. All was silent save for his heavy breaths.

He crouched and opened his knapsack to situate its contents

better and stuffed the pistol down the side. A far-off sound began to rise and fall from the direction of the house. Dykes stood and strained to hear it. After another moment it grew louder and unmistakable: hounds.

"Damnit." He weaved both arms through the pack's straps and cinched them tight as he started running again, hard toward the creek.

As he entered the woods he lost the light under the dim canopy. He stepped high and put his hands in front of him to fend off low branches, but they still lashed at his face and arms as he ran. The barks and frantic bays of the hounds grew clearer as they broke out into the stretch of field nearest the creek. He wasn't sure where its steep bank began but braced for a fall as he pushed forward. And then the canopy opened up, the creek lay exposed in what light remained, and he slid down the loose slope into the cold pull of its current.

He turned north and moved with the flow of the creek, half-swimming and kicking off from the bottom when he could. As the sound of the hounds neared the bank where he'd entered the water, he silently loosed a log from the far bank and clung to it, kicking lightly to propel it along with the creek. The baying hounds were shrill and wrecked the still of the woods around him, but they seemed to hold at the bank. He saw a few flashes of lantern light through the tops of trees from where he'd come and heard shouts of men as they joined the hounds.

The temperature was dropping and he began to shiver as the sound of the dogs grew fainter behind him. He stared up as he glided under the dark bulk of the turnpike bridge. All was quiet from the road above.

One item he regretted not having now was his wool coat, which had been left hanging from a nail in the barn loft. Had he been slightly more prepared against the elements, the creek passage could take him through much of the county — all the way through to the Potomac. But it was too cold, and he didn't want to travel that far anyway. He needed information. He was aware of two mills upstream from the bridge, the second of which stood along a road that could get him to Lincoln. That would be best. He could dry off a bit, perhaps borrow a coat from Cassius, and plan next steps from there.

* * *

THE SECOND MILL — his point of exit from the creek — dammed a portion of the flow and sluiced it through a wooden channel and into its water wheel. He navigated the log along the edge of the dam structure and grabbed at the slippery planks, pushing the log out and away from him. He shimmied along the slick dam wall and over to the bank. No light could be seen from within the mill. He moved past it quickly toward the road, his pants heavy with water.

At the road he turned toward Lincoln, remembering the route from the map he had studied countless times in familiarizing himself with the county. Once a ways from the mill, he took the shirt and pants out from his pack, damp but not soaked. Pausing a moment to listen for any travelers coming along the road, he removed his wet pants and shirt and wrung them out. His shivers were violent. He put on the clothes from his pack, and put the wet shirt on over as an extra layer. He tied the wet pant legs around his neck and shoulders. And then he donned his pack and started off, hoping a brisk walk would serve to both dry and warm him.

The sky was clear, affording him some light from a bright moon when not under the cover of trees. The road was quiet as he walked. He was slightly unsure of his exact route; stretches of road seemed to go on far too long between turns. If he couldn't find a path by memory, he'd have to wait until morning before consulting his map; he hadn't packed so much as a lucifer match to make a light.

His doubt grew along a particularly long stretch of road that he had turned onto following little more than a hunch. It seemed never-ending. As he began considering the possibility of making a camp off the road bank for the remainder of the night, a glow ahead lifted his spirits. Walking more quickly, he soon confirmed what he'd hoped: the warm lights of an ordinary, marking a spot along a main road a few miles outside of Lincoln. He crossed to the side of the road opposite the inn and held his brisk pace.

A few lamps burned from behind the ground floor windows, but the clatter of plates and low din of socializing had long since faded as its occupants retired for the night. A pipe glowed on the dark porch as its handler puffed at it lightly. Dykes felt eyes on him, but walked on.

The road he trod now would run into the heart of Lincoln, and he knew Cassius' cabin was somewhere southeast of town. He knew the small creek that cut a curved path around the back of the cluster of cabins, a creek Dykes assumed the road spanned ahead. He came to the low wooden bridge outside of town, his heels beating out his gait as he crossed, and stopped at the other side. It was his best option for navigating the town at this hour. He stepped off the road and followed along the bank, picking his way carefully to avoid plunging a boot into the dark water.

On its meandering path, the creek repeatedly coursed toward shadowy buildings on the outskirts of town and then back into woods. Over ten minutes or so he passed what he guessed to be a barn, a cluster of houses, and a cluttered open shed — perhaps a blacksmith's forge. After another stretch through a stand of trees, the creek emerged into an open area, and his plan bore fruit: the outlines of a familiar gathering of trees and cabins grew visible. And there with them stood the church, its white walls near glowing in the moonlight.

He passed near the structure and under the cottonwood trees where he had breakfasted not so long ago. The cabins were all dark, but Dykes found Cassius' without any trouble. The small porch creaked as he stepped up onto it. He knocked on the door lightly.

"Cassius," he whispered, hoarsely. All was still. He knocked again, a bit louder. "Cassius. It's Solomon."

The door opened enough for Freeman to peer out at him.

"Solomon?" He looked him up and down. "What have you gotten into?"

CHAPTER 29

FREEMAN KNEW the look of a man in need of refuge, and in those early morning hours he had taken Dykes in without question. He also knew that whatever troubles had befallen him would be better explained after rest. He gave Dykes a change of clothes and a fresh blanket, and let him sleep the rest of the night on his bed; Freeman made a pallet on the floor.

Dykes was hard asleep when the rooster crowed, and Freeman rose and dressed quietly so as not to disturb him. He would see what news he could gather. He did have one utterance to go on, which Dykes had said before being reassuringly hushed by his host: "They're in pursuit, and I don't know why."

Miss Patience was the only one yet up beneath the old cottonwood, stoking a cook fire to ready breakfast for the others under an awning erected against one side of the church building.

Freeman lightly doffed his hat at her in a greeting. "And good morning to you, Miss Patience. I trust you rested well?"

"Mr. Freeman, I can always count on you and that old rooster. I slept just fine, thank you. Can I fix you some coffee?"

"No thank you, not at the moment," Freeman said. "I need to speak with Mr. Tyson before he's carried off with the day."

"Well maybe when you get back. Give my best to Mr. Ben."

"I will, and I will take you up on that coffee upon my return." Freeman hooked his thumbs in his front pockets, as was his habit when he walked, and after a good-bye made his way into town.

Ben Tyson rose early, but typically had a full schedule. Freeman knew he started with a cup of coffee on his porch before making rounds in the community, and he hoped to catch him there. In repose, with his coffee and his Bible.

Freeman turned down the road to his house and was relieved to see him still there, rocking with Bible in hand. He hated to interrupt this moment of peace in his day but felt the circumstances justified it.

Ben looked up from his reading as Freeman approached. "Well good morning to thee, Cassius Freeman. 'Tis a pleasure to see thee so near the dawn." He reached for his coffee mug and raised it. "Can thee join me for a moment?"

"As a matter of fact, I would like nothing better than to share a cup of coffee with you this morning, Mr. Tyson. I am much obliged."

They exchanged pleasantries as Freeman ascended onto his porch, and Mr. Tyson disappeared into the house to prepare another cup. When he returned, Freeman was seated in the second rocker, a small table with the open Bible between them. Freeman gladly accepted the steaming coffee.

Ben eased back into his rocker and took up his own mug once more. "To what do I owe the pleasure of this visit?"

Freeman sipped his cup and stared out onto the road beyond the porch. He thought for a moment. "You remember Mr. Solomon Dykes, the man who passed through last spring?"

Ben nodded. "Yes. A fine man. The champion of your new worship house, correct?"

"Indeed he is."

"He is settled where, now? Aldi?"

"Middleburg. Or nearabouts." Freeman took another sip of coffee and savored it. He turned to make eye contact with Mr. Tyson. "I believe he is in some trouble."

Ben straightened a bit and set his mug on the table. "How so?"

"He came to me last night — the dead of night — looking a mess. Wasn't properly dressed, clothes all damp, pants around his neck to keep warm. He said someone was pursuing him. But he doesn't know who or why. At least as far as I can gather."

Ben sat back in the chair. "I see."

"Now all is quiet this morning, so I think it's safe to say he eluded his pursuers," Freeman said. "But I believe what he needs now is some information. I know the look he gave me. He was scared but didn't know why. And if he came here from Middleburg last night," he paused. "He's in some trouble."

Ben nodded and took a sip of coffee. He looked down at the worn floorboards of the porch and drew a breath. "How can I be of help?"

"I just need some information — something for him to work with. Do you get news from that part of the county?"

"I do. I have a warm relationship with James Duncan, who pays a visit from time to time. It sounds to me thee needs this information sooner, though. Is Solomon Dykes about?"

"He's asleep in my cabin, unless he's been awoken by Miss Patience's cooking. She sends her regards, by the way." Ben nodded. "But I suspect he'll lay low. And yes, I would like to enter a conversation with him armed with something more than whatever he knows. Because I don't believe it's much."

Ben thought a moment. He rocked gently and put his hand on the pages of the Bible as he did so. "So," he spoke slowly. "There is this. I typically send a written report, or note, to James Duncan in the neighboring township each week. By horseback. There is not much in it. It is quiet here, as thee knows. But it does present an opportunity to get a bit more information on happenings further afield. Wils Jasper is prepared to take news tomorrow. I can send him this morning without raising any ... wariness ... from James Duncan. Will that be of help?"

Freeman shook his head. "Yes. That is promising news, and I do appreciate it."

"Fine then." Ben placed his mug next to the Bible in a final sort of way. "I am happy to oblige. Where can I find thee around noontime?"

"Noontime? So soon?"

"Wils Jasper rides a fast horse."

"I see. Well, I plan to be at Oakdale at that time. He can find me there," Freeman said. "I do certainly appreciate it."

Ben raised his large, steady hand. "No appreciation necessary. We will see if the effort bears any fruit in making some sense of Solomon Dykes' predicament." He picked up the Bible and rested it over his crossed leg. "Is thee familiar with the book of Acts? Amazing tales of growth and transformation."

The pair rocked and spoke quietly as the morning light slowly broke the dawn's chill from the air.

* * *

FREEMAN WAS ORGANIZING a pile of books in a back corner of the Oakdale School when a knock on the doorframe broke the silence of the empty room. Last he had checked, Dykes was still asleep, and he didn't expect to see him here. He turned to see who might be calling. Wils Jasper stood in the doorway.

"Cassius Freeman. A word?"

Freeman placed the two books he held in his hands on a shelf and motioned for him to enter. Jasper closed the door behind him.

"Mr. Tyson said you may be back by this time, but I didn't think it possible," Freeman said. "Were you in Middleburg this morning?"

"Aye, I was." Jasper was as old as Ben Tyson but small and boyish, making him look a good many years younger. He brushed a loose lock of gray-brown hair from his eyes. "And I have news that will be of interest to thee."

* * *

FREEMAN RETURNED to his cabin having eaten lunch, but he'd stowed a wrapped piece of cheese, an apple, and a small loaf of bread in his satchel for his guest. When he entered the cabin he saw that Dykes was awake and up, studying the newspapers plastered to the back wall of the little room.

"Good morning," Dykes said, turning.

"More of a good afternoon." Freeman opened his satchel and offered him the provisions. "You've slept well, I hope?"

"Yes, thank you. I apologize for the intrusion — this is an imposition, I know, but I wasn't sure of where else to go in the dead of night."

"Think nothing of it," Freeman said, pulling a chair out from a table near the door.

"I just need to collect my thoughts a bit before returning home. To confront those men and whatever grievance they may have with me."

"Men came to your home?"

"Yes, at dusk. Harlan Kirkbride, I believe, and others I do not know. I'm sure they have some quarrel with me. I was caught on the defensive and feel the need to approach that crew from more a position of strength."

Freeman sighed and motioned to the edge of the bed nearby. "Sit."

Dykes did as told, and placed the food by his side on the quilt. He leaned forward, hands clasped between his knees. "You have some news."

"I do. We are blessed to have quite a resource in Ben Tyson. He is well connected and respected in the county, and as a result we have come by information that may make you reconsider your ... approach."

"Okay then. What is their quarrel?"

"I will speak of the subject lightly because I fear you have little knowledge of it. Have you heard news of Mr. Mosby? Your neighbor, Jeb Mosby?"

"No. No, I have not heard from him in some weeks."

"I am sorry to say — he has been killed."

Dykes sat up stiff and froze, his eyes searching the air, before putting a hand to his forehead. "Jesus, no. No I had not heard that news." He pulled his hand down his face and rested it over his mouth, drawing a deep breath.

The muffled ticks of a pocket watch could be heard from Freeman's vest. He leaned forward and lowered his voice. "Mr. Mosby was murdered in his own field. And you are suspect."

"You have got to be ..." Dykes checked his agitation and lowered his voice to a whisper, taking a cue from Freeman. "On what grounds? On the count of me being from Connecticut?"

"There is some evidence. They have a weapon. It's unique. Apparently someone in town had some familiarity with that weapon, associating it with you, which gave cause to pay you a visit. And last night they found a match to that weapon in your home. So now you get to tell me what's going on."

Dykes studied the floor and thought a moment. "I have my pistol here. In my bag. What's left at the house is an old flintlock I'd found, I assume left by the former resident."

"A unique old flintlock?"

"Yes, I suppose. Damnit. So they think I shot my neighbor and fled when they came to question me."

"Seems so. They've got two weapons that make a pair. One was near Mr. Mosby and one was in your house. That's a good start for evidence."

"That does look bad." Dykes looked up and locked eyes with Freeman. "I did not kill Jeb Mosby. He was a friend — one of my few here. Damnit. Jeb was a good man."

"You don't have to convince me, Solomon. I knew from how you showed up here last night that you were an innocent man on the run. But I'm not the one who needs convincing."

"Right." Dykes drew a long, contemplative breath. "So I need to collect what evidence is in my favor and present it for trial. Lay low for a bit and gather my case."

Freeman shook his head lightly. "That's not how it works."

"How do you mean?"

Freeman thought a moment and sighed before answering. "They aim to hang you."

"Hang me? I'm sure Kirkbride would like nothing but. What of a trial?"

"Okay. So they aim to try you. Then they aim to hang you. They've got you where they want you and there's no working within that system. That's a bottom fact."

"Well then what do you suggest?"

"I have some notion, but I can't speak of it now. I need to speak with Mr. Tyson once more."

"And what will I do until then?"

"You'll be safe here," Freeman said. "My cabin is small but it makes a comfortable home. I have some books …"

"Hold on now." Dykes reached to put his hand on Freeman's shoulder. "You're a fine man, Cassius. Don't let me be a burden. Say the word and I'll flee elsewhere."

"You're safe here. From here on out you keep the door latched when I'm out. I'll announce myself with one rap followed by two quick raps." He knocked it out on the tabletop. "Like this."

Dykes nodded. "One and two quick. Understood." He leaned back on the bed and gazed at the ceiling. "How did it come to this?"

* * *

THE LIGHT outside the cabin was fading. Dykes had kept low over the course of the afternoon, reclined on the bed and reading with the curtains drawn. There was one simple, rectangular window in the one-room cabin, above the bed. A small fireplace occupied the wall opposite the bed. The beams peaked to a shallow point above, with some planks laid across to make a small loft space. Cassius used the area for storage, from the looks of it, but Dykes had flagged it in his mind as a hiding place should someone unknown approach the cabin.

In the quiet of the cabin, Dykes thumbed through a book absently while mulling over his predicament. In piecing together what evidence there was, it was fairly apparent to him what had come to pass. John Stibbs, clearly in no right mind after his wife's accident, had visited Jeb for whatever reason and shot him. Had Dykes known that pistol was a match for another, he would have burned it with the rest of the refuse from that damnable mess. But it was unique. It intrigued him. And here he was.

He wanted nothing more but to return to his land, having grown somewhat accustomed to his new home. But the more he thought on it, the less that seemed a likely outcome. Still, there was a chance. There was a case to be made. A guilty man roamed free, while Dykes had both his innocence and his knowledge of Stibbs and the murder weapon on his side.

He busied himself by hanging his damp clothes over chair backs in an attempt to air them, and sorted through the contents of his pack. There were no surprises. His current possessions were whittled to what he had hastily gathered some twenty-four hours prior. The revolver with a box of ammunition, his pocket watch, canteen, a small knife, the Yardley-Taylor county map, a tin of sardines, and two tins of oysters.

He was replaying the night over in his mind when he heard footfalls on the porch. There was a pause. And then a knock. And two short knocks.

Dykes stepped over to the door and quietly opened the latch. Freeman moved in without opening the door too wide.

"Evening, Mr. Dykes. I trust your afternoon was uneventful?"

"Thankfully yes. Being alone with my thoughts is not the best place at the moment, although I know there are worse. I appreciate the use of your admirable library."

"I hope it could be of some distraction." Freeman sat down in the chair with Dykes' pants thrown over the back. "We have an option for you."

Dykes took his seat on the bed.

"I was able to find Mr. Tyson at the Meeting House. It was nice and quiet, and we were able to talk frankly. After some thought, he became sympathetic to your position in a most generous way," Freeman said. "Your prior work for our community is still much appreciated, I'll add."

"Well, it has always been my pleasure. And it is clear to me now that I should have settled here, in Lincoln, rather than further afield in the county."

"Ah, but your heart yearned for farming, and good land drew you elsewhere. You can't doubt past actions based on sound judgment. Misfortune finds men anywhere."

"Fair enough. So what of your option?"

Freeman cleared his throat. "Do you know the history of this place? Lincoln and its people?"

"I'm not sure I follow. Its name was changed from Goose Creek, correct?"

"Yes, but I mean more of its unspoken history. These people here, men like Mr. Tyson, helped men like me in a most noble way. This was a station — a safe place along the journey north. You've heard of the Underground Railroad?"

Dykes' face lit with surprise. "Of course. I didn't realize ..."

"This whole county was a major thoroughfare to get folks over the Potomac and up to freedom. People like Mr. Tyson made it happen."

"I did not know that part of Lincoln's history. But yes, that makes sense to me."

"So here is what Mr. Tyson proposes." Freeman leaned back in his chair. "We can get you north."

Dykes sat silent for a moment. "Get me north. What does that mean? How far north?"

"You're in a bad spot. Heading back up to home in New England won't do it, but we can get you to a good place farther north. Canada. For a new start."

Dykes shook his head. "No, that's mighty generous, but I just can't see that as a feasible option. There must be some other way out of this."

"I'm telling you, Solomon, there's not. I know you're an innocent man, but you know how Mr. Kirkbride and his cronies feel about you. They're not going to let this one go. And with Virginia soon occupied no more — it's speculation, but I feel the law will reach beyond the borders of our Commonwealth. They'll find you, and they'll bring you back."

The pair sat quietly before Freeman broke the silence once more. "Where are you going to go otherwise?"

Dykes looked at the worn planks of the cabin floor, swept clean. "I don't know."

"I know this is not what you want or expected. But I think it's your best option. And it's fortuitous you came to it." Freeman stood. "If it's going to happen, it's going to happen tonight. No good will come of waiting another day. I will return in an hour. You have an answer ready by then. Either you escape tonight, or you tell me a better plan."

Dykes nodded. "Thank you, Cassius. I'll give it some thought."

"You're a wise man, Solomon. Give it some good, objective thought. I'll see you in an hour."

Freeman stepped sideways through the door and into the cool of the evening. The sound of laughter pealed in from under the old cottonwood where a group had gathered for supper.

Dykes closed the latch behind him and sat heavily on the bed once more.

CHAPTER 30

THE LUMPS of the mattress moved up around his sides to ground him as his eyes traced the rafters above. In the far corner, a spider web. How did Cassius reach up there? A broom? Would that clear the rafters during a cleaning? Perhaps so, if aided by the added height of a chair.

A journey north would mean failure. Failure to achieve a goal, to start a new and more fruitful life in the welcoming climate of a Virginia he barely knew. Failure to learn and master agriculture. Failure to work the land up from neglect, with little but his hands, his tools, and his horse, yet unnamed. Failure to start a family, perhaps. To put down roots in this place that held such promise but a day ago.

Yet the thought of staying afforded little hope. Cassius was right — any trial would be a farce. Dykes was an interloper, an intruder into a way of life he didn't fully understand. He was a symbol of the force that had undone what was sacred to the Kirkbrides of this place. They would not let this opportunity for justice, or what they perceived as such, pass.

Dykes turned the options over in his mind, but could not reason through what he knew to be his cold lot: This was a true

Hobson's choice. There was Mr. Tyson's plan, or there was nothing at all.

A departure would seal his guilt in their minds, dashing any chance of reckoning for Jeb Mosby's true killer. But there was great risk in staying for the sake of his untenable plea of innocence.

The knock came again, one rap and two short. Dykes stood and turned the latch. He faced Cassius as he stepped into the room. He had never noticed their difference in height until this moment. He looked up to meet the man's eyes.

"You know my answer," Dykes said. "North it is."

Freeman nodded solemnly. "I wish it weren't so, Solomon. We have not known each other long, but I consider you a good friend. No doubt that friendship would have grown all the more over time."

"I feel the same." Dykes glanced at his belongings strewn about the room. "What is expected of me now? How do we proceed?"

"You must move quickly. We've already given up a day for word of the crime to spread through parts of the county. There's a full moon up tonight, or near enough to travel by. The night makes for a friendly road."

"I discovered this last night, as much as I loathed it."

"That should be the worst of it. You have friends now to lighten the journey's load." Freeman motioned to the belongings scattered about the cabin. "Now let's get you packed up, and we'll await a visit from Wils Jasper. He's a fine man who works for Mr. Tyson and is no stranger to this road. He'll give you safe passage to Washington, and from there further north to Baltimore. And from the port of Baltimore, a ship to freedom."

"You make it sound easy."

"God willing, it should be," Freeman said. "The railroad won't be watched the way it was when I traveled by it." He held out a hand and Dykes shook it. "You'll be fine."

The pair pulled in for a hug. Dykes was surprised at how tightly Freeman held him, but found comfort in it.

* * *

DYKES DUCKED INSTINCTIVELY as he passed from the porch through the surrounding cabins and out to the road where a cart waited. As he neared he saw it loaded with hay, and he wondered where exactly he would be carried. Surely not on the bench up front.

Freeman followed behind and greeted Jasper with a silent nod. The pair slid the back gate of the cart up to reveal a space, two feet high at the most, between the floor of the cart and its base above the axles. Freeman motioned to Dykes.

"This is your ride. You'll be safe. I recommend you lay face up — there's room for your pack as a pillow."

Dykes thanked him quietly, pushed his pack in and began to follow after it. He hesitated just as he was about to duck his head in and turned to Freeman.

"Cassius."

"Yes, Solomon?"

"John Stibbs. You don't know that name, but it was John Stibbs who killed Jeb."

Freeman stared back, surprised. "Yes, Solomon. I will carry this with me and do with it what I can."

"Thank you." Dykes found a hold on the inside of the cavity and pulled himself in headfirst, sliding on his back into the darkness. It smelled of fresh earth and hay. He heard the gate slide down behind his feet. A moment later the cart lurched forward. He stuffed his pack under his head and closed his eyes to protect them from the sting of dust jostled loose from the boards above.

* * *

DYKES COULD NOT MOVE, let alone see to check his watch, but it seemed hours passed on bumpy dirt roads. He dozed some, often waking with a start as a cartwheel hit a rock or a rut. There was no stopping, just slowing before turns were made.

During a moment of wakefulness, the rhythm of the road quickly turned to a hollow thumping. A bridge. Dykes envisioned a map in his head. A bridge, but what bridge? As the thumping drew on, it became clear. So long a bridge must be crossing a river — no creek. Quite possibly the Chain Bridge, at least he hoped it, spanning from Virginia to north of Washington near the Maryland border. He could almost see its broad beam arches passing on either side as they traveled. After a minute or so the cart slowed, and then stopped. Dykes heard a muffled exchange between Jasper and an unknown. He held his breath. The horse stamped impatiently on the worn deck of the bridge. All was quiet. And then the cart lurched forward once more.

Dykes exhaled and settled his head into the soft part of his pack, hoping to doze again before reaching the Federal City.

* * *

SOMEONE WAS SHAKING HIS FOOT. He woke with a start and instinctively sat up, hitting his head hard on the boards above. He let out a short bark of pain and rubbed his head, feeling for wet. There was none.

"Shhhh … Solomon Dykes. We've arrived." Jasper had a hoarse whisper and maintained a hold of his foot. He shook it again. "Time to come out."

Dykes felt stiff as he shimmied out from the cart into what he perceived to be early morning light. He stretched as Jasper arched his back to do the same. It had been a long ride for both of them. They were standing in an alley. The backs of row houses faced them on both sides, with small fenced yards standing between them and dark windows and closed doors. The only light burned faintly from the upstairs window of a house to their right. A quilt hung on a line in the yard.

"This is a station to us — a place where thee can stay a bit while I prepare for the next leg," Jasper whispered.

"What have you to do?"

"I am to deliver this hay, change horses, and pick up a new load to carry north. I should be back within an hour or so." Jasper opened a gate in the short picket fence and stood aside for Dykes to pass. "Go on in through the cellar there, then upstairs to the inside door. Just go on and knock. We are expected."

Dykes gave a nod as he fed his arms through the straps of his pack. "Thank you, Mr. Jasper."

"Just sit tight." He turned and mounted the cart once more.

Dykes passed through the dark yard as the cart clattered off down the alley. The reassuring smell of wood smoke hinted at a well-tended fire still burning from the night, or a stove lit early. He gave the cellar door a pull and it opened broadly to expose wide stairs lit by an unseen lamp somewhere down below. He descended, unsure of what to expect from within; more unsure of every moment, from one to the next, than he could remember.

CHAPTER 31

THE CELLAR WAS WELL-STOCKED but tidy. The floor was a jigsaw of
worn brick, kept clean and dry. A wall of narrow shelves held
preserves organized by, at first glance, color and size. Three
barrels occupied one corner, and in another was a curious set of
wide shelves three high. Perhaps bunks. But there was no
mattress or bedding to indicate such. A table by these shelves,
complete with two simple chairs, held the oil lamp that had
served as his beacon down the stairs and into the place.

Dykes dutifully crossed the room to the narrow set of
wooden stairs leading up into the house. He mounted them
slowly and stopped at the top, perched on the small landing
before a dark door. He took one step backward, down a step,
before he knocked.

He waited. There was no sound from within. He knocked
again, a bit louder. No sound. He looked back into the cellar
behind him. Hesitantly, he turned the knob and opened the door
into a hallway. He stepped in and closed the door softly
behind him.

To his right was a back room, perhaps an office. To his left, a
foyer and stairway to the upstairs. It was somehow familiar to
him. He walked quietly into the foyer and turned into a front

parlor. Rows of books. Four painted ships hanging. A small brass clock ticking quietly. It chimed.

"Oh, my." The voice was soft but strong behind him. He turned to see Beth Tompkins draw a hand to lightly cover her mouth but drop it quickly. "First Lieutenant? You're my passenger?"

Dykes stared in disbelief, suddenly embarrassed by his situation. He was a mess, his clothes rank, dusty, and covered with bits of hayseed. He hadn't shaved in days. He looked to see if he'd tracked anything in with his boots.

"Ms. Tompkins — my God. I don't quite know what to say. I apologize for ... the imposition."

"No imposition, but my goodness. How did ..." She stopped and suddenly seemed to collect herself a bit. She smoothed the apron over her dark blue skirt. "Let me take your bag. I have some coffee on. I should be the one apologizing for not hearing you come in sooner."

"I just did walk in, it's no trouble." He handed her his pack. It was filthy. "I am so sorry to intrude under these circumstances."

"Can we be done with the apologies, First Lieutenant? I was expecting you." She fitted his bag over the back of her correspondence desk chair. "Well, not *you*. But someone in your position. Mr. Tyson sent word of someone in need, and I was certainly happy to assist. I had not heard from him in some time." She motioned to the sofa as she moved into the kitchen. "Please, sit."

Dykes did as told, brushing the back of his pants off before taking a seat. He looked around the room once more. He could not believe the chance that brought him here. His heart raced lightly at the thought. The room felt wholly safe. He gazed at the cracked ceiling as the sounds of coffee cups clattering on saucers and being filled came from the adjacent room. "Sugar?" she called out. "I haven't any cream."

"None, thank you."

After a moment she reentered, offered him his cup and saucer, and took a seat across from him on the edge of a cushioned chair beside a reading desk. She turned a nearby lamp up a bit and sipped her coffee, eyeing him over its rim. He took a sip as well.

"This is good. Thank you."

"It is my pleasure." She took another before placing the cup and saucer on the table, careful to not clatter it. She folded her hands in her lap. "Now tell me. Why are you here, in this position?"

Dykes looked for a place to set his coffee. Seeing none, he held it, rested in his lap. "I must say, Ms. Tompkins—"

"Call me Beth."

"Yes. I must say, Beth, I find it fortuitous that I have returned to your home, although these circumstances are ... well, they're terrible."

Beth continued her gaze and gave a half-nod that Dykes interpreted as sympathy. He continued. "It's best if I start at the beginning." He thought a moment. "Did you receive my correspondence, by any chance?"

"Yes, I did. It was kind of you."

The words stung a bit. "Kind. Yes." Dykes glanced at the floor but determinedly returned his eyes to meet hers. They were piercingly hazel. He had not noticed before. "So you know that I settled in Virginia, not far from Middleburg. Again, I thank you for the use of your map. It was invaluable."

"I'm glad to hear it. And it sounded as if you were making a happy life for yourself there."

"I was, yes. Starting to, at least." Dykes shifted in his seat a bit and took a sip of the coffee, wanting to finish it before it cooled too much. "The land I settled on, I purchased it from the county due to some back taxes owed. I didn't think it particularly honorable at the time, although I didn't truly reason through how it might affect those settled there. They were evicted. I later found that it caused them some sorrow."

"I can imagine it might, yes."

"I'm not exactly sure how it transpired, but from what I can gather, that former owner returned and ... you would think he would seek some vengeance on me, but he returned to murder my dear neighbor. A man named Jeb Mosby."

Beth's eyes widened. "Oh, good heavens. How terrible. A Loudoun Mosby, no less."

"Oh, yes, well I don't believe they were kin. But he was a good man, and had become a friend to me. Now as best I can gather, the weapon used, dropped at the scene of the crime, was a match to a pistol left behind, in my kitchen as it happens."

Beth's expression indicated she was following but waiting for further explanation.

"A few men in town, over my time spent there, had become a bit aggressive toward me based on my being ..."

"A Yankee."

"Yes, well, that's how they would put it."

"I can't say I'm surprised to hear you received some rough treatment," Beth said. "I have read of those seeking to exploit the Southerners' situation following their surrender."

"And I, too, although I never gave them reason to doubt my intentions. Regardless, these men did happen to associate that make of weapon with me. They used it as an excuse to peg me as a suspect. Not fully understanding the situation, I fled lest confront them initially. They subsequently searched my home, found the matching weapon, and here I am."

He took another sip of the coffee. It was beginning to cool. "I've been told any trial would be a farce. I happen to agree, given the circumstances."

Beth nodded and considered the information for a moment. She stared at his cup. "Would you like more? Coffee?"

"No, thank you."

"Well let me take that for you." She rose and quickly ferried his cup and saucer into the kitchen. He remained in his seat and studied the rug. It was nice. A blue and maroon Oriental pattern, worn but still intricate in its detail. "What of the man who did this terrible deed?" she called from the kitchen. She came back and leaned against the door frame. "What of him? It seems he's now free to roam the countryside."

"I've considered this. I mentioned his name to Cassius Freeman — do you know Mr. Freeman, in Lincoln?"

"I do not," Beth said, still leaned against the frame.

"He's a good man and may do something with the information. I believe it was a man named John Stibbs. He is the former owner of my property."

Beth nodded. "It seems your property will be back in the hands of the state."

This fact had stuck in his mind during the hours he lay awake in the belly of the hay cart. The house, his land, his horse — all that he had worked for is left behind. Tools, clothes, books, all of it. The chickens would be stolen or scatter to be eaten by dogs; the fields would return to weeds.

"Yes." Dykes sighed and leaned back, deflated, against the curve of the sofa. "This is not how I wanted things to go."

She entered the room and sat down next to him, her knees angled toward his. She placed a hand on his leg. "I am so sorry, Solomon. Ours is a complicated world now. This likely couldn't have been avoided."

He appreciated her sympathy. "I feel it could have been at any number of steps. But perhaps I was foolish to venture south. A return north was likely inevitable."

She patted his leg and folded both hands in her lap. She was sitting so straight and proper; he returned his posture to match and angled slightly to face her.

"I did consider a visit in response to your correspondence," Beth said. "I do believe I would have made it down, before winter set in."

"That would have pleased me very much. I feel we're kindred spirits, Beth. I felt it after we first met. I feel through the map you gave me you were guiding me along my path." He looked away from her. "That sounds foolish."

"That sounds lovely, and I should like to think the same." A faint burning smell drifted through the room. "Oh my — I've a loaf in the oven that's gone too long." She stood up quickly and returned to the kitchen. Dykes sat back again, exhausted from the night and the unfolding exchange with Beth. Their conversation was turning to a place he had often visited in his mind in recent months.

She called from the kitchen, "Just the top, it can be cut off!" She returned to the doorway with a gleam in her eyes. "Mr. Jasper likes my bread."

"I see." Dykes laughed a bit at her enthusiasm. "I hope I'm lucky enough to enjoy it in his company."

"Oh, you are. Whenever he returns."

Dykes stood and took his pack off the chair. "I have your map. It has been dear to me, and it was one of the few things I did think to take from the house as I was leaving."

"Well, keep it."

"No, it wouldn't do me any good." He pulled the rolled linen from the pack and presented it to her. "Perhaps it will help another down the line."

She hesitated but took the map. "I'll return it to its hideaway in the office then." She gave him a double tap on the shoulder with it as she passed and walked down the hall. He followed her, stopping at the door back down to the cellar to watch as she moved about the back room.

"I do have something for you, though," she called. "For what may come next." She returned to meet him in the hall and stood before him. "You'll have to open your hand."

He did as he was told. She carefully placed a small, oblong silver coin in his palm. He studied it. What appeared to be a holy man, with a staff and tall hat, stood in a boat to fill the oval.

"St. Nicholas," she said. "Patron saint of sailors. Pray to him, and he will provide for you." She closed his hand around it and held her hand there.

"I admit I'm not usually one for prayer, but I shall cherish it. Thank you." They remained standing before each other in the hall. "Beth, you have been so generous with me, but I know so little of you. You're from Boston. What else?"

"Oh, there's not much to know." She looked down for a moment. "I do love music. You speak of Boston — they held a national jubilee there last summer. I didn't make the trip up, but I so would have liked to have been there. Ole Bull was concert-master. Do you know ..."

She trailed off, feeling a heaviness grow between them, his gaze so intent into her eyes. She looked down, slightly embarrassed by the intimacy of the moment. He raised a hand and tenderly moved a stray bit of hair from her face.

Three loud knocks echoed out from the cellar door next to them, jolting them apart. "Beth Tompkins!" a voice whispered from the other side. It was Wils Jasper.

She smoothed her apron and opened the door.

"Beth Tompkins. Everything is ready." He looked at Dykes. "Thee looks ready to go. Was thee about to descend to the cellar?"

Solomon and Beth exchanged a glance. "Yes. I need my pack," he said.

"And you need your breakfast, the both of you," Beth said. "I have your bread, Mr. Jasper."

"Oh, Beth Tomkins. I so have missed thy kindness and thy bread."

The three separated, Dykes to retrieve his pack and Beth to ready breakfast while Jasper loitered in the foyer. After a moment she returned carrying a tray with a plate of bread, butter, fried eggs, and two fresh coffees. Jasper's eyes lit at the sight. "Oh, this shall do me good, Beth Tompkins. We shall take it in the cellar before departing."

"By all means." She passed them and carried the tray

through the open cellar door and down the steps. Jasper followed her down.

Dykes paused a moment in the foyer. As the footfalls on the cellar stairs receded, he was left in the quiet house once more. The small clock in the parlor ticked softly. He walked over to it and peered at its delicate face. After a moment he had a thought and slung his pack around to open its flap. Rummaging through it, he pulled out his brass pocket watch. He smoothed his thumb over its glass face and checked its time against the clock. Off by a bit. He turned the knob on the watch. Its hands swept forward.

CHAPTER 32

JOURNAL *of 2nd Lt. Solomon Dykes*

Thursday, January 15, 1863

A day like this burns bright in a man's mind and sticks tight — no doubt I will carry it with me for some time. This war is providing its share of surprises.

After venturing further south late yesterday, we rejoined our own regiment and others led by a General Weitzel, onshore from our flotilla of gunboats and just south of the crippled bridge spanning Bayou Teche. The rebels had given our fleet its share of trouble, it seems, with torpedoes snarling the waterway and making maneuvers treacherous. Nonetheless, the Confederate steamer Cotton was cornered.

My company was positioned on the western bank, nearest what had once been the bridge — the property of a nearby landowner named Corney — which was now merely a span of debris. The river was somewhat wider here but still tight for our gunships, which stood at the ready for the Cotton's return.

Though I had not laid eyes on her since witnessing her turn further upriver, it seemed another appearance of the rebel steamer was inevitable. Her crew was pernicious and unrelenting, having made two runs at our ships throughout the course of a day. But as the light faded from the evening sky, we began to wonder what had come of her.

Perhaps her crew had abandoned her and scattered into the thick of the forest. Pickets could tell the tale come morning light.

We had orders to hold our position, so we dug in a bit and settled into the calm of the night. The nocturnal bayou, even in these winter months, brought forth a cacophony from unseen insects and reptiles marking their presence. Though this broken symphony typically kept me awake, I was overpowered by sheer exhaustion after a long and somewhat harrowing day, and soon found sleep against my pack.

I awoke with a start. The sky was bright, though not from the moon — what sliver had been in the sky set hours ago. I sat up and stared in disbelief at what was approaching from upriver: the Cotton, returning for a third run as predicted, though engulfed in high-licking flame. The whole of the craft was a waterborne inferno, dropping bits of fiery refuse into the water as she sailed. It was an eerie sight to behold.

It seemed we had bested her crew.

The vessel soon lodged itself into the bridgeworks, spreading rings of flame through the mess and providing some help in clearing it. We watched over the next hour as it burned itself out, towering flames soon reduced to the deep glow of slow-burning coals. Though we stood at the ready to meet its crew or other land forces coming down river, there were none in the night. Morning came, and we began to assess the fate of the Cotton.

Gen. Weitzel ordered a contingent of men to board the wreckage and gather what information they could. My company being the nearest to the wreck, I joined a group tasked with accompanying the party. We were rowed out on several light boats and hefted over her starboard side, the craft leaning slightly down toward the water where we boarded.

There were few bodies on board — what we saw were charred but had likely fallen in combat over the course of yesterday's engagements. We picked our way over the blackened deck, much of it still smoldering. Any remaining cotton bales were charred black on the outside; some had split open to reveal seams of white glinting in the sun.

The pilot house was still intact, and the general's scouts had descended on it fairly rapidly, a pair of them emerging with a metal box and some singed papers tucked underarm. *After their group cleared, I went in to have a look for myself. The ship's wheel was blackened but standing, though little else of the space afforded any clues of its former prominence. There was a desk sitting with its drawers hanging open and empty. It had been slid partially away from the wall, and I instinctively approached to peer behind it. There, on the deck, was a thin metal chain snaking its way under a fallen bit of timber.*

I slid the desk back further from the wall and crouched behind it to finger the chain. Moving the timber aside, I exposed what was tethered to its other end: a brass pocket watch, pristine amongst the surrounding wreckage. On its back was a small eagle in relief and the initials "J.L.R." Its face was unblemished, and its fine hands still ticked out the seconds. I ran the meat of my palm over the glass and revealed not one crack.

Although I am not predisposed to collect spoils of war — and I do not foresee myself seeking out trophies from my enemies hence — this watch seems somehow special to me. It pains me to think who may have checked its time mere hours ago, who may have glanced from its face out to my comrades firing upon the vessel from the banks of Bayou Teche. But whoever it may have served in the past, it now serves me.

CHAPTER 33

I⊤ WAS SNOWING IN BALTIMORE. It seemed too early in the season, but Dykes heard the unmistakable softness of it falling on the canvas above his head. He lifted a corner and peered out from his shelter among a cluster of brandy barrels to verify what he already knew. The flakes were small but steady, creating a haze over the harbor. He threw the canvas back over the barrels and stretched his arms and back from a crouched position. A row of docked steamers swayed gently across the channel.

He was on a long dock that ran parallel to a cobblestone road dotted with indistinguishable storefronts, their features smudged by the falling snow. A sign nearest to him and most visible read: Federal Hill – Ship Chandlery. He turned to look back out over the quiet of the water. Looming overhead were the dual masts of a schooner, its riggings creaking lightly but rhythmically. This was to provide passage north, or so he had been told.

He glanced at his watch. Wils Jasper had brought him to this place an hour ago with instructions to remain hidden among the load he had left on the dock. The owner of the vessel was wise to the scheme, Jasper had explained, and would allow him discreet passage onto the ship and below deck before she got underway.

But this transition was taking longer than Dykes had hoped. Perhaps the captain was delayed by the weather.

Dykes studied the dirt under his fingernails, deposited there from a land that now seemed impossibly far away. His departure from Beth Tompkins' house had been disappointingly decorous. She served him and Jasper a lovely and sustaining breakfast in the cellar, but once plates were on table, she excused herself politely and returned upstairs. Dykes exchanged a good-bye with her as if a stranger before watching her figure ascend into the warm familiarity above.

Jasper had spent his morning delivering the load of hay, exchanging horses at the same stables, and retrieving a load of brandy to deliver to the Port of Baltimore. After breakfast, the pair returned to the alley and the waiting cart. Before sliding the false back up, Jasper pulled the canvas covering the barrels down over the back wheels. He glanced around cautiously and motioned for Dykes to climb under. Although the scene certainly would have puzzled any watching intently, Dykes supposed it was better than him scrambling into the hidden cavity in broad morning light.

Surprisingly, it took less time to reach Baltimore than it had to navigate the dark roads of Virginia the night prior, and after a final jolting stretch of cobblestone, the cart pulled to a halt. The back slid open and Jasper jostled his foot in the now-familiar way.

"This is it. Almost there now."

Dykes inched his way out into the light and breathed in the fresh, briny air. He pulled out his pack and dusted himself off. Jasper was hitching the horse and preparing to unload the cargo. Dykes began to help by untying the tarp.

"Not necessary, friend," Jasper whispered. "Take a seat here by the wheel and I'll do the work. Any here in the harbor need to see me and me alone."

Dykes took his seat as told, but was somewhat surprised when Jasper abruptly whipped the tarp off and let it crumple around him. Nonetheless, he remained still, listing to the sounds of Jasper heaving barrels off and onto the dock. After the unloading was done, there was a moment of stillness before Jasper pulled up a corner.

"Just move with me as I go," he whispered. He slowly dragged the tarp over the dock, lifting it up over the cluster of barrels, which he had arranged in a U shape, creating a cavity. Dykes shuffled right in and continued to sit under the tarp. Jasper gave it a pat from the top. "Good luck to thee, friend."

Dykes pushed back up to meet the hand above. "Thank you, Wils. I will never forget this." His words felt inadequate for what had just been accomplished. He hoped the man would find some well-deserved rest at a nearby inn before venturing south once more. He would have loved to have joined him for a beer.

* * *

THE SNOW WAS FALLING HARDER NOW and sticking to the dock. Dykes felt he should return under the tarp and began inching back.

"Oy! You there!" A rough voice called out from down the dock and heavy boot steps came rushing toward him. Dykes stood to face the man.

"What are you doing under that tarp?"

"Getting out of this snow a bit."

The man glared at him. He was stocky, with a weathered face framed by a pale blue tattoo that traced under his jawline.

"Now that's some bollocks. You want to get out of the snow you'd be heading indoors." He motioned to the row of buildings nearby with a club he'd pulled from his belt. The man eyed Dykes and then the schooner behind them. "You're sneaking on, ain't you?

Dykes began to shake his head and put his hands out nonthreateningly. "No, not at all — in fact I'm here to meet with the captain about this cargo."

"Bollocks again! I've met with the man who delivered these. You're a would-be stowaway." He looked somewhere off behind Dykes. "The harbor master will deal with you." He reached for Dykes' arm.

"No!" Dykes pulled back. "Now just listen … hold on. What can I do — what can I offer you? I need passage on this ship."

The man stepped closer. "What can you offer me?" His breath was laced with a trace of onion. "Don't know that you have anything I want."

Dykes thought through the contents of his pack. All worthless, and the pistol would only escalate the situation. He patted his pants front and put a hand in his pocket. His fingers traced over the small oval medal. St. Nicholas. And then the smooth of the watch face.

"Here." Dykes held out his open hand. Snow fell lightly on the brass eagle and melted away from its warmth. "Take this watch."

The man looked at it indifferently. "A watch, eh? That brass?"

"It is. Keeps perfect time. Not a crack on it."

The man looked over his shoulder and back at Dykes. "Fine." He grabbed the watch with his mittened hand, holding it close to his face for inspection. "Stay out of sight." He clubbed at a barrel as he walked past, soon becoming a shadow in the falling snow.

Dykes exhaled and stared out at the water, vacantly. There was no sign of the captain. But no other option. He shook the exposed underside of the tarp to free it from snow and crept back in among the barrels. Pulling the tarp down, he returned to the quiet darkness and sat flat on the dock, his knees bent toward his chest. He shifted to pull the medal out of his pocket, careful not to drop it through the cracks of the dock.

Water sloshed below. A harbor bell rang out, muffled, somewhere in the distance. Dykes rested his head on his knees. Eyes closed, he traced his thumb over the relief of St. Nicholas and mouthed a silent prayer.

EPILOGUE

THE LAMP FLICKERED and snuffed itself out, a final wisp of greasy smoke coiling from the nub of the wick. The change in light caused Dykes to stir. Under the quilt he was still wearing a sack coat over his shirt and drawers. He sat up and rubbed a palm over his face, getting his bearings. It was dinnertime. He had dozed off.

He blew his nose into a handkerchief, folded it, and wiped his beard. He was not accustomed to wearing a beard, but shaving seemed so unnecessary now. He rarely saw another soul. A monthly trip down to the village yielded what provisions he needed, but on those visits he would keep to himself. He suspected the store clerk had come to recognize him, though they never exchanged introductions.

He rose stiffly and opened the stove door. He lit a candle from the embers within and fed in a few bits of wood. A skillet was already warm on the stovetop and he scraped in a hunk of lard, guiding it around the pan with the tip of his knife to ensure an even melt. He added some salt cod from a tin and sliced a bit of onion in after it, stirring it all with the knife.

For a moment, Dykes became lost in the sizzle of pork fat and cod, staring absently into the pan. And then he snapped to attention, remembering. He moved quickly over to a journal he kept and thumbed through recent pages. "Tuesday last, Wednesday," he muttered aloud. He flipped blank pages and mouthed days of the week. "It's Friday. Friday evening."

He hurried about the small cabin, pulling on heavy trousers that had been left on the floor, their bottoms cold and wet. He wrapped a wool scarf round his head and neck and donned a coat hung among traps and ice tools. It was snowing hard now, so he pushed through the door and quickly closed it behind him.

The wind was low, the hillside still, save for the eerie muted patter of heavy snowfall. He squinted through the thick flakes, out to the sea. Around this time each week, a little ferry would steam up past his line of view, around a spit of land, and into the wharf of the village. The same ferry that had deposited him here so many months ago.

It was difficult to see anything. The horizon was a haze of white. But after several minutes of standing there, his back to the door, he spotted it. A speck of gray in the storm. The little ferry, steaming to port.

It stood to reason, as he saw it, that she knew he was here. She knew the means by which he had come to this place, surely she would know of his final destination. With that came a chance, a bit of hope he nurtured gingerly like the stove fire inside, that one day she would come calling.

The little ferry steamed on and out of view. He leaned back against the door, snow caking on his beard, and smiled.

ACKNOWLEDGMENTS

Although the characters in this book are completely fictional, if my grandfather, Jimmy Rouse, were alive to read it, he would catch glimpses of himself in more than one of them. It was through Pop and his wife, Emma Lou (Granny to me), that I learned so many life lessons, including the value of a good story and the importance of family history. My parents, Darryl and Martha Gates, instilled in me a love of writing and reading, and encouraged me to take *Hard Road South* from a few pages to what you hold in your hands. Although my father is another who is not alive to read this, I carry his words of encouragement with me to this day. Thank you to my brother, Craig, for talking through endless plot possibilities and for his devoted interest in all manner of rough drafts—not to mention his work on the cover. Thank you to my wife, Kelly, for her unwavering patience and support, as well as for encouraging me to attend the workshop where I first met the marvelous Sherry Torgent and Amanda Gawthorpe at Blue Ink Press. To that end, thank you to Sherry, Amanda, and the whole Blue Ink Press team for recognizing this book's potential and polishing it into something fit for public consumption.

This being a work of historical fiction, I took certain liberties with details of the era and region while still striving to ground the world around its characters in historical fact. Thank you to Mosby Heritage Area Historian Emeritus Richard Gillespie and Civil War era enthusiast Lester Adams for providing feedback on the history of the time.

An invaluable research tool was loudounhistory.org, which includes material from the Waterford Foundation and local historian Eugene Scheel. I also drew inspiration from the Loudoun Museum in Leesburg, as well as the Loudoun Heritage Farm Museum and its lovely *It's Just a Way of Life: Reminiscing about the Family Farm*. The museum, in Sterling, is also where I stood before Yardley Taylor's impressive county map for the first time.

ABOUT THE AUTHOR

Scott Gates grew up in Montgomery, Alabama, and has worked as a writer and editor in Colorado, Virginia, and North Carolina. He currently lives near Raleigh with his wife, Kelly, and their three children. *Hard Road South* is his first novel.

facebook.com/ScottMGates

instagram.com/scottmgates